Ladybug,
Ladybug...

Other Books
by W. O. Mitchell

Who Has Seen the Wind
Jake and the Kid
The Kite
The Vanishing Point
How I Spent My Summer Holidays
Dramatic W. O. Mitchell
Since Daisy Creek

Ladybug, Ladybug...

W.O. Mitchell

⟦A DOUGLAS GIBSON BOOK⟧

M&S

Canadian Cataloguing in Publication Data

Mitchell, W. O. (William Ormond), 1914–
Ladybug, Ladybug

ISBN 0-7710-6075-0

I. Title.

PS8526.I88L33 1988   C813'.54   'C88-094316-5
PR9199.3.M59L33 1988

Printed and bound in Canada by Friesen Printers
Design by Linda Gustafson

A Douglas Gibson Book

McClelland and Stewart
The Canadian Publishers
481 University Avenue
Toronto M5G 2E9

For my brothers,
Dick, Bob, and Jack

With thanks to Dr. John W. Fair, B.Sc., M.D., C.R.C.P.(C)
and with gratitude to the University of Windsor

1

HIS IMMEDIATE RESPONSE WAS A STIR OF IMPATIENCE WITH the careless idiot who must have shoved it into the wrong mail slot. It was addressed to a D.J. Chatterjee, DIRECTOR OF SPACE PRIORITY PLACEMENT. Wrong recipient! Wrong department! Yet it was signed: 'Dr. Tait, CHAIRMAN ENGLISH DEPARTMENT,' and in the bottom left-hand corner it did say: 'cc Dr. Lyon – Dean Taylor.' After looking over the pink phone slips he had come to the memo halfway through the mail that had been piling up all the time he'd been away in Cambridge, Detroit, and Hartford. The flu he'd picked up in Connecticut had graduated through bronchitis to viral pneumonia by the time he'd got off the plane and made it to bed at home and then into Western Hospital for two weeks.

With growing disbelief, he read the memo. 'As of June 30th, end of inter-session, English Department Office number 273, which has been allocated to Dr. Lyon, will no longer be occupied by him, but by Dr. Halstead, who is at this particular point in time returning from sabbatical. Office number 281, which was Dr. Taylor's office prior to taking sabbatical leave and which has been during that period of time occupied by Professor Skeffington in Dr. Taylor's absence will continue to be Professor Skeffington's office. A new office allocation for Dr. Lyon will not be necessary since he is leaving Livingstone University English Department at the end of inter-session.'

It simply couldn't be true! He read the memo again, his incredulity still vivid, though gut shock was contradicting it now. He drew in several breaths, but even with the fourth he couldn't quite touch bottom. He sat back in his chair. So! Now that office number 281 had at this particular point in time returned from sabbatical leave, Dr. Lyon would no longer be in the English Department he had founded at Livingstone University twenty years ago. Three weeks from now, end of inter-session, clear out, old man! Bugger off!

How he had looked forward to the emeritus years, when he would be free from teaching responsibilities. There would be more time with Sarah, and he could totally commit himself to the Mark Twain biography, a project just as important to her as it was to him. Maybe even more to her. He'd have given anything to have accomplished it before she died. How lovely it would have been to have shared and celebrated it with her. The Mumm's champagne bottle still lay on its side in the back of the cold-room shelf, where she had put it, waiting to be popped only when the advance copies from the publishers arrived in their hands. They would toast and celebrate the book together.

Five years ago Sarah had stopped waiting.

All his scholarly life he had been so lucky, a flake of insight here, a flake there. After retirement Sarah had been sure that even more would fall, and she had assured him that his winter years were going to be warm and sunlit with discovery, that all the storms would be creative ones. They had been, until her death five years ago.

He could never have made it through the next few years if he hadn't been able to get out to the university and away from a house reminding him of his loss every time he turned around. At first, he had thought he could escape the pain and loneliness by immersing himself in the biography, which had meant so much to her, but in fact it had turned out quite the opposite, bringing her back with more pain.

He had finally got rolling again. There were still blocks more often than not, but at least he was trying with some consistency, going to his office to work every day. Last year the momentum had been damn fine, and he had felt that with luck another year or year and a half would get him close to completion.

That was a shattered hope now that Tait had pulled the Livingstone rug out from under him. God only knew when that champagne bottle would be opened. If ever.

The memory ache for Sarah, for their little Susan, for his brother Henry, and the faster-growing number of friends who had reached the finish line ahead of him, would never leave him. Now it was going to be even lonelier here in the twilight. But it could have been a damn sight worse in the company of ghosts and demons, gods and angels, heroes and villains of both sexes. Long ago he had decided for himself that myth and religion, parliament and congress wouldn't do any more, belonged only to religious and political demagogues and their brain-dead victims. He had not wasted much of his diminishing time on them. Nearly bedtime now. Storytelling's over.

One good thing about reaching seventy-seven next February eleventh, if he did reach it, age had smartened him up some, more than it had Sam Clemens, whom he had already beaten by two years. Despair was lurking no more and no nearer than it had in childhood or adolescence or middle age. Couldn't say the same for Sam, with his dark and lonely last years.

He did think of death more often, now that the mortal promise made at his birth was so much closer to being kept. The new perspective did sadden him a little, but the simple and proper response was: so what?

Goddam Tait!

———

He stood in the doorway and looked out over the cartons the movers had just carried up into the office. There was hardly any clear space left on the floor between the couch, the library table, the desk and the bookcase wall. He'd have to crawl over a jam of cardboard boxes to get to the other shore!

The expected discomfort and confusion of getting all his stuff from the Livingstone University office to this one had turned out to be no superhuman task after all. Bev had found him the cartons; she had helped him pack them and label them with a stencil pencil; she had arranged for the moving truck to come, for the driver and his helper to dolly them down the English Department hall to the freight elevator and then onto the truck and across town. They had worked swiftly and efficiently at both ends.

Now, after twenty years, he was, in rude fact, separated from Livingstone University. From any university. And was it only the mothers who suffered post-partum depression? Couldn't it also visit the infants after birth had been accomplished?

He was going to miss coming down the hall from the elevator, rounding the corner to see the English Department office door always open and Bev framed there at her desk to look up and smile and wave to him as he went on to pick up his mail and then to his own office. He was going to miss the stir and nudge of university life all around him. Breaks from work would not be true breaks if he could not drop in on a colleague and waste some time for him in conversation. He was going to miss sandwich and tea for lunch at SUB with Alistair or Colin or Ed or Herbie or Charlotte. He'd miss having a drink at the end of the day with them in Sarah McNair, sitting by the glass window and looking out onto the close where junior fellows played croquet in spring and fall and summer.

Six-twenty. About this time he'd be in the Faculty Lounge having dinner with someone. Now? Eggs and toast in the kitchen alone. Forget these cartons for today; get to them first thing in the morning. After supper there might be something in the conservatory to be repotted or pruned or sprayed or planted. Maybe some snooker in the basement. Hell no! Solo pool or solo life wasn't worth a good goddam!

That's right, Lyon, you keep right on feeling sorry for yourself. Isn't as though this is the first time you've had this happen to you. It's called dump shock. The old Henry trick, behind the cottage at the lake. Remember how he could creep up on you, without a broken twig to crackle and warn, with more stealth than even a James Fenimore Cooper Indian could manage? This time it isn't a younger brother sneaking through warm and humming August beneath the birch tree, but you are still the unsuspecting victim who hung and swung in childhood and who has once more been tipped, this time after drowsing for twenty years in a university hammock.

———

So. Going to be another bad day. He turned off the hum of the typewriter, sat back in his chair, and stared at the fan-tailed, pop-eyed goldfish swimming follow-the-leader round the scarlet and silver thermos. Dear Chao Lien had brought it to him all the way from Beijing; how could a visa student have known that the professor had been owed a tea debt since birth? Slender and lovely and peasant mother of two; how she must have missed her children during that year.

Behave, Lyon; well over a month now since you left Livingstone, and next to nothing done on the Mark Twain biography. You can't drift like this forever. Just look at those sheets eddied on three sides of your typewriter, and the archipelagos over there on the table. You haven't found a trustworthy map for him yet, just a time chart. Research has given you that. So what? Any hard-working idiot can find lineal sequence, but by itself chronological structure is not enough. Not nearly.

What about the life weather of this literary Columbus? Find some sort of Beaufort scale to measure the calms and storms he lived through; those periods more intense with accomplishment or failure, with grief or delight. How does that seagoing, Amsterdam boomer of a metaphor strike you? A little on the fancy side, you reckon? Not mixed, but a touch laboured? Dead on, all the same? Always remember that restraint is my best writing weapon, and keep my eye peeled for smart-ass self-indulgence, you say? The way you always did.

No, I wasn't snickering, Sam. Honest.

Let's take another run at it. How about your childhood years, November 30, 1835, until you become a printer's apprentice at fourteen. Your first four years are in Florida, Missouri, at the forks of Salt Creek. Then the family moves to Hannibal, right on the Mississippi. These early years are your litmus years, isolated in the centre of North America. Same goes for you too, Lyon. Sure, three-quarters of a century separate the two of you, but seventy-odd years is just about the historical difference in frontier time between the Canadian foothills of your boyhood and the Mississippi Valley of his.

You and young Clemens smelled and tasted and touched and saw and heard a similar New World before man could badly scar your patch of the earth's skin. Both of you obeyed and disobeyed the same Lockean schoolmasters, were slate children upon whom adults could write whatever they pleased. In church and Sunday school you listened to Calvin's voice dipping to hell and soaring clear to heaven. You heard Tom Sawyer's voice too: again and again in the school yard, on the prairie when you drowned out gophers, flew kites, lit candles in caves, made the white moon rise in Daisy Creek, marvelled at spiders, and respected privy wasps. Both of you saw what today's child has seldom seen: the rust tracks of chewing tobacco from the corners of male mouths, and sparrows dining on road apples. Cutthroat trout equals catfish; saskatoons equal huckleberries; the smell of wolf willow that of wild grape; jack rabbit and coyote, coon and 'possum. . . .

'Hold on a minute, Lyon! Whose biography is this anyway?'

'Mark Twain's.'

'You seem to have forgotten. Inside every biographer there's an autobiographer struggling to get out. Not quite so troublesome as that bad novelist you've got inside you, but keep your eye peeled all the same. Constantly.'

'Who the hell are you?'

'Your literary conscience.'

'Go bug Sam, wherever he is, while I have a cup of tea.'

'You've just had one, Lyon. Forget the old cup-of-tea-delay trick. As it is – by Greenwich Sphincter Time, there will come a bathroom interruption in about one hour and seven minutes –'

'So what?'

'So – you drink one more cup of tea now and it will happen in half an hour and two minutes, to be followed seventeen minutes later by another trip down the hall to the toilet to decant the second cup of tea.'

'Have a cigar.'

'Ricardo's Urination Law of Increasing Returns.'

'I said have a cigar.'

'Oh, I'm wise to that old cigar trick too. I have one, so will you, and you promised yourself and Dr. Gallstone you'd limit yourself to three. Remember? One at breakfast – one at noon – one after supper in the billiard –'

'Bugger off!'

'With no inhaling, and you also made a promise to clean up your foul –'

'I intend to –'

'– a promise you have not even tried to keep. You have – in the past month – achieved a new high, even for you, in both obscenity and blasphemy.'

'I got my ass kicked out of the goddam University by a son-of-a-bitch –'

Wasn't that just great! One thing to carry on internal

conversations with yourself, but not out loud! And in more than one voice, for Christ's sake! Hadn't done that since he'd been yanked out of school for a year because of the TB wrist. He'd come around full circle: lonely child ends up lonely old man.

You know what I'm talking about, don't you, Sam? Sad insight for both of us. "Age has left only limited oxygen supply, so the interior life flame grows weaker and weaker, the need for exterior warmth stronger and stronger. When the candle gutters low, power and fame and wealth can kindle no longer, only outer love can warm."

So. What to do about it, Lyon? How about getting somebody to move in here with you? Perhaps a visa student in need of help, one as lovely as Chao Lien.

Shouldn't have looked up 'emeritus' in *The Shorter Oxford Dictionary* first thing this morning: 'honourably discharged from service.' Short and bitter. And Tait had not discharged him honourably at all! By memo copy, and without warning. No longer welcome in the Livingstone community. Bad mistake, going to the *Webster's Third International Dictionary* and finding 'emerita: a genus of anamouran decapod crustaceans (sub-order Repantia) widely distributed along sandy shores of both coasts of No. America and the Western coast of S. America – see BAIT BUG.'

Must be something you can do about it. How about a housekeeper so you won't be robbing time from the biography? Someone besides yourself and Sam to talk to. Maybe shoot a game of snooker with. Might help heal the exile wounds so you can get back to work and regain momentum, make it in here every morning, every week, every month, every year, however many of those you may have left. On the dot of nine, after breakfast, you can fill this silver and scarlet furnace and carry it up here and sit down. . . .

Furnace! You are in great shape! Not so bad that spoken words come out crippled now and again, but *thinking* them is another matter! Silver and scarlet *thermos*, you silly old bastard! Right now – you write out an ad!

He rolled a new sheet into the typewriter. After three drafts, he felt he had one he might use.

WANTED: ONE HUMAN

By slightly vulgar, occasionally foul-mouthed, literate, impatient and self-centred, senior citizen male, desiring good companion. Drinking and smoking, non-laconic agnostic preferred, but will consider pool-playing practising Druid with green thumb if necessary. Unmistakably female and skilled at back and neck rubs. Room and board and $500.00 a month for light housekeeping duties.

Now – what sort of person in her right mind would answer an ad like that? Well, it did signal clearly what she might be letting herself in for, and it could interest a woman who was curious, who appreciated candour. Or was desperate.

Maybe he ought to tone it down. Better idea: phone it in just as it is and see how the classified woman responds to it.

He dictated the ad slowly and distinctly and when he had finished, she said, 'I'll read it back to you.'

'Please.'

'WANTED: ONE HUMAN BY slightly vulvar –'

'Slightly – *vulgar*.'

' "Slightly vulgar –" '

' "Vulvar" is vulgar,' he explained.

'I thought it might be. "Slightly vulgar –" '

'Comma.'

' "Comma occasionally foul mouthed –" '

'Hyphen.'

' "Occasionally foul mouthed hyphen –" '

' "Occasionally foul hyphen mouthed." '

'Got it,' she said. 'Comma literate comma impatient and self hyphen centred comma senior no hyphen citizen male comma desiring good companion period Drinking and smoking. . .'

She had stopped.

'Go on.'

' "Non-ionic agnostic?" '

' "Non hyphen *laconic* agnostic." '

'English is my only language.' He heard her sigh. 'You some kind of professor?'

'Yes.'

'Well, I think we're going to make it all right from here on in, Professor.'

She was right, had even spelled Druid with a capital 'D.'

How long did he want it to run? Would he like to take advantage of the extra two days given by their weekly rate?

Let it run for a full week.

Did he want his telephone number listed or did he want a box number for replies?

Box number.

It was too late to make the Saturday edition but would be in on Monday. They'd bill him.

'Which section?' she asked.

'Pardon?'

'Help Wanted?'

'What else?'

'You do say good companion – pool-playing – unmistakably female,' she said.

'So?'

'Smells a lot like Personals to me.'

17

'What do you suggest?'

'Up to you.'

'Would you answer an ad like this one?'

'Twenty-five years ago I might have. Before I married a foul-mouthed, snooker-shooting alcoholic who desired lots of good companions skilled at neck and back rubs. Female. Have a nice day, Professor.'

———

It had happened again. In his usual daze on waking, he had showered, shaved, and dressed, and was halfway down the stairs before he realized he wouldn't be going out to the university this morning. Or any other morning. He added water and stirred up the Prairie Maid cereal left over from yesterday, put it on a front burner. He filled the kettle for the day's tea.

It took him a while to find the paper in the dwarf juniper at the end of the planter under the living-room window. When he got back to the kitchen, the kettle was whistling. He poured it into the teapot, dished out his porridge, opened the paper to the Classified section.

He had never, ever read the Personal columns. He should have.

'SIXTYISH BALL-OF-FIRE finds middle age the greatest adventure of them all! If you are a male whose flame just burns brighter with the years, let's set the world on fire together.'

Next.

'SLIM, HANDSOME, VIRILE, SENSUAL, SIX-FOOT WASP, 41, foot fetishist with divergent interests, seeks highly attractive female desirous of wining, candlelight dining, tennis, delightful erotic role play and mutual fantasy fulfilment.'

Oh, shit!

'TEACH ME JOYCE AND DOSTOEVSKI, share tennis, theatre, music, laughter on weekends.'

And this one right on top of him: 'GAY ORIENTOPHILE, tall, fair, bearded and professional seeks Asian man for relationship. Interests must include travel, tennis et les arts.'

Up Yours!

Under him lay: 'DIVORCED MALE PH.D. Red-haired and bearded with considerable success in eclectic areas of the fine arts and sex. Has had herpes, seeks attractive, tennis-playing woman with vibrant imagination, tall, spunky and Rubensesque.'

He did not belong in this exotic, tennis-playing and candlelit crowd; he'd have to get them to shift him over into HELP WANTED.

Even though they promised they would do that, they gave him three more Personal insertions. The gay orientophile was replaced by 'sensual blond, 38, seeks integrity, spirit and mad romance.' 'Walking encyclopedia with heart and witty as hell' took over from the PH.D. who'd had herpes.

They were sad, really, all these lonely people day-dreaming perfect companions for fictional selves, but was he all that different? Maybe he did belong in PERSONALS with them. The next to last day he had made it into HELP WANTED.

There were seventeen replies.

'In answer to your ad, you sound like an exceptional man ready to share with an exceptional woman who is happy, fun to be with, gourmet cook, lover of fine wines, the ballet, travel and tennis. I'm young, vibrant and sixtyish and ready to share with an unthreatened man, who yearns for hugs, laughter and tender attachment.'

No!

'My friends describe me as a handsome woman with sensitive face, deep feelings and soaring spirit, energetic body, intense vision . . .'

Next.

'. . . lover of dancing, French language, travel, hiking, chamber music, tennis, who also savours quieter, home-based pleasures . . .'

'. . . widow, 73. Attractive and elegant and in excellent physical condition. I don't play pool, but I am eager to learn how . . .'

'I am replying to your ad for someone to do light housekeeping duties in return for room and board and $500.00 a month. I smoke and I drink. I have no idea whether I have a green or grey thumb, but I can play stripes and solids, billiards, pea pool, snooker. My father said I was the best back and neck rubber going. I am occasionally foul-mouthed. I am an actress, but don't let that bother you. It is the reason that I have to apply to your ad. My phone number is: 287-1192. Ask for Nadya.'

Well, now. Placing the want ad had not been such a bad idea after all. A snooker-shooting, foul-mouthed actress! Exactly what he'd been looking for!

———

'Nadya?'

'Debbie. Nadya isn't in.'

'When do you expect her?'

There was a very long pause. 'Who is calling, please?'

'She answered an ad of mine.'

'Oh!' It was an exclamation of recognition. Also of relief.

'She'll be about an hour. I'm on the phone! Kimberly! Can I take a message for her?'

'Have her call me. My phone number is 253 –'

'Shut up, Kimberly!'

In the background Kimberly shut up.

'Sorry. My daughter. Your phone number?'

'253-7346. My address is 4931 Livingstone Road. That's South West. She can phone me, or if she wants to she can drop by for an interview. My name is Lyon – Kenneth Lyon. I'll be in all day – and this evening.'

'I'll tell her as soon as they – she gets back, Mr. Lyon.'

It took him until lunch time to tidy the place up. At two o'clock he heard the front-door chimes.

She had dressed for the occasion. The cape coat that flared from her shoulders to her ankles was red. Her dark eyes looked up at him from under the brim of a shallow scarlet derby. Her purse, her shoes were red. His front-door step had just grown one small, formal red poppy.

As soon as she was seated on the couch under the living-room window, she opened her purse and got out a cigarette package.

'All right with you if I . . . ?'

'Of course.'

He watched her light up. She gestured to the cigarette package on the coffee table.

'Just cigars,' he said. 'You – ah – you'd – you're interested in – working for me?'

'Yes, I am.'

'You act.'

'Yes, I do,' she said.

'Full time?'

'Not as full as I'd like to. Whenever I get calls. I do three mornings a week at the Peter Pan Kiddy Garten, part-time work at the Sock and Buskin, props, promotion, box office. I'm Equity. I've done a few commercials. I still get residuals from a coffee thing I did two years ago. And I was the waitress in a series of network beer ads, serving all those guys with perfect teeth and broad shoulders and flat stomachs, who never belched or – and who'd just been surfboarding or building a log cabin or playing slow-pitch. What do you do for a living?'

'English professor. Was. Do you play tennis?'

'Is it a prerequisite for the job?'

'No,' he said.

'Do you?'

'No.'

'Why d'you ask, then?'

'Just trying to come to a conclusion,' he said. 'Can you cook?'

'To beat hell.'

'That answers my next question.'

'Which is?'

'Whether or not you're foul-mouthed.'

'I said I was, for Christ's sake!'

'Ah – blasphemous as well.'

'Okay.' She leaned back in the couch. 'I answered your ad for a housekeeper. You suggested this interview. I am a good cook. I can dust, vacuum, wax floors, wash dishes, carry out garbage, shoot pool.'

'I believe you. It's just that I don't want to get stuck with someone who has herpes and a vibrant personality or is a foot fetishist with divergent interests –'

'God damn it, Doctor – what is this? You may not be – but I am playing for keeps. I need the job!'

'Sit down. Sit down, Nadya.'

She sat, leaned forward to pick up the cigarette package on the coffee table.

'Now you have a slight idea of what you might be letting

yourself in for,' he said. 'How about telling me more about yourself?'

To begin with, she said, she had been an army brat, her father a paratroop officer in the NATO forces so that she had been born in Lahr, West Germany, and had grown up in Cyprus, Orimocto, New Brunswick, Rome, and Ottawa. As she relaxed, it became evident that she was well qualified in regard to another of his ad's requirements. She was not laconic. She had a BFA in drama with a minor in English.

'I'm quite a mix. Scottish and Lunenburg Deutsch on my father's side, Danish and Ukrainian on my mother's.'

'Unusual recipe.'

'Yeah. Ukrainian's the great spice.'

If he hadn't known it before the interview, he certainly did now as he looked at her on his living-room couch: he was still an eye man. Out on the front porch his first response had been to those lovely dark eyes, so large in such a delicate face with high and articulate cheek bones. It was a face that could be quite ordinary one moment, surprisingly beautiful the next.

Sarah's had been like that.

Probably this interview was heightening that chameleon quality. She'd meant it when she said she really needed the job. A week ago she'd given up her own apartment and moved in with a friend named Debbie, who lived in the same building. She did not say why this had happened, but as she told him he noticed a cloud come over her face. Strapped for money? Fallen behind in her rent? Evicted? More to it than this. Something was missing. He guessed she was holding something back, something she did not care to share with him. For now.

Debbie had given her a ride to the interview, she said, was over in the park with her little girl, Kimberly, and would be picking her up in an hour or so. Again, he sensed inner ten-sion. He had a feeling that she usually had a much easier way with people than this. He recalled that when he'd phoned and Debbie had answered, there had been unusual caution in her voice too, until he'd identified himself.

Whatever the answer might be, he'd made up his mind. She needed him: he sure as hell needed her. It would be nice to have her move in with him, if only to watch the Sarah candles light up within her.

The front-door chime went up and down its brief scale, startling Nadya to her feet. 'That'll be Debbie now!'

He got up. 'Okay, Nadya. You've got it. Move in any time.'

One thing he knew about her acting: she could sure as hell project emotion to the last row in the house.

Debbie was wearing a kerchief over all the curlers in her hair. Debbie was dark and Debbie was large. Slacks had not been intended for women like Debbie, or her daughter, Kimberly, when she grew up. Somehow he felt that Debbie could read palms or tarot cards or tea leaves. He guessed her to be, for one reason or another, a single mother, who had her hands quite full with Kimberly. Yes, she promised Kimberly, they would come back again to play on the rings and the monkey bars and the teeter-totter and the merry-go-round you pushed, but not today. Not right now. Maybe tomorrow. No. Not right now. Or this afternoon. Perhaps when they brought Nadya to move in with the Professor. Tomorrow possibly. Depended if that was when they brought Nadya to move in. Yes, she could go back to the park then.

He stayed behind on the step as they went down the walk, watched as they got into Debbie's car parked across the street, Kimberly in the front with her mother, Nadya in the back. Just as he turned to go into the house, he caught a glimpse of a face in the back seat window. Not Nadya's. It was a child's face.

But Kimberly was in the *front* seat of the car!

No mention had been made by anybody that they'd brought along a little friend to play with Kimberly in the park. Unless Debbie had *two* children, he smelled conspiracy. Didn't this mysterious child explain Nadya's flashes of anxiety during the interview? Of course it did.

Well now.

He had promised himself he'd get a few hours in on the biography today, but the interview and the child's face in the car window had put him off stride. No doubt about it. She had a child up her sleeve, hadn't levelled with him, probably because she didn't want to handicap herself in getting the job. Question: did he want her – and a child as well – to move in with him? Have to think about that. How old? Boy or girl? Whatever sex, certainly have to be an improvement on Debbie's little Kimberly.

Damn it all! He wished she'd told him during the interview. Or when Debbie and Kimberly came to pick her up. Should he wait until she showed tomorrow? No. Phone her this evening and . . . No. At least see the child first. Sleep on it, Lyon. Sleep on it.

Easier said than done because, as usual, sleep was reluctant. Each year drawn curtains depressed him more and more. Fall had become simply winter's shadow for him now, and made him wince against the shrinking days and growing nights to come. Age needed light. Just walk down any town or city street and count the incandescent houses with their windows blazing all night long: senior citizens' homes. Soon enough the final lightless time would come for return to earth and darkness.

Snicking on the memory light helped some. First sight of Nadya's changing face, those large almond eyes, had reminded him of Sarah's. The child in the car window had summoned Susan's, too, and the loss ache that could never be erased. To the end it must have stayed with Sarah, too; till his own death he would ask himself the same old questions for which there could be no answers, for which he did not want the answers.

———

It had happened almost forty years ago, during his tenure at New York State in Buffalo. He had been thirty-eight, Sarah thirty-two, Susan three. For six weeks, from the middle of July to the end of August, he would teach creative writing at the Fine Arts Centre in the Canadian Rockies. It would also be little Susan's introduction to flying squirrels, and chipmunks, and marmots that whistled, to camp robbers and chickadees that would eat out of her hand, to antlered deer and elk with their does and fawns, mountain sheep and their little lambs, and black, brown, grizzled, or cinnamon bears, that would rattle the garbage cans at night. There would be all the would-be artists too, who could play golf and tennis, swim, fish and hike and ride, at the same time salving their consciences by taking up dance, painting, sculpting, writing, weaving, pot-throwing, drama, or music. Including mime, glass-blowing, and mastery of the bagpipe chanter, not an art or a craft had been overlooked. For everyone, animal or human, it would be a picnic summer in mountain wilderness.

The first three weeks had been.

Susan had loved the place at first sight and smell, the menthol of pine, the snow-capped mountains, all the promised wild friends great and small.

She had been unwilling to leave her red trike in Buffalo; they had brought it with them in the back of the car. They had been wrong in assuming she would pedal it only inside their A-frame chalet or on the broad deck out in front. She quickly mastered the gravel parking areas, and even conquered winding dirt paths bumpy with roots and rocks. No slope up or down was too great a challenge for her. She preferred to ride naked, leaving clothing spoor behind her, sandals, socks, shorts and skirts and shirts for Sarah to retrieve.

They had finally managed compromise, but it had not been easy. From Costumes, Sarah had got a beaded headband and fixed in it a raven feather, and had done a lipstick war-paint job round Susan's bellybutton. Mounted on her trike, she made a striking little aboriginal Lady Godiva, who promised her mother she would not shuck her britch-clout.

Almost as soon as she had begun to talk, Susan had picked up the habit of echoing the last three or four words spoken to her. Now she discovered that her very own voice would always come back to her, bounding off the side of a peak called Devil's Thumb, across the narrow lake like an aquamarine fragment of cloisonné at its foot. Just as devout and relentless as Music's baritones and altos, tenors, sopranos and coloraturas doing their scales and arias from the crack of dawn till sunset, Susan practised voice-bouncing daily. Students, staff, and instructors called her Little Miss Echo.

He told Sarah that he foresaw two wonderful futures possible for their child. She could grow up to be either the world's greatest diva or its leading lady bulldozer driver. If she were to develop both her evident talents and found the right composer and librettist, their gifted daughter might star in La Scala's first opera celebrating the joy and anguish of an orphaned gipsy girl, who operated a heavy-duty backhoe. Sarah preferred the New York Met and something more in the line of *Rose Marie*. Sarah meant it.

The first three weeks had been sunlit and wonderful.

Between classes and tutorials, he had plenty of time to spend with Sarah and Susan, or, quite often, just with Sarah while a young Helen Hayes or Keats or Monet baby-sat for them. There had been lots of holding hands and canoeing and beer, and at the end of the third week Sarah's sister Kathleen came up from Portland to spend a few days with them. On her arrival, the two sisters celebrated their reunion by going to the Château Trois Soeurs for a posh dinner and reminiscence, leaving Susan in his care while he caught up with manuscript reading.

That was the night it happened.

That afternoon he had told the blonde poetess he didn't care to go skinny-dipping with her, that he was flattered by her invitation, but had no intention of being disloyal to Sarah. To be honest about it, he did have other reasons for refusing: she couldn't write worth a damn; she was fat; and the lake was fed by glacial run-off.

After three stories, two trips to the bathroom, another glass of milk, and another hug Susan had finally gone to sleep. He had caught up with his manuscript reading and just started on notes for tomorrow's seminar, when the knock came on the chalet door.

It was the skinny-dipper.

She had just come by to drop off some poetry for him to read. He stepped outside and closed the door behind him, explaining that he did not want to wake Susan up. Also, she said, she wanted to talk to him about this terrific idea she had for a poem about a woman in the third term of her pregnancy, who kept having dreams about an albino hippopotamus . . .

Not tonight; he had to prepare seminar notes; she ought to bring it to class tomorrow so she could, ah, benefit from the response of others as well as himself. She pressed her sheaf of poetry on him and left. He stayed out on the deck for a cigar, which lasted until the car lights told him Sarah and her sister had come back.

So much for any strange flesh interlude this summer. In or out of the water.

Already high on Château Trois Soeurs wine and after-dinner brandy and reunion anecdotes, Sarah and Kathleen kept right on remembering childhood and adolescence over nightcaps. Their conversation was subdued, their laughter quelled, so as not to waken Susan.

Sarah got up, went into the bedroom, came out, went into the bathroom, came back into the living room. Susan was not in her cot nor was she in the bathroom. Little Miss Echo was nowhere in the chalet!

———

He was upstairs in the office with Mark Twain the next morning when the phone rang.

'There's something I have to tell you, Doctor. I should have yesterday. I'm sorry –'

'You mean about your child.'

'Oh. . . . You know.'

'I guessed it – as you drove away.'

'I'm sorry, Doctor. That's why I've phoned. I didn't play square with you. So . . .'

He waited for her to go on. 'So?'

'Aah – if you want to call it off –'

'Is it a boy or a girl?' he asked.

'She's a girl. Rosemary. She's five.'

'All right. Now you've told me, I'd still like you to come –'

'You don't have to –'

'Of course I don't, but I want you to. I would also like you to bring Rosemary with you.'

'Oh, Doctor –'
'Any time today.'

———

Just as he finished the lunch dishes, the chimes sounded. He opened the door to find that this time his front step had grown one scarlet poppy and one small buttercup. The little girl was a ringer for her mother with the same delicate yet strong face, same large eyes, black hair. One look and all doubt was gone; he knew – oh God, how he knew – that Nadya and Rosemary must move in with him.

As soon as they were seated in the living room, Nadya apologized again for not telling him about Rosemary right from the start.

'Let's not worry about that any more,' he said. 'I've had all night to think about it and now I've met Rosemary I've made up my mind. It will be very nice to have a little girl . . .' He stopped himself before he would say '. . . again.'

It was obvious that Rosemary was not going to make her mind up about him as quickly. Her arm and her cheek seemed welded to Nadya's waist. She spoke just to answer a direct question and then only if she had looked up to her mother. Yet her eyes were never still as he showed them the house upstairs and down, especially when he told her that this room would be her very own. She wasn't missing a single thing, and in the solarium, where she left her mother's side for the first time, she went to smell the scarlet hibiscus flowers, to touch the yellow globes of the Persian lime, and to be enchanted by the Bird of Paradise and the purple Portia orchid.

They ended up in his office with its bookcase wall and the sliding glass that allowed him to look down upon Jamaica in the solarium below. Rosemary was fascinated with the Greek comic and tragic masks over the couch.

'I spend most of my day in here with Mark Twain,' he said. Then as Nadya looked startled, 'I'm writing his biography. Trying to. I spend a lot of time in the billiard room in the basement, too. Probably more than I should. You want to see the billiard room, Rosemary?'

'Sure.'

'You shoot pool?'

'Mom does.'

'Want me to teach you how?'

'Sure.'

'Okay. You drink tea?'

'If you put a lot of sugar and a lot of milk in it,' she said.

'Great. Just happens I'm an unrepentant tea drinker. I always keep cups and a loaded thermos in here, so how about we have a tea party? You and I and your mother.'

'Sure.'

'And if it's all right with you I'll have a cigar. Not you, though – you don't –'

'Mom does.'

'I know.'

'Cigarettes.'

'And a cigar sometimes,' Rosemary said.

He looked at Nadya. She grinned sheepishly and nodded.

'Hey! That's great. Something else you've been holding back on me.'

She nodded again.

When they had finished their tea, he went to the bookshelf, found what he wanted, and came back to the couch. 'You familiar with the Russian writers at all?'

'Ukrainians aren't the same as Russians at all,' Rosemary said.

'I've made sure Rosemary knows the great difference,'

Nadya explained. 'Yes. In spite of their being Russian, I have read some. In a short-story course I took at university, we hit a few of them. In drama we really got to know Chekhov. Matter of fact I played the lead in his play, *The Cherry Orchard*.'

He looked up from finding his place in the anthology. 'Tolstoy?'

'*War and Peace*.'

'Ever come on a folk tale of his, "The Three Hermits"?'

'No,' Nadya said.

'Is it like "The Three Little Pigs"?'

'Not exactly, Rosemary. They're three fellows who live all alone on an island. There isn't a big bad wolf but there's a bishop.'

'Is he a bad guy?'

'Not really. The bishop, while he's on board a ship passing the island, hears about the three hermits who live there and he has the captain stop the boat so he can bless them. One of them is very old –'

'Like you?'

'Rosemary!' her mother chided.

'Damn near,' he said. 'One of them has a beard clear down to his ankles –'

'So he trips on it all the time.'

'Look – whose story is this – yours or mine?'

'Tolstoy's,' Nadya said.

'You guys want to hear this story or not?'

'I do,' Rosemary said.

'Me too,' Nadya said.

'All right then. The third hermit's beard has bird-nested round and round his mouth so he has difficulty getting people to understand just what he's saying. Ah! Here we are!'

"But how do you pray to God?" asked the Bishop.

"We pray in this way," replied the hermit. "Three are ye, three are we, have mercy upon us."

And when the old man said this, all three raised their eyes to Heaven and repeated:

"Three are ye, three are we, have mercy upon us!"

The Bishop smiled.

He closed the book.

'Is that all of it?' Rosemary asked.

'No. The bishop explains to the three hermits that this is not the proper way at all to save their souls, so he teaches them the Lord's Prayer. With difficulty. They aren't very bright. When he thinks they've got it down right he leaves them, but before the ship gets under way he sees something coming out from the island. It's too small to be a whale, too big for a small boat, then he sees it's the three hermits running across the water.

'They stop out there and look up to the bishop and tell him they're awfully sorry, but after he left them the Lord's Prayer fell apart on them and would he please teach it to them again so they can save their souls. He stares at them standing out there on the water and says, "Carry on, boys, you're doing just great without the Lord's Prayer I tried to teach you." '

'What a great story,' Nadya said.

'Will you tell me lots of stories when we come to live with you?'

'Yes,' he promised.

'Better than that one?'

'I'll try. Nadya, what I wanted to let you know was how much it means to this old hermit to have you and Rosemary move in with him.'

'You made your point, Doctor.'

'Three are ye – three are we –'
'– have mercy upon us,' she finished up for him.
'Can we go see the billboard room now?'
'Sure, Rosemary,' he said.
'And another chocolate chip cookie?'
'That too, dear.'

———

After supper he shot a round of pool. Even though he was on tonight, he put the balls in the basket and hung up his cue early. No more one-man snooker or billiards now, not after they'd moved in tomorrow afternoon. For the first time since he'd left the university he felt a stir of eagerness to get up to the office and onto that typewriter. Wait up for me, Sam.

Been quite a while since I checked in to see how you're making out. Forgive me; I know you will; you've always been such a forgiving fellow. Mind if I trespass on your private correspondence again? Here we are: 'London, January 25, 1900.' That makes it Boer War time. It's Dear Howells again and you're wondering 'Why was the human race created? Or at least why wasn't something creditable created in place of it.' Oops! Missed a question mark there, Sam.

Let's see now. If it's 1900 you've just turned sixty-five and that's a bad one all right. Seventy's worse. Believe me, I know what I'm talking about. You point out to Howells that 'God had His opportunity, but no, He must commit this gross folly – a lark which must have cost Him regret when He came to think it over and observe the effects. For a giddy and unbecoming caprice there has been nothing like it till this war.

'It was my intention to make some disparaging remarks about the human race and so I kept this letter open for that purpose, and for the purpose of telling my dream wherein the Trinity were trying to guess a conundrum . . .'

I know just how you feel, Sam. The sadness never leaves you. Look at this earlier letter to Howells, the one you wrote him from Vienna, January 22, 1898. You were in Europe when your Susy died of spinal meningitis. Howells had just lost Winnie. I lost my Susan too. I named her after your daughter, Sam. I do agree with you that a lot of Heavenly tomfoolery does go on. Always has. Always will. Bothered Aristotle. Gave St. Tom and St. Augie great concern as well. I'm not saying for one moment they got the blame and credit right either, but they did make a lot better stab at it than you did in this letter.

Your Susy's birth was not the beginning of a practical joke, her death a dirty trick played on you by that Great Prankster in the Sky. Our own Susan's birth was a marvellously magic act performed for Sarah and me. We did not, as you say here, '– enjoy one long stretch of scented fields and meadows and shady woodlands; and suddenly Sahara.' We were granted just a niggardly three years '. . . of the glorious days of that old time.' No trap was set for Sarah and me when our child was born, '. . . given in miserable sport and then taken away.'

Should have kept your eye peeled, Sam. Long before you were this far downstream you should have discovered the Greeks were right again: Fate has the deal every time and sooner or later she flips out the same old hole card: mortality for all. You can bet your life on that. She made the rules; she doesn't have to deal off the bottom to win. You feel she did that to you and Livy; meningitis, madness, epilepsy were losing cards for your daughters, all right, but death is not exclusively an adult matter. Enough of scapegoats, human or divine.

You too, Lyon.

———

At some time when he had been out on the chalet deck with the poetess or was having his cigar, Susan must have wakened and slipped through the back door. They'd called and they'd called, but just their own voices bounced off the side of Devil's Thumb. He left Sarah and Kathleen to continue the search while he ran over to the Centre to phone the park warden. As he did he noticed that the red trike was still by the side of the deck.

It must have been just before dusk that she had left the chalet, and she was such a devout little traveller sudden mountain night could have caught her a considerable distance away. Had she climbed? Had she slipped and dropped to her death? Had she fallen into the river to be carried through the fury and anguish of the rapids below?

⟨All that long night the forestry and game wardens could find no trace of her. Through drip and drizzle and low, wreathing mist the next morning,⟩ human chains of faculty and staff and students moved out in all directions as the mountain weather mourned. On the second and third day they dragged the river. On the sixth day the sun came out and all caring by others ceased.

The search was abandoned. Rehearsals for *The Devil and Daniel Webster* and *The Happy Journey from Trenton to Camden* took up again; the bunheads went back to their wool-pant warm-ups, grands jetés, pirouettes and entrechats, the singers to their opera, the writers to their fictions. World without end and without Susan.

Kathleen drove back with them to Buffalo. They left the red trike behind. In a best possible script, if there really had been a green station wagon with Colorado licence plates, Susan would be a few years older than Nadya by now, might even have a Rosemary or two. Might even be an opera star today. Or a bulldozer operator. Or both. If it had been a foraging bear, though, or a cougar: a small skeleton hidden in some mountain crease.

Good night, Susan and Rosemary. Good night to you, Sam, and your dear Susy, too.

2

FROM THE FIRST SIGHT ON HIS FRONT STEP HE HAD BEEN right about Nadya. He had never before seen a face that faded and shaded so. Whenever she smiled or frowned it was with no holds barred, and very soon he knew how it was with her: no in-between, either way, up or down. Every time he looked up at the Greek comic and tragic masks over the couch in his office, he thought of her.

Rosemary was a little ringer for her mother; the face that wedged from broad cheeks to fragile chin had the same bone structure and strength as her mother's. She had shed her initial shyness quickly, and he had a pretty good idea now of what her mother must have been like as a child.

When he brought up the striking resemblance, Nadya said, 'Ukrainian. Straight down from old Nadya, my great-grand-mother. She lived to be ninety-four. I was Rosemary's age when she died.'

Nadya hoped the child did not take after her father.

'Her father?'

'A down-under son-of-a-bitch – exchange graduate student majoring in Sociology. He's gone back to a wife he hadn't bothered to mention and whom he'd forgotten to divorce in Australia. I hope the Ukrainian blood that came down to me through the female line is strong in Rosemary.'

'Maybe it is,' he said.

'My great-grandfather came over a couple of years before my great-grandmother to homestead, and then she came with their two children – boy and a girl. All the way from Kiev, to London, to New York, to Toronto, then out west without being able to understand or speak a word of English. If I have any weapons, I got them from my great-grandma Nadya. I'm glad I have her name. Also her ham genes.'

'Rosemary may have them too.'

'I hope so. My grandma told me once, they didn't have the money for horses and she and the other women wore the harness and *they* pulled the plough, till they could afford a team. They built their home out of cottonwood logs, and found this stuff in the bottom of a slough, and then she and the kids tramped it and crushed it with their bare feet to make plaster out of it for the walls and ceiling of the house. I never saw it, but my grandma said it was white as snow inside there. She told me a lot about old Nadya, about how she used to make kutya.'

'What's that?'

'Cakes – like biscuits – Christmas-time or maybe it was Easter. When she'd mixed the batter with honey and crushed poppy seed and walnuts – I think there was wheat in there, too – and it was the consistency of thick porridge she'd take the ladle and bring it up and back and take aim and fire it up at the ceiling.'

'What for?'

'If it stuck up there then it meant they were in for a lucky year. If it dropped off – look out for drought, or hail, or smut, or sawfly, or grasshoppers, or rust.'

Very early after they'd moved in with him, he could tell that their life together was not going to be dull.

———

They had choreographed their days. Nadya would be up first to prepare breakfast; after the dishes she would take Rosemary to the Peter Pan Kiddy Garten seven blocks away. She worked with the children there three mornings a week, and when she had finished with mime and finger painting and games and story telling, she would catch the LRT across town to the Sock and Buskin. After breakfast he would go upstairs to the office to check in with Mark Twain. At three in the afternoon he would pick up Rosemary at Peter Pan, and more often than not, while the indian-summer days lasted, he would take her over to the park.

The evening ritual had soon become established: Nadya would cook a fine supper, which would be followed by Rosemary's bath, followed by tucking her in and a story. Then to the basement for a game or two or three of snooker or golf or fluke. She'd said in her answer to his ad in the Personal Column that she was good. She wasn't bad, and she'd refused to let him spot her, which was all right with him. He managed to break her habit of grabbing her cue too tightly and too far back, got her to lower her head more so that she would sight, not from above at a distorting angle, but through her hand bridge to the cue tip to the target ball. He wondered if Sam had taught Susan or Jeanie or Clara the art. Not their mother, Livy, certainly. Nor, on second thought, his daughters.

His own foul mouth was at its best over the pool table, but Nadya could mark up one hell of a lot of scatological points herself, especially if she missed a sure black ball. He was not about to teach her to look more carefully beyond her immediate shot to later possible Gestalt. Any more than Sam would have.

So many times, when he came downstairs to shoot a game, he would remember his Manitoba undergraduate years and Dr. Lodge, piloting classes and seminars through human thought from Thales on, with side trips into billiards or sailing. Probably had a good hand on both the tiller and the cue. What a witty Platonist he had been, could teach almost as well as Socrates. Up there leaning on the corner of the lectern in Theatre B, gowned and long and thin and stooped, with those thick-lensed glasses, he was an academic stork. Or Aldous Huxley, with one elbow up on the mantelpiece. He reminded them many times that they were not meeting simply to play an entertaining game; they must commit themselves to being good Greeks for the rest of their lives. As he racked up the balls or waited his turn, he had often made silent upward apology for turning out existentialist, which Lodge, if he were listening, would consider a euphemism for pragmatist. In his book on Socrates, he'd used a frog analogy for philosophers; high-hipped and pop-eyed, the idealist frog kings squatted on land to contemplate green algae patterns and judge that garter snakes were not just or beautiful; deep

in the empirical water the materialists swam through the
submarine world of the many. Hopping and plopping in, then
out, then in again, the amphibian pragmatists couldn't make
up their minds.

'Some say there are three keys,' he once said to them.
'Ideal, Empirical, and a third: Phenomenalist. That last one
won't open anything for you, because contradiction makes it
silly. Take this ideal cue down from this imagined rack. Line
up your shot. Try to strike that ivory ball of matter. It won't
move for you – to kiss or miss, bank off the cushion, drop into
a pocket – and don't blame it on the chalk, for it is blue or
green, and empirical chalk cannot leave powder on the tip of
this imagined cue. You, therefore, have not got three keys
really, just two that will unlock truth. Logically. The choice
is yours.'

He wondered when Mark Twain had first listened to the
crack and click of the balls. He himself could remember the
staccato cluck and chuckle, the dying, pocket spiral whirr all
the way back to early childhood, when Mr. Bean would hoist
him up and onto the board across the arms of the chair, would
fasten the cloth around his neck in the Soo Billiards and
Barber Shop. Even now he could feel himself shiver with cold
recall of those hand clippers, their needle bite at the back of
his neck. In there with perfume of Tiger Balm, the ripe
spittoons, the fall smell of cigar smoke, with his chin down he
had looked up from under his eyelids at the men crouched
over the green baize. God bless Mr. Bean for freeing him
from the asexual Buster Brown haircuts his mother had loved
and he had hated. God bless the Soo Billiards and Barber
Shop.

There was a price tag tied to the comfort of their company. He soon discovered that Nadya had a bad habit of interrupting him long before he'd reached his point. Get there quicker, she said. She also went on at great and repetitious length about unimportant things: cigar ashes and butts, tea stains she had to scrub because he forgot to rinse out his cups, missing the bowl again and leaving the rim up, dirty socks, shirts, and underwear on the floor instead of in the laundry basket, not bothering to wear his rubbers when he went out so that she had to get down on her hands and knees to clean up his goddam mud tracks all over the goddam house she was trying to keep clean for him.

Look who was talking, the long-haired sink and bathtub drain-plugger, couldn't tell one end of a plumber's helper from the other. Then there was her purse; he had come to hate the very sight of it, a bulging saddlebag hanging at her hip. Part of the time. She left it all over the house, on tables, on counters, on couches and on chairs, against his thigh on the car seat and several times – when she was behind the wheel – in his lap. How in hell she ever found a house key, a cigarette package, parking-meter change, or a credit card in there, he'd never know. And another thing, which an actor should never fail to do – she didn't project. She mumbled; she spoke with her head down or turned away, or from the other end of the goddam room.

Very early on she suggested that perhaps he had a hearing problem, and wouldn't it be wise to mention it the next time he had a medical check-up? He admitted there might be a slight hearing impairment, but it was normal for his age, and only in the left ear. Nothing at all to get excited about. She kept bringing the matter up, but eased off after he quit asking her to repeat herself. He also stopped turning up the volume on the television set, even though it lost him most of the evening news. Given the quality of television and the news – small goddam loss!

By mid-October the hot and cold thermostat war was well under way. A hundred times, his hands cramping in the sub-Arctic chill, he tried unsuccessfully to explain to her the simple cut-off principle of thermostat control, that if she insisted on sixty-five degrees, she must set it at sixty-five degrees. The desired temperature would not be achieved one damn bit more quickly by turning the needle down to forty-five. Or lower.

God, she did remind him of the years when Sarah had been at his side. And dear little Rosemary kept reminding him of . . .

———

For the first time since he'd been kicked out of Livingstone, he found the biography growing well, particularly when he returned to the earlier years. Sam's voice was coming to him so much clearer now, and more and more the act of writing was one of conversation with him. Yesterday's had been a dandy one:

I never did hunt '. . . the deceitful turkey' as you did with your cousin Fred, but I did go out with my brother Henry, and we also took turns with '. . . a single-barrelled shot-gun intended for younger boys.' Ours was a single-shot .410 Couey. You say yours '. . . was not much heavier than a broom'; ours weighed in pretty close to a fence-post maul. and just as you and your cousin did, Henry and I took turns carrying it. It had a kick any Missouri mule would envy; set Henry right back on his ass the first time he pulled the trigger. Also the second and third, as I recall.

In this piece copyrighted by Harper and Brothers, you say

that your uncle and his big boys hunted only with a rifle, would not be found dead with a shotgun, also that they were good shots, killed hawks and wild geese on the wing. With a *rifle*! Come on; even Annie Oakley wasn't that good. Or Natty Bumppo. I won't say anything about this to Jim Cooper. Trust me. You were dead on target with him.

My brother and I were after prairie chicken, partridges, mallards, pintails; our Canadian foothills grew no oak or beech trees, so we never hunted wild turkeys, with a '. . . call made from the leg bone of a turkey.' We tried to seduce wild geese with a caller we made from cigar-box cedar.

You say, 'When a mamma-turkey answers an invitation and finds she's made a mistake in accepting it, she does as the mamma-partridge does – remembers a previous engagement and goes limping and scrambling away, pretending to be very lame; and at the same time she is saying to her not-visible children, 'Lie low, keep still, don't expose yourselves; I shall be back as soon as I have beguiled this shabby swindler out of the country.'' At first I had a little trouble buying this dishonest mamma-turkey you followed '. . . over a considerable part of the United States one morning, because I believed in her and could not think she would deceive a mere boy . . . ,' but I'm no wild-turkey expert and I do trust your powers of observation.

I didn't know that Missouri mamma-partridges did this, too; our Canadian ones in the foothills don't, though the ruffed grouse can get pretty hysterical when her young are threatened. Our great dissemblers were the killdeer that pulled off the old fluttering, broken-wing trick on Henry and me again and again. Watch out for mamma-goose, though; she can break your arm with one wing tied behind her back. One of them almost did with Henry.

I remember a mamma-killdeer who tried to fool Henry

and me. A tender-hearted, summer-fallowing farmer had moved her nest over to the grass at the outer edge of the field, and Henry borrowed one of her eggs and hatched it, cuddled in a pillowslip in the wood-stove warming oven. Wherever Henry went, that little cheeper stilted after him; for the next ten days he fed it grasshoppers and ants, flies and butterflies as well as oatmeal. Mother made him return it to the nest and all its brother and sister chicks, and we watched its mother welcome it back into the family.

Henry sure printed that killdeer baby with love for him. Damn near as deeply as he did me. He grew up to use a shotgun on much bigger game.

———

Ever since Sarah, Christmas had been difficult for him to handle; with the pressure of mid-terms off, and students and teachers gone for the holidays, the university became an empty and echoing shell, the house just as bad. It didn't help at all to see everybody bouncing around, stuffed to the gills with goodwill and jingle cheer. He hadn't bothered with a tree or any decoration all the years since Sarah had left him. This time round, thanks to Nadya and Rosemary, it was going to be a lovely one.

Because Nadya was busy with rehearsals for the Sock and Buskin's annual pantomime, in which she was playing Sinbad, he had Rosemary pretty well to himself, which was fine with him. He took her downtown for the Santa Claus parade, and to the Sears toy department to sit on Santa's fat knee and tell him everything she wanted for Christmas. She wouldn't. This was more than one of the shy retreats she sometimes made when confronted by strangers. Santa could have coaxed and persisted longer, even though the waiting line of parents and children stretched clear over to Unisex Hair and Skin Care, but it probably wouldn't have worked. Her refusal to say a word to the jolly old bastard had disappointed him, for he had planned to eavesdrop and get an idea of what he might give her for Christmas himself. Several times he had asked her to give him a hint, but she had said if she told him it would spoil it because it would stop being a surprise any more, and you were only supposed to tell Santa what it was you wanted.

'I don't think that's the way it is, Rosemary.'

'Yes, it is,' she said.

'How can you be certain of that?'

'Kimberly told me.'

'Kimberly could be wrong,' he said. 'You could tell *me*, couldn't – '

'She said if you told anybody else but Santa then you wouldn't get what you wanted. Maybe nothing at all.'

'I see.'

'Then when she told me that I wouldn't tell her either.'

'Good for you. But why wouldn't you tell Santa when he asked you?'

'Because he wasn't Santa.'

'He sure looked like – '

'You weren't close up to him on his knee the way I was,' she said. 'I could tell right away he was just a guy pretending to be Santa so he could find out what I wanted and spoil it so I wouldn't get what I wanted.'

'Are you sure?'

'Sure I'm sure. Real Santa has a real beard he grows out of his face – not one that hangs off of both his ears the way that guy's did.'

'Then maybe we better go find the real one.'

'Nope. He's still up there at the North Pole with Mrs. Santa and all those beardy little dwarths in his toy shop helping him get ready.'

'You could be right.'

'Can we get a soft ice cream now?'

'Yeah.'

'Santa doesn't drink beer either.'

'Right again,' he agreed. 'Up at the cold North Pole only Napoleon brandy will do the trick.'

It had been a cinch deciding what to get for Nadya; he'd found the perfect gift for her, the billiard cue, short, four-teen-ounce, classy with ivory and mother-of-pearl inlay, two come-apart sections nestled in a red velvet lined case. He knew she'd love it. As for Rosemary's present, he'd asked Nadya for suggestions and she'd been no great help.

'A nice dress,' she said.

'You don't give people things they need for Christmas.'

'Not just because she needs a dress – which she does – she loves clothes.'

'They are a utilitarian present. When I was a kid, clothes for Christmas were a rip-off.'

'Maybe for you,' she said. 'This is for Rosemary.'

'You're her mother. You ought to know. But I'm the one giving the present and I don't want to give her clothes. Help me out.'

She considered for a moment, then her face lit up. 'There is one thing – I know – she was nuts about Kimberly's!'

'Kimberly's what?'

'Trike.'

If only she hadn't said that!

'I even know the colour she'd like it to be.'

Anything but that!

'Red.' She waited for his response. 'What's the matter, Doctor?'

'I – I don't think – so,' he got out. 'You have any other sugg – '

'But why not a trike? I know she wants one. Why don't you – '

'Not right now, dear. Some time – I'll – I'll – might – be able to tell you why.'

And now Kimberly had really complicated things. The evening of the visit to counterfeit Santa, when Nadya got home from the Sock and Buskin, he said, 'We've got a problem. Both of us.'

'Yes?'

'Rosemary.'

'Something happen this afternoon? What's she done?'

'No – no,' he said. 'She wouldn't tell the Sears Santa what she wanted for Christmas.'

'Why not?'

'Because he had false whiskers.'

'So, what's the big problem?'

'The big problem is – she won't tell anyone else what she wants,' he said. 'Has she told you?'

'No. But I'm sure she will.'

'I don't think so. Evidently dear little Kimberly told her if she did tell, it would wreck any chance she had of getting what she wanted or getting anything at all.'

'I would like to kick Kimberly's two front teeth out for Christmas!'

'Me too. I wasn't able to persuade – '

'I'll talk with her.'

'She's pretty stubborn about it,' he warned her.

'I'll phone – get Kimberly to recant – '

'First, let me talk to her again about it. Set it up for you and then you – '

'What are you going to say to her?'

'That Kimberly doesn't have it quite right. That there is one person – besides Santa – she can tell with no penalty, her own mother. Then you break your vow of silence and tell me what she wants. Think it might work?'

'Might. If it doesn't I'll take a run at Kimberly. But not tonight,' she said. 'I need you for something – '

'What?'

'Cue me on my lines for two scenes I got to have down for tomorrow. I've always been a slow read, damn it.'

'Okay. What will I be feeding you?'

'Mostly Dame Twankey.'

'Oh, shit!'

———

He'd bought the flat tin case of watercolours and a bubble-blowing set for her stocking. He'd thought he'd get her the skates she'd mentioned to her mother, but Nadya wanted them to be her gift, as well as the clothes. To hell with Barbie and Ken, who must be bland senior citizens by now. Probably have to settle for the miniature sewing machine, and *Treasure Island*, *The Wind in the Willows*, *Tom Sawyer*, *Alice in Wonderland*, *Through the Looking-Glass*, *Robinson Crusoe*, *Peck's Bad Boy*, and all the other books he'd gotten so many years ago for another little girl, to be read to her or by her, when she was old enough. The full set of tiny china cups and saucers was nice, also the two-storey doll's house; yet somehow he felt he could do even better.

Partly because it would interrupt his momentum on the biography, which was going well now; partly because the

Christmas Day opening of *Sinbad* was so close that rehearsals were being called for morning, afternoon, and evening, they had to leave the tree and decorating later than he or Rosemary would have liked. Nadya had said to go ahead without her, but he didn't want to; all three of them should do it together.

He did pick out a fine tree with Rosemary's approval and Nadya's later, when she got home late from rehearsal. He tracked down a tree stand in the corner of the garage, not in the basement, where he was sure he'd left it five years ago. Rosemary had gone with her mother to Food Vale for the turkey and whatever else was needed for Christmas dinner.

Finally, five days before Christmas, the yuletide spirit made its way into *Sinbad*'s director and he gave the cast an evening off.

'Let's get that tree in while it still has some needles left,' he said after supper. 'Get going on the decorating.'

'Can I help too?'

'Of course. You're going to be the boss. The light strings for outside and inside and the tinsel and – '

'They're in those two big cardboard boxes under the shelf,' Rosemary said, 'in the cold room.'

'Thanks for reminding me.'

'In the basement.'

'I know where it is, dear. Nadya – if you'll bring them up – '

'I'll help you, Mom.'

'No,' he said, 'you can help me figure out how the tree stand works while – '

'You said I was the boss.'

'So I did. Suit yourself.'

'I'll help you,' she said.

They were both on their knees in the middle of the living-room floor, trying to figure out how the goddam tree stand worked, when he heard Nadya behind them.

'Look what I found – on the shelf, in behind all those empty Mason jars.' She was holding the gold neck in one hand, the bottom cradled in her other palm. 'You all right, Doctor?'

It was going to take a moment to answer her. 'That's a bottle – of – Mumm's.'

'I can see that. Judging from the dust on it – been lying on that shelf for quite a while.'

'Yes.' He'd managed to get to his feet. 'Sarah – put it there – long time ago. When you go back down – please put it back.'

It had been pretty decent of her to leave it at that. He'd probably tell her about it. But some time later on. Also about the little red trike.

With Rosemary's help he was hanging icicle threads from the pine branches. 'One by one, dear. Don't just throw them at the tree. We're not decorating the floor.'

He heard Nadya calling from the hallway. 'What's she want?'

'She said come quick and see,' Rosemary said.

No wonder he'd been feeling chilly for the last few minutes; she had the goddam door wide open, was out on the step and looking up. 'Aren't they beautiful!'

She was right! High over the park escarpment across the street, the night sky was hung with a rippling curtain of light.

Rosemary was entranced. 'What is it?'

'The Northern Lights,' her mother said.

'Is that what the three wise guys saw?'

'No, dear. They saw the Star of the East.'

'Then what's that?'

'I told you. The Northern Lights.'

'But who's doing them?'

'Your turn, Doctor.'

'A lovely thing that happens at this time of the year,' he said. 'It's a magnetic – uh – the North Pole – '

'I get it.'

'You do?' Nadya said.

'Sure. Santa Claus, he's – '

'Not really,' he said.

'Shut up, Doctor. Quit while we're still winning. In a way, Rosemary. He's hanging up his Christmas lights too.'

The afternoon before Christmas Eve, he hit pay dirt in the novelty and gift store beside Ye Olde Pipe Shoppe, which in spite of its name carried the Cuban cigars he was addicted to. He had looked in next door and spotted it on a high shelf over the counter. Just one up there. The clerk stopped enthusing about the very expensive video game children wanted more than anything else in the world. Reluctantly. She got up on a chair and pulled the doll down. It had been quite the rage four years ago, she said, but was passé now. Not with him, it wasn't.

It was soft to his hands, a puppet of dove-grey velvet, with a lugubrious face that could change as fast as Nadya's or Rosemary's from sad and vulnerable to silly to happy to startled to angry, at the finger bidding of a hand shoved up his rear. He had never seen anything so magically gifted with empathy for all moods of all children. His name, the woman told him, was Wrinkles. Rosemary was going to love him with all her heart. But she had better not nickname him Professor.

Until Rosemary's stocking, and Nadya's, and his had been hung from the living-room mantel, a saucer of chocolate-chip cookies and a glass of milk left on the hearth for Santa, Rosemary's gift to Kimberly wrapped (a bottle of perfume, which was just about what Kimberly deserved), and Rosemary off to bed, he didn't have a safe chance to show Wrinkles to Nadya.

'Oh – he's a real doozer! She'll love him!' She looked away from Wrinkles and up to him, then back to Wrinkles again. 'You know something – '

'Don't say it, Nadya. I'm warning – '

'Okay, Doctor. Come in the kitchen with me, I can use some help with a thousand things I have to do yet before opening matinée tomorrow afternoon.'

———

Wrinkles did win the Christmas sweepstakes, and the billiard cue was a winner, too. Thanks to Alistair and Herbie and Colin and a couple of other former colleagues out at Livingstone, he now had damn near enough cigars to last till next Christmas. If he stuck to Dr. Gallstone's brutal limit. He opened last the small box Rosemary brought to him from under the tree. The card said, 'Merry Christmas to Dr. Wrinkles from Rosemary and Nadya and Old Nadya.'

Inside, in a nest of pink excelsior, they lay, three of them, brilliant and exquisite examples of Ukrainian egg-painting art.

'Thanks, Rosemary – and Nadya.'

'Old Nadya too,' Rosemary said.

'That's right,' Nadya said. 'She did them, and my grandma gave them to me.'

'They're real eggs,' Rosemary said, 'so you got to be careful you don't bust them.'

'I will,' he promised. 'I'll be more careful of these than I've ever been of anything else all my life.'

They went into a crystal brandy glass, that was going to sit on his office desk for the rest of his life.

After breakfast Nadya left the kitchen and came into the

family area. She was carrying a bowl and a ladle. 'All right, you guys.' She dipped the ladle into the bowl. 'Kutya.'

'What's that?'

'Don't you remember, Doctor? Old Nadya? My grandma?'

'Oh, yes.'

'You and Wrinkles stand back, Rosemary.' She lifted the ladle out of the bowl. 'I'm going to fire a dollop of this batter up to the ceiling and it's going to tell us what kind of year we're going to have. If it doesn't stick, look out. If it does we're in for good times.'

'Starting with *Sinbad* this afternoon?' he said.

'That's right. And the Mark Twain biography.' Now she had the handle back and over her left shoulder, the spoon end hooked in the tips of her fingers. 'One – two – three – fire!'

It was not a good launch; her release timing had been a split second too late, so that the dough blob flew off the ladle, not straight up but in a shallow arc that missed his right ear by inches. It also missed its ceiling target and plastered itself high against the family-room wall, over the sliding glass door to the conservatory.

They watched. They waited. It stayed.

'Does the wall count too?' Rosemary asked.

Nadya returned the ladle to the bowl.

'Mom?'

'I think maybe,' Nadya said. 'Old Nadya never told me about that.'

'Probably because she never missed the ceiling,' he said.

'Thanks a lot, Doctor.'

———

Maybe the wall did count in kutya omen forecasting. How that audience of young and old had cheered her cocky young

Sinbad. Even though she couldn't be bothered to do it for him in the house or anywhere else, she had sure as hell projected from that stage, and wasn't her timing just great! Look at the way she'd picked up every cue. Five curtain calls and five bouquets, including the freesias he and Rosemary had got for her. Then after he'd read to Rosemary and Wrinkles and kissed them both goodnight, she'd taken him in stripes and solids for the first time since they'd started to play together. Maybe that new cue hadn't been such a hot idea after all. All the same, keep the kutya up on that wall or ceiling; there's a Mark Twain biography coming.

It had been such a lovely Christmas, he told himself as he lay in bed. It had retrieved so much for him: Sarah, Susan, Henry, his own childhood long gone. For the first time in decades, just before he dropped off he remembered how, as a child, day or night he had often dreamed his Gulliver dream. In the dream he wasn't twenty times bigger than all the others, but he was a lot smarter, for he found himself in a primitive past with a seven-millennium advantage over the uninformed innocents around him. These B.C. people (Before Clothespins) had never held a hockey stick or a baseball bat or a kite string, heard or smelled a firecracker, struck a match, popped corn. They didn't know about balsa wood, piano wire, rice paper, all needed to build the elastic-powered model airplane he would wind up and release so it would fly and amaze. They wouldn't have a clue about how to use a safety-pin, and he'd have to show them what an egg-beater was for. Maybe even an egg. He'd brought back in time a whole suitcase full of these clever wonders. The bar of Ivory Soap and the toothbrush had left them cold, but they had been quite enthusiastic about learning to read and write and do arithmetic.

But for the past ten years of his life, whether he was awake or asleep, the dream had reversed itself; *he* was a bewildered primitive in a strange and time-advanced country, where even the very young were not awed by robots, mushroom clouds, trips to the moon or other planets, vacations in outer space. Now he was the illiterate when it came to computers, word processors, micro-chips, floppy disks, whatever the hell they were. He was reasonably sure they didn't mean condoms when they spoke of software.

Goodnight, Sam.

3

STRANGELY NOW, IN HIS PURSUIT OF MARK TWAIN HE FOUND himself spending much more time on inner rather than outer research. At first, the realization had been disconcerting; he had been doing it without knowing he'd been doing it, damn it all! Recapturing personal past to inflict it upon bored victims was the well-known maundering symptom of old age; Clemens had got fine milage out of that one; look at 'The Jumping Frog of Calaveras County' and 'Grandfather's Ram.' He had grown quite impatient with himself; what possible relevance to the biography could his own rebel and rural childhood, his own Southern adolescence, have? Behave, Lyon.

But he hadn't. He found he couldn't. It had been frustrating to come in here brimming with good intentions and sit down at the desk, only to find himself drawing a bead on the wrong past: his own. Every single time he tried to concentrate on Clemens, unbidden voices, incidents, emotions, sensuous fragments took over. Sarah visited him often, or little Susan did, or Henry dropped by. Why in hell should he find himself back in the Samuel Clemens Chair at New York State in Buffalo with that old retired brigadier general, who had only one oar in the water; in the Canadian Rockies, beating the bushes for a little girl lost; out at the lake cottage with a hot right wrist that squished if he squeezed it; on the edge of Tampa Bay with a prune-faced old Civil War veteran beside him on the stage of the Williams Park bandshell, missing the spittoon to spatter all over the white elocution pants his mother had bought especially for him to wear at the Decoration Day celebration. It had been the palsy that had spoiled the old man's aim, and palsy must be highly infectious.

That tobacco-chawing bastard had been the reason he had forgotten the Gettysburg Address to be declaimed in front of all those Americans, who had stolen the tune of 'God Save the King' for 'My Country 'tis of Thee,' waving their fans out there under the turpentine pines and banyan trees hung with Spanish moss so that the whole goddam park had palsy.

And of course there was dear Henry and the blue-black barrels of the . . .

None of this stuff belonged to Mark Twain. Or to himself any more, for that matter.

And then, only God knew why, about the time that Nadya and Rosemary had come to him, so too had the beautiful insight. He saw that his own remembered feelings of delight, disappointment, impatience, grief, bitterness, rage were the true way to recognize and understand Sam Clemens, and just possibly might give life resonance to the biography he had promised Sarah decades ago. A bonus for you, darling, not one but two: Sam's; my own.

Now, Sam, let's look at this letter to your brother, Orion, 'November 29, 1888.' He's older than you, five – eight years. Look it up. You're fifty-three or is it fifty-four? Orion is considerably older than Henry was when he . . .

> Jesus Christ! It is perilous to write such a man. You can go crazy on less material than anybody that ever lived.

Henry did. The booze helped.

> What in hell has produced all these maniacal imaginings? You told me you had hired an attendant for Ma. Now hire one instantly, and stop this nonsense of wearing Mollie and yourself out trying to do the nursing yourself.

I could have written one like this to Henry. Probably did. Several times.

> And don't write any more rot about 'storms' and inability to pay trivial sums of money and – and hell and damnation! You see I've read only the first page of your letter; I wouldn't read the rest for a million dollars.
>
> > Yr Sam

So much for brotherly love, Sam.

> P.S. Don't imagine that I have lost my temper, because I swear. I swear all day, but I do not lose my temper. And don't imagine that I'm on my way to the poor

60

house, for I am not; or that I am uneasy, for I am not; or that I am uncomfortable or unhappy – for I never am. I don't know what it is to be unhappy or uneasy, and I am not going to try to learn how at this late day.

Sam

Shame on both of us.

———

He had often wondered just how many hours of writing each day, whatever the mode, a person could suffer. Unrepentant romantics said there was no limit; the creative act, according to them, was unwilled, either for art or for erections. Made them half-right. Coleridge, Wordsworth, and their euphoric ilk claimed that fine poetry always bubbled up out of the breast like nightingale song, a lyric statement that must have done just that too. Aldous Huxley told Percy to get out from under that tree with the blithe spirit perched on the branch above his head; Blake didn't need any warning, probably wasn't a romantic in the first place. Damn few of them were devout about getting a good grip on the truth.

The truth was that the beginning of each writing day hurt like hell; overnight inertia had become well established; pessimism took over, and more often than not what bubbled up was pedantic nightingale piss. If not that, it was bitterness and gloom; the sun wouldn't come out till noon, and there was no warranty on that. Hot or cold, four hours was the absolute limit, so put down the quill pen, leave the typewriter or the word processor and shoot a game of pool. Or else go into the conservatory for some sweetness and light.

Athletes and dancers and today's pregnant women know the importance of warm-ups, and he should have too, much sooner. Necessary for artists as well. Through the long gestation of *East of Eden*, Steinbeck worked out every morning, sharpening four times as many pencils as he'd ever need to do all those letters never sent to his editor. Just bet Sam did most of his correspondence in the mornings. As for himself, what a life-saver it had turned out to be, discovering how these autobiographical knee-bends, sit-ups, and push-ups could loosen him up.

Where are we this morning? At the lake, of course. Morning there too, and you've got to fetch the two buckets of water from Sandy Beach well, empty going downhill, slopping full coming back, damn it. 'Henry never swears the way you do, Kenny!' Well, Henry did, but never for the benefit of adults. Twice a week deadfall must be dragged out of the bush behind the cottage. Henry didn't help with that, but he did with laying the trunks and branches in the sawhorse for an older brother who could be trusted with a bucksaw. Henry's other jobs were to stack the result and carry a supply into the kitchen. He wasn't all that industrious, but what a little entrepreneur he was; it had been his idea to capture lard-pails of frogs and sell them off the hotel dock for a cent apiece in the late afternoon to guests heading out into the bay for evening pickerel and pike.

What was trying to break the surface here? Oh yes. The wrist. How old had he been that July? Twelve? No, ten and a half, and that made Henry nine. It was the peanut-butter summer, when they took a break from the fuel chore to go into the kitchen. 'You boys through with the wood?' Nope. Just getting some razzberry vinegar and bread and peanut butter, Ma.

At the time both of them would have killed for peanut butter. That day there had been enough left in the bottom of the jar just for three pieces, not four. Halfway through his own first slice, he told Henry the peanut-butter truth that had been kept secret by the world peanut-butter cartel. It explained why peanut butter was light brown, why it pasted itself under the base of the tongue, in the back of the throat, between the teeth, on the roof of the mouth. There was a very good reason each jar had a squirrel coffee-potting on the front of it, Henry. Just as there are people who make good money gathering lead and copper, pop and beer bottles, duck and goose feathers, there are those who salvage squirrel turds to be weighed and paid for in collection depots run by agents of peanut-butter manufacturers.

Henry had not finished even the one slice of bread and peanut butter. That left three and a quarter all for himself.

Wait a minute. What was it that he'd – that had slipped away on him. Ah! The right wrist. That was the summer he'd haywired and spiked up the peeled birch bar between the close-together twin cottonwoods behind the cottage. He supposed he'd put it up so high for two reasons: so that his performance on it would look circus dangerous, and so that Henry, even with the help of the sawhorse, couldn't make it up there. How quickly and easily he had learned to do the sideways pinwheel with ankles locked, legs rigid, both hands clutching the bar through his crotch. Taken much longer to master both forward and backward spins with the bar under one kinked knee. He had not quite made it all the way round when he finally got up the nerve to try a backward double knee circle, lost his grip, and dropped. He missed the saw-horse but his right hand took the full shock of the ten-foot fall. Acute pain speared from his wrist to his elbow, but nothing had been broken.

The bar came down; the wrist continued to ache through the rest of July and all of August. It stayed hot and swollen; if he grabbed it and squeezed it close to his ear, it squished. He didn't ask his mother to listen to it until summer holidays were over and he was back in school. She got him down to Dr. McKibbon. There were x-rays, then all the way to the orthopedic clinic in Winnipeg.

It seemed that he had been born too soon to have benefited from the universal pasteurization of milk; the outrage to his wrist had activated bovine-tuberculosis bacilli. He must take afternoon lie-downs, daily sun-lamp sessions through winter, sun baths in spring and summer, cod-liver oil probably for the rest of his life. He would have to wear a series of plaster casts for three months and for the next six years a leather padded brace, which meant the end of hockey and baseball, and the loss of any skill at all for knife, poison, chase, or plunks. He could swim if he didn't overdo it and took the brace off and let his right arm trail by his side. He must learn to write with his left hand. In time, he had. Badly. For the rest of his life. Right or left. He would be permitted to tie his own shoes. But it had been humiliating to have his mother or even Henry button up his fly for him, and very quickly he had mastered doing it by himself with the good left hand.

The injury altered the course of his life forever. Taken from school for a year, he became from nine to four, week-days, the only boy alive in town or in the whole province or Canada – or the world. Exiled. More and more he walked the seven blocks out Lafayette Street to the town edge, but now it would be alone and not for the old commercial reason of drowning out gophers and clubbing them to death in order to cash in their severed tails for bounty payment at the municipal office or the junk dealer's. He traded tame for wild, and sought not town but foothills companions: killdeer, meadow-lark, goshawk, red-winged blackbird, ground owl. He had found much sweetness and much light out there, but there had also been the dry husks of dead gophers, with or without their tails, crawling with ants and carrion flies and undertaker beetles. The black margins were ruled by the barbed-wire fences, impaled with butterflies, grasshoppers, perhaps field-mice, the shrike's supermarket. In winter bird prints in the snow, the alternating dog-tracks of coyotes, the domino ones of jackrabbits – all signalled bird or animal life to him, not human.

He discovered the wind to be a fine ventriloquist; although you could feel the general direction it was coming from, you couldn't really pin it down, and it had so many voices: winter blizzard, spring chinook, the one in grass, another through leaves, or over a whitecapped lake, and when it plucked foot-hills telephone wires, it saddened but fascinated. Indeed, one evening just after supper, excused by the brace from helping with the dishes, he went into the living room, sat down at the piano bench (the brace also granted a reprieve from piano lessons, for which Henry envied him), and finally tracked down the actual notes of the wind going through telephone wires.

He had made another trade as well: outer for inner. During weekdays, when his mother was down at the clothing store, Henry and other young properly in school, he had no other choice but conversation with himself, very soon aloud, though that could embarrass you if someone caught you at it. As a child or as a senior citizen. It had been after Sarah's death that he'd found himself doing it again, and once he'd started the Mark Twain biography, Sam had showed up, wanting either to listen or to talk. Interesting enough company there in the office. Most of the time. He would probably never stop hearing Sarah or Susan or Henry. Till death.

From Grade One on, he had always been the smallest in his class. This was his mother's fault, for she was a small woman, who had told the boys again and again what a large, fine figure of a man their father had been. Just his luck he had to inherit his mother's slight build; Henry had been given the shoulders, the height, and the generous chest cage of their father. After the wrist accident, it seemed as though his growth had slowed down even more while his brother's had speeded up, and by his own thirteenth year, Henry had overtaken him in both height and weight. Even though you've been denied the use of your right arm for a year you are not supposed to give your younger brother a near-concussion, when he holds your left arm and pokes you again and again in the chest, in the face, in the nuts, till you have to crown the bugger with a looping swing of the metal brace crating your right arm from the elbow down. There had been a very large and interested beach audience watching.

In September, after another trip to the clinic in Winnipeg and advice from the orthopedist, his mother rented their house to the new CPR station master and, for the summer months, the lake cottage to the McKibbons. Mr. Sweet took over running the store for her, and they moved to St. Petersburg, Florida.

Going south with the ducks and geese that fall had been another unexpected bend in his life, almost as important as the wrist injury. From their train window Henry had seen the orange tree first, also the palm tree just like in *Boy's Own Annual*. Henry didn't spot the first flamingo, though. They'd both known about the everglades, and the black porter said they were dead right, that was swamp out there and those were cypress trees sure enough, and underneath them was just loaded with alligators and swarming with coral snakes and water moccasins that were way more poisonous than rattlers. When Henry asked him, the porter said there were frogs too. He also told Henry they did have peanut butter in Florida.

There were just shacks in the first part of St. Petersburg

that they rolled through; everybody was black, and judging from the clotheslines and the washtubs and the women over scrubbing boards out in the yards, they must be very clean people. The town ran out of black citizens further on, but poinsettias had taken over the whole place. Americans seemed to be a lot older than Canadians were. And not as healthy; Henry counted up seven in wheelchairs between the station and their apartment. Down here it smelled different, much more alive and fruity to their western foothills nostrils.

The ones that had lived here all their lives were called crackers, had never felt a flake of winter, though the snow-birds from the North did their best to explain it to them, whether they wanted to hear about it or not. His mother right off the bat established that there was a Presbyterian church; Americans had heard about John Knox, though they probably thought he'd been born and raised in Virginia like the minister, said zee for zed, and carved the Thanksgiving turkey on the wrong day of the wrong month.

The church entrance, like all the concrete curbs, was sloped to make it easier for wheelchairs; it did have stained-glass windows, but there were cardboard fans, with real-estate advertising on them, along with the hymn and prayer books in the pew racks, and the whole congregation chatted right out loud while they waited for the choir and the minister to show up, again during the passing of the collection plate and also the announcements intermission. All through hymns and prayers and sermons they waved their fans in a most irreverent manner.

Another thing: John Philip Sousa let his band blow their horns every Sabbath in Williams Park; Lou Gehrig and Babe Ruth swung their bats and to hell with the Fourth Commandment: Fatty Arbuckle, Buster Keaton, Charlie Chase, Andy Clyde, William S. Hart, Lon Chaney, Pearl White, and Hoot

Gibson didn't care a hoot whether it was Sunday or not. Up in Canada they did. The 'thee-yaters' and the shuffleboard courts were just as crowded as on any weekday. His mother never shuffled a Lord's Day game in Mirror Lake Park for the first two years they were down there.

School was different, too. For starters the first day when he went past the monitor, who wasn't looking, and climbed the 'down' stairs instead of the 'up' stairs, he was sent to Captain Lynch's office. In his knee pants he must have looked funny to the other students; American boys all wore long pants and had their shirts open and sleeves rolled up tight above their elbows and bow ties that weren't tied, hanging down in front. They swore just as bad as Canadians did, maybe a little worse. Southern teachers could be called by their first names with Miss in front of them, even if they were married.

Classes took a lot of getting used to. Ovid and Horace ate grits, and corn bread, and must have been born and raised like Mr. Knowlton in Tennessee, which had the funniest dialect of all. Caesar started up each of his Gallic wars after explaining the outcome of the previous one, with the help of Mr. Drake's Mississippi ablative absolutes; the next year, when Miss Dumas orated for Cicero, it was quite evident he was filibustering from the floor of the Louisiana State Legislature. Miss Dumas could have destroyed Carthage much sooner and with one hand tied behind her back if its citizens had persisted in not doing their ten lines of translation each day. Just like Mr. Weldwood, Virgil had been raised in Mobile. In spite of all his voyaging, Monsieur Perrichon never lost his Georgia accent.

Just before their second Christmas without snow, his mother decided that recitative talent was genetically sex-linked. Embedded in the minister's eulogy for his paternal grandfather's funeral in East Flamborough county, Ontario,

September 18, 1902, was the statement: 'Some of the finer selections from the poets took on new meaning under his recitation.' Add to this the fact that his father had been an elocutionist at the turn of the century as well as a men's and ladies' wear drummer, later to own his own store out west, and the inescapable conclusion was that at least one of his sons must be elocutionally gifted.

He had put up resistance, but it didn't work against his father's scrapbook, which she had brought south with them, filled with recital announcements: 'Lawn Social at the Manse Christie'; 'A Peach Festival Under the Auspices of the Ladies' Aid of Balmoral Church'; 'Young Men's Literary Society of Dundas Street Concert'; 'Gore Street Methodist Church Social and Concert under the auspices of the Epworth League of Christian Endeavour.' He had been unable to deny that the Dundas *Banner* had said his father's 'humour is clean, wholesome, and refreshing', though it had occurred to him later in life that there could hardly be any other kind of public humour in the first decade of the century. 'He is an elocutionist of rare ability,' the Perth *Expositor* said. 'His splendid voice and attractive stage presence at once command your attention.' Henry was the one more likely to grow up fustian; wasn't fair at all to pick on little Kenny, the horn-rimmed-spectacled kid with the stage presence of an introverted chameleon on a palmetto leaf.

She was not faint-hearted. She turned the scrapbook pages listing his father's recitations: 'Caleb's Courtship and What Come of It,' 'Trouble in the Choir,' 'The Flag,' 'The Heelin' Man's Prayer,' 'Never Forget the Dear Ones,' 'The Romance of a Hammock,' 'Casey at the Bat,' 'When Father Rode the Goat.' She closed the scrapbook, put it away, and enrolled him in Madame Brocklebank's School of Dance, Drama, Music, and Elocution.

Against his will each Saturday morning, when he would rather have been down with Henry and the sand spurs, floating in Boca Cieca Bay, he roller-skated to Madame Brocklebank's; fifteen blocks of cathartic grind and crack-clicks under the lace of pepper trees and Spanish moss, past the stubbed trunks of palms, the arterial red of poinsettias, shoving on the skates with indignation and anger and rage. At ten blocks' distance he would hear Apryl Symington's cornet. By the time he was two blocks away, he would hear some piano student practising 'Robin's Return,' a nice enough piece the first few times round, in which the robin had a rough time making it uphill, hesitated at the top, then made it over and down the other side to beat hell. In front of Madame Brocklebank's with all her doors and windows open for advertising purposes, he could generally hear 'Tiptoe Through the Tulips,' which seemed to be the only piece the school's students could tap-dance to once they had mastered 'East Side, West Side.' He would skate the length of the long hall with cribs down both sides, in which a woman teacher was closeted with a client. His own assignation was with Miss Dora Finch, who waited for him in a doll's house under a pecan tree in the back yard.

Miss Finch came from Birmingham and anticipated Tennessee Williams's sad heroines by some twenty years. He suspected that she also had tuberculosis, for she had the palest skin he had ever seen, transparent ivory. Decades later, when he was Visiting Professor in Turin, he would see her again as he looked at the bust of Queen Nefertiti. She moved always as though she were wading through a lagoon and the illusion was heightened by the gauzy gowns she wore. She did not get up out of a chair; she bloomed from it. She did not sit down in it; she sank to rest with all the drifting grace of dandelion down. She was his idea of a very spiritual woman – about 99 per cent

70

spirit to 1 per cent flesh, as opposed to Madame Brocklebank, an ample woman with monocotyledonous bosom, who was about 99 per cent flesh to 1 per cent spirit.

He was allowed one hour under Miss Finch once a week, during which she would give him gestures and facial expressions and postures to go with such pieces as: 'The Fool' by a guy named Sir Henry Newbolt. 'And I called him a fool. . . . look from the window . . . all you see was to be his one day . . . forest and furrow – lawn and lea – and he goes and chucks them away – chucks them away to die in the dark. Somebody saw him fall – part of him mud – part of him blood – the rest of him . . .' (LONG LONG PAUSE – PUT OUT THE LEFT HAND IN THE SPURNING GESTURE AND CLOSE THE EYES FOR THE–PAIN–TOO–GREAT–TO–BEAR–EXPRESSION – LOWER THE VOICE BUT DO NOT FORGET THE CHEST CHAMBERS) '. . . not at all!'

When he was through he would leave her, passing the next student coming in to her, just as he had earlier passed a previous one coming out. Madame Brocklebank would be waiting for him then, and just before he strapped on his skates he would give her the two-dollar fee. He had wondered in later years if the women who worked for her were not possibly culls of white slavers.

After eight weeks he had qualified for the twice-monthly recitals held at the school, incestuous affairs attended only by blood relatives of the performers. Madame herself was the star artist; she came on stage at the beginning to open the concert and report on the progress of the school; again and again to lower a gangplank for each student.

She had a dandy introduction for Apryl Symington, who never missed a concert. He disliked Apryl as you would any girl who played the cornet, had you by two inches, and was built blockily enough to make you think she could put you down quite easily. At his first performance – and every one after that – she played 'The Eagle and the Rabbit.' Madame Brocklebank would explain that the cornet solo about to be played for them by Apryl Symington depicted 'a little rabbit startled from cover and going lipperty-lipperty-lip over the green meadow. Then high in the cloudless blue, an eagle wheels and soars and hangs effortlessly. Far, far below he spies the rabbit and down he plummets, pounces on the rabbit, clutches it in his talons and bears the furry little creature grunting and kicking and squealing helplessly – aloft – higher and higher in ever-decreasing concentric circles until he disappears. . . .' She never did pursue that eagle to its logical anal destination.

Apryl would march squatly to centre stage with the cornet mouth resting on her fat hip; there she would stop and come about. You could hear the first inhale clear to Jacksonville as she raised the cornet to seat it on her mouth. This inflated Apryl, and her cheeks would puff out like two balloon fish attacked by simultaneous enemies. He had known then and he knew now that a woman playing the cornet must be among the most astonishing things in the known world. A woman playing the harp was honestly funny, too, but not nearly so incredible as a woman blowing a cornet.

His mother had not been too impressed with these concerts; in her opinion she had expensively loaded her son, and it was time to discharge him publicly at strangers. This she did regularly during the following year. At the Canadian Club it was 'Giuseppe Goes to the Baseball Game'; at the Shrine Club, 'A Negro's Prayer.' He also appeared for Captain Holly's Boys' Sunshine Club to raise funds for the purchase of barrel hoops and canvas for the construction of canoes. Very tippy sons-of-bitches, they had turned out to be. This was his first outdoor concert, held at the base of the Million Dollar

Pier, and he found himself in staggering competition with a seven-year-old boy, Palm Beach Tippy. Tippy was a little fart with a head of hair like a bleached dust-mop, and he dived unfairly from a fifty-foot tower, which his Dad forced him to climb, into Boca Cieca Bay, after his old man had dumped out and ignited a drum of gasoline. Following all that 'The Bald-Headed Man and the Boy and the Fly' had to come only as anticlimax. He told Henry that Palm Beach Tippy was a twenty-three-year-old midget.

By this time he had an elocution suit – a double-breasted blue serge jacket with brass buttons, and cream flannel pants. Shortly after the Sunshine Club engagement Miss Finch told him and Apryl they had been selected to take part in the Decoration Day Program in Williams Park. He was to deliver Lincoln's Gettysburg Address, and had less than a month to work on it. Apryl would blow guess what on her cornet.

Almost two weeks went by before he truly appreciated the enormity of what he had agreed to do. He had agreed to perform an act of treason. Before accepting the honour he should have remembered he was a Canadian, and Abraham Lincoln had not been one of the Fathers of Canadian Confederation. He owed allegiance to the king, the beaver, and the Maple Leaf; every time he turned around down here, he knew he stood amid alien corn. These people said 'die-van' for chesterfield; 'napkin' for serviette; they accused Canadians of saying 'eh' instead of 'huh,' 'hoose, moose and loose' for 'hayouse, mayouse and layouse.' They even denied Canada's smashing victory in the War of 1812.

His patriotic conscience had ached for almost a week before he took the matter up with his mother. She said, 'Don't you dare get up there on that stage in front of a bunch of

Americans and disgrace your country, because that's just
what will happen if you don't hurry up and memorize Lincoln's Gettysburg Address.'

He had put it off for another week, thus disappointing but
not surprising Miss Finch, who gave him three more facial
expressions and seven new gestures, and told him to skate
home and get the thing memorized by Wednesday so he
wouldn't let Madame Brocklebank's School of Drama,
Dance, Music, and Elocution down. He also had a Solid
Geometry test coming up on Monday morning.

He'd got a 92 on the test but more importantly, right in the
middle of it, he found a solution that would logically satisfy
all given allegiances in the treason problem. He spent Monday
afternoon and evening memorizing Lincoln's Gettysburg
Address – but with thirty-nine very slight changes. Wherever
Mr. Lincoln had said 'we' or 'us' or 'our,' he changed it to
'you' or 'your' so that the amended version's opening sentence
started out: 'Four score and seven years ago YOUR forefathers
brought forth . . .,' and the adapted ending: 'With malice
towards none, with charity for all, it is for YOU – I repeat –
YOU to resolve that YOUR nation, under God . . .'

He didn't try it on his mother, let alone Miss Finch. The
next morning he knew it wouldn't fly.

Decoration Day afternoon the Williams Park band shell
was frighteningly crowded: one Tallahassee senator, who was
to be master of ceremonies, forty-nine Daughters of the
American Revolution, which was a sort of Imperial Order
Daughters of the Empire, Mr. Sousa and all his band, Madame Schumann-Heink, an internationally famous contralto,
Babe Ruth, who just had to sit up there to make the greatest
Decoration Day contribution on any stage in America that
year, Apryl Symington, the Canadian-born Abraham Lincoln, and a turtle-old Confederate Civil War veteran. He was

one of only eleven left alive, the Tallahassee senator explained. His field uniform was faded grey; his forage cap was tipped forward; he had a bitter aura of mothballs and also smelled like overripe figs. It had taken a moment to figure that out; then he saw the trail of tobacco juice down the old man's chin, and the morning-glory mouth of the brass spittoon between the veteran's left foot and his own right one. The Decoration Day Committee had arranged for it to be placed there, and the old man needed it, though it wasn't doing him or the stage floor much good. His medals kept on clinking because he had palsy, which jigged his feet and jumped his knees and trembled his hands and rippled through his shoulders to jerk his head with such crack-the-whip violence that it ruined his aim. Apryl moved her cornet over to the other side of her chair; there was nothing he could do about his cream-flannel elocution pants.

Madame Schumann-Heink and Mr. Sousa did 'The Star-Spangled Banner' well, but he could recall little else, except for Apryl and her hysterical cornet. For the very first time he could go along with Madame Brocklebank and that squealing, kicking, terrified rabbit borne aloft in the eagle's triumphant talons. The Civil War veteran wasn't the only guy on that stage who had palsy now.

Apryl and the eagle landed; she bowed, knocked the spit from her cornet mouthpiece, and marched back to her chair. The senator was looking over at *him* and nodding and smiling the invitational and pitying smile of someone asking you to step out onto a tightrope stretched over Niagara Falls. Deliberately he pulled himself together, tightening chest and shoulder muscles to still the tremors, reminding himself of Apryl's nerveless approach to public performance, rose smartly, and stepped firmly into the Civil War veteran's spittoon. It was exactly his shoe size.

To get a spittoon off the foot, it does no good to tip the toe forward ballet-style, for doing so thrusts out the heel so that it hooks up under the flange of the spittoon collar. Turning *up* the captured toe stops the spittoon from being disengaged too. After this impasse was established in a whispered caucus of two, the senator asked him if he didn't wish to forgo his part in the Decoration Day 'progra – yam.' He had been tempted to, but he told the senator no, he'd just wear the goddam Confederate spittoon and deliver Lincoln's Gettysburg Address the way his mother and Miss Finch had promised he would do. To this end he anvil-chorused his way to the front of the band shell.

The green benches must be empty all over town, the cochina-shell beaches and the shuffleboard courts deserted. Everyone white had brought or been issued a fan coming into Williams Park, so that made three with palsy: the Civil War veteran, himself, and the whole goddam park; the impatient breath of a thousand fans set every mango and banyan leaf dancing, stirred and trembled the hanging tendrils of Spanish moss. Also, as predicted by his mother and Miss Finch, he had forgotten Lincoln's Gettysburg Address.

Not in the opening paragraph but from there on, Mr. Lincoln had forsaken him. Forced to go it alone, he ad libbed in a Lincolnesque way. Then he caught up with the bugger for the last paragraph '. . . shall have a new birth of freedom; and that government of the people, by the people, for the people, shall not perish from the earth.'

The fans stopped; the leaves and Spanish moss were stilled; then every Northerner and Southerner in Williams Park, in or out of a wheel chair, cut loose with applause that made Palm Beach Tippy in his death-defying dive into flaming gasoline look like a piker!

The proper method of extricating a foot from a spittoon is

quite simple: unlace shoe or boot first, then withdraw foot from shoe or boot. Shoe or boot may then be taken from spittoon quite easily. If spittoon was not empty, wash foot, sock, boot or shoe – thoroughly. In the washroom behind the band shell, he and his mother had done this. She said she was very proud of him, that if his father could have been here today he would have been proud of him too. It was then he realized that she thought he had actually delivered Lincoln's Gettysburg Address. So had all those Americans out there. He had just learned a rather sad truth: everybody had heard about Lincoln's Gettysburg Address; nobody really *knew* Lincoln's Gettysburg Address.

He said he still didn't think it had been proper for a Canadian to have done the thing, but she said yes it was, Kenny, for Mr. Lincoln belongs to the whole world.

———

Now then, I've had a good warm-up, and I think I know how you felt after the Sandwich Island trip in 1866, when you delivered your maiden lecture in San Francisco. You say in the following January you were in New York and had just completed your thirty-first year, when the recurrent dream came back again.

'In this dream I was again standing on the stage of the Opera House in San Francisco, ready to lecture, and with the audience vividly individualized before me in the strong light. I began, spoke a few words, and stopped, cold with fright; for I discovered that I had no subject, no text, nothing to talk about. I choked for a while, then got out a few words, a lame, poor attempt at humor. The house made no response. There was a miserable pause, then another attempt, and another failure. There were a few scornful laughs; otherwise the house was silent, unsmilingly austere, deeply offended. In my distress, I tried to work upon its pity. I began to make servile apologies, mixed with gross and ill-timed flatteries, and to beg and plead for forgiveness; this was too much, and the people broke into insulting cries, whistlings, hootings and cat-calls, and in the midst of this they rose and began to struggle in a confused mass toward the door. I stood dazed and helpless, looking out over this spectacle, and thinking how everybody would be talking about it next day, and I could not show myself in the streets. When the house was become wholly empty and still, I sat down on the only chair that was on the stage and bent my head down on the reading desk to shut out the look of that place.'

I ran across this bit in your dream piece, 'My Platonic Sweetheart,' a euphemistic version, I suspect. Albert Bigelow Paine says you were 'always interested in the psychic phenomena which we call dreams' and your own 'sleep fancies were likely to be vivid' and that it was your habit 'to recall them and to find interest, and sometimes amusement, in their detail.' All of us do, Sam; it comes with the human territory; I don't know how many times I've dreamed panic on stage, in a lecture theatre, back in the Williams Park band shell with that old bastard and Babe Ruth and the senator: not just without my lines or my notes either, often sans britches. Take my word for it, Abe had those same dreams. Just like you, he was one hell of an elocutionist too.

4

SHE HAD GONE OUT TO THE UNIVERSITY TO GET HIM ANY-
thing she could find to support his theory on the genesis of the
Bret Harte feud. Jealousy. She had brought back the Bernard
deVoto biography so he could check out the letters to Dean
Howells again. As well she had run across one of the rare
copies of a limited edition published privately in Ohio, an all-
male banquet address given in Paris. Evidently Livy had kept
it quiet, and it hadn't come to light until after Clara's death in
Detroit in the thirties. The title explained why: 'The Joy of
Onanism.' It was the first time he'd seen it, though he'd read

quotations from it in an historical survey of nineteenth-century medical and moral attitudes toward masturbation. He had long forgotten the name of the journal publishing the article, but now, thanks to Nadya, that didn't matter; he had the real thing.

She hadn't seemed all that excited about the find; indeed before and during supper he could tell that something was bothering her. She really wasn't with them; several times he had to repeat questions to her.

After supper and with Rosemary in bed, he said, 'Help with the dishes?'

'No.'

'Sooner they're done sooner I can give you a chance to get even in the snooker – '

'Not tonight, Doctor.'

'Come on, Nadya. Ever since you came home you've been obviously distracted by something. Maybe it's none of my business but from the look on your face – '

'What look?'

'To use an old foothills expression, like you'd been eating punkin through a wove-wire fence.'

'I ran across someone out there,' she said.

'Yes?'

'A guy.'

'Yes?'

'Somebody I'd just as soon I hadn't run across. That's all. No big deal.'

But it was. He could tell that it was. Not her ex of course. Highly unlikely; neither Livingstone University nor its library were in Australia. 'Old boyfriend?' Even as he asked her he wished he hadn't. Wasn't any of his business.

'No way,' she said. 'Just a passing acquaintance with a son of a bitch.'

'Sorry I asked.'

'That's all right.'

'None of my business – '

'Of course it is. Remember? Three are we? O.K., I had a bad experience with him – back just before we moved in with you. Some time – later on – I'll – I may tell you. Here.' She was holding out a dishtowel to him. 'I wash. You wipe, and we'll go downstairs and then I'll wipe you.'

Maybe, as she had said, it was no big deal, but it was big enough to put her right off her game. A couple of times he had to remind her it was her turn to shoot; she was still out at the university with some fellow she had hoped never to see again. Whatever it might be there was no point in distressing her further by bringing it up. Let her call her own shots.

Just before he was going up to the office to get in an hour or two on the biography, she said, 'Tell me, Doctor, when you were in the English department, did you ever know a graduate student named Slaughter? Charles Slaughter?'

He thought for a moment. 'Name rings a bell. Just a tinkle, though. Last few years I was there but I wasn't there. In a teaching sense. Pretty big department. What was the name?'

'Charles Slaughter.'

'Names never did stick well for me. I have a fine memory for faces, though. I imagine if I were to see him I might – '

'If we're lucky neither one of us ever will, Doctor.'

'That bad, eh?'

'I'm afraid so.'

He left it at that.

———

Now then, Sam. You were really flying with them that night at the Paris banquet. I am impressed with your convincing and well-structured defence of your chosen topic, though I'm pretty sure Livy wouldn't be.

Anybody who publicly praises a Pope for jerking off his mitre can't be all bad. You do have a slight Presbyterian bias, of course, the large majority of your Popes being Catholic, but we both know the practice to be a Protestant hobby too, and you certainly were not treating it in a pejorative sense. By this time in your life you believe that the human bag is a mixed one of all sorts of faiths, prejudices, and professions, and that Popes are no exception to the rule. I'm sure you'd agree with me that any man who abuses himself is less likely to abuse others; the Pope you mention would never have sizzled larks blind by running red hot wires into their eyes, then released them for the great sport of watching them fly straight up and up from the Vatican porch to their doom.

Let's get back to Bret and the shabby way you treated him after the jumping-frog caper. You are on record as saying he was your beloved mentor in the California days, that you'd always be grateful to him for teaching you how to write. Now you know very well where you first heard about that bullfrog with a load of bee-bees in his white belly. It's a dandy. My guess is that you came across that story by a mining camp fire, in some saloon or press room, or over a poker or billiard table. Frontier oral tales are public domain, so neither you nor Bret could be a plagiarist, and it wasn't Harte who said you were one; it was that fourth-rate journalist on the New York *Post*, who gave your ass the heartburn by accusing you of being a literary thief.

Of course you didn't care to know that Harte never made the accusation, did you? You were busy looking for any excuse at all to get your vanity off the beholden hook. Let's consider the way you handled Harte's consular appointment to Germany.

Heidelberg, June 27, 1878.

'My dear Howells:
What do the newspapers say about Harte's appointment? Billiardly speaking, the President scored 400
points on each when he appointed Lowell and Taylor –
but when he appointed Harte he simply pocketed his
own ball.'

Three of them scoring ahead of you, Sam.

'Now just take a realizing sense of what this fellow is when
one names things by their plain dictionary names – to wit:
Harte is a liar, a thief, a swindler, a sot, a sponge, a coward, a
Jeremy Diddler, he is brim full of treachery and he conceals
his Jewish birth as carefully as if he considered it a disgrace.
How do I know? By the best of all evidence, personal observation.'

And everything he eats turns to faeces. You also overlooked
comma splicing.

More to come: 'I don't know him myself, to be a thief, but
John Carmany, publisher of the *Overland Monthly*, charges him
with stealing money delivered to him to be paid to contributors, and the defrauded contributors back Mr. Carmany. I
think Charley Stoddard, said Harte had never ventured to
deny this in print, though W.A. Kendall, who published the
charge in the San Francisco *Chronicle*, not only invited him to
deny it but dared him to do it. O, the loveliness of putting
Harte into public service, after removing Geo. H. Butler
from it for lack of character . . . .

'I don't deny that I feel personally snubbed, for it seems
only fair after the letter I wrote last summer the President
should not have silently ignored my testimony, but should have
given me a chance to prove what I had said against Harte . . . .

'Now there's one thing that shan't happen. Harte shan't

swindle the Germans if I can help it. Tell me what German town he is to filthify with his presence; then I will write the authorities there that he is a persistent borrower who never pays. They need not believe it unless they choose – that is their affair, not mine.'

Boy oh boy! That Aw-shucks-didn't-you-know-I-was-only-fooling brand of humour may have fooled Howells. Not me, Sam. Not me.

———

That name Nadya had mentioned, Slaughter. Wasn't a name a person would likely forget, unless he'd been born south of the Mason-Dixon line. There'd been a Jack Slaughter in his senior-year Trig class; maybe that explained the faint memory stir. Came from Tennessee, didn't he? Played fullback on the Green Devils. My God, Lyon, you're maundering worse than the old fellow told Sam the jumping-frog story. Keep it up and you'll be as bad as the one in 'Grandfather's Ram.'

Wait a minute. Why should he be remembering the smell of smoke that greeted him as soon as he stepped out of the elevator in Wapta Tower that morning early last April? He'd asked Tait about it in the hallway, and of course Tait, as usual, had responded with one of his would-be witty answers: that it must be accumulated smoke from all the cigars the Professor Emeritus had burned over the years in his office.

Bev had given him a proper explanation. There had been three dissertation defences scheduled the day before, and during the third one the fire-alarm system had been set off and Wapta Tower had had to be evacuated. It had been a creative-writing thesis, a novel called *The Red Messiah*, and the graduate-student author had war-painted his face and arms and chest and stomach, worn only a porcupine crest and britch clout, and had set up a four-foot cross hung with a red Christ in eagle-feather bonnet. But more importantly he had lighted and scented the TA room with four small bonfires of wolf-willow twigs. The student's M.A. Degree was being withheld from him.

Now he remembered. That young man had been named Slaughter.

5

CHARLES SLAUGHTER, M.A! NO MORE THREES FOR YOU, BOY!
Three lates, march right up to the Principal's office! Three
strikes, you're out! Three on a match, you're dead! Three's a
crowd, get lost, Slaughter! No more threes – no more threes –
no more threes for Slaughter, MA, future Nobel Prize winner
in War and Literature!

What a day! Caught up with that Nadya and paid off that
bursar son of a bitch as well! His M.A. would be granted next
month at Spring Convocation. Should have given it to him last

fall. It was his, and they had no right to hold it back, steal six years out of his life. Tait had given permission for the crucifix and Indian costume and miniature campfires. English department head ought to have thought of the fire alarms, but didn't. That was the real reason they'd withheld the degree, not the fee balance, he'd promised he'd pay when he had it. Tait hadn't lifted a finger to help, and the bursar wouldn't listen. After Harbottle turfed him out of the research job he'd got in Psychology, just where in hell did they think he was going to find the dough!

And all Ellen had been able to do was whine and whine about when was he ever going to come up with some grocery or rent money, and no, she was not about to go to her bank or any other loan outfit for a measly six hundred and fifty to pay off the bursar to release his M.A.

'But I'll pay you back as soon as – '

'I've heard that a thousand times,' she said.

' – Psychology pays me the fifteen hundred they owe – '

'Dr. Harbottle stopped payment on that when he fired you. Get a job. Any job. Sell your bloody cycle! Pay your way or get out!'

Her giving *him* an ultimatum. He had moved out with his sleeping bag and the rest of his stuff, to sleep in the storage room in the apartment basement. But not before he'd thrown her against three walls and a window, shoved her head in the toilet bowl three times, then dragged her by the hair down three flights of stairs. The buck-toothed bitch!

Squared with Harbottle too. Rode the Triumph all the way out to the guy's hobby ranch, where he'd done so much week-end work for the ungrateful bastard. Surgery to be done on the Duke of Downsview. Sorry, Duke. Sometimes innocent, bovine bystanders do get hurt. And Professor, I did leave the prairie oysters for you in a dish on the ranch-house kitchen table.

Two weeks in the apartment storage room until he'd run across that Nadya woman doing her laundry, then helped her with all her garbage and house cleaning and she'd let him move in and use the hide-a-bed couch. Her kid was staying over with a friend that weekend while she caught up with her spring cleaning. So what was wrong with a little bedtime bingo? For weeks after, it had still swelled up and hurt to beat hell and throbbed him awake, and taking a piss was like having somebody run a red hot needle up . . . Some sweet day he'd promised himself he'd catch up with her and even the score.

He'd holed up in the Chapel at Kathleen MacNair, the sleeping bag behind the organ till Security kicked him out of there. Thank God for Clyde, letting him have a corner in Wapta Tower basement and getting him a gym mat from Human Kinetics for a mattress. But what the hell, he always helped Clyde a couple of hours each night shift with garbage bagging and mopping and polishing and dusting. After Clyde had showed a little compassion things had improved. He'd managed to hang onto the Triumph. There'd been regular jock-strap sessions in Fine Arts: they liked having a muscular 200-pounder to pose for them. He'd turned a few faggot capers, and today he'd finally managed to pay off the bursar.

After Spring Convocation it would be Charles Slaughter, M.A.!

What sweet chance he'd run across her, waiting for the bus, being able to tell her to lock up every night wherever she was, to instal a dead bolt on her door, bars on her windows. Also, he advised her just as the bus arrived, get herself a good, vicious guard dog. He had ridden alongside the bus for three blocks, just for fun, and from the look on her face in the window, he knew he had gotten his message across.

————

Surprise – surprise – surprise, Miss Tree. Aren't you sorry now for picking and picking and picking on Charles Slaughter, M.A., in the third desk in the third row, pointing me out to all the other Grade Threes. Fooled you too, Ms. Cogswell in Student Counselling, sending me to Dr. Laurence Rosner for professional help. One-two-three-a-lary, Larry was a little fairy. You could tell by the lilt in his voice. Black was the untrue colour of his hair.

Three times a week he had ridden the Triumph across town to the Foothills Clinic. He would cut off Third Avenue and onto Poundmaker Drive, turn just before Stampede Road, down into the ditch and up and out again to turn and tilt his way through the bush along the west side of the Foothills Clinic parking area.

Three lates: you just march right up to the Principal's office! Three strikes: you're out! Three on a match: you're dead! Three's a crowd: get lost, Slaughter!

Halfway in he would lean the bike against a cottonwood trunk, pile brush against it, then walk the rest of the way to his session with Rosner. As usual, even though she knew just as well as he did that his appointment was every Monday and every Wednesday and every Friday at three-thirty, there would be surprise all over Miss Simmons's monkey face as she looked up through the potted plants that banked the front of her desk in the reception area. Her thin eyebrows would lift and her mouth drop open.

'Oh!'

Just who in hell had she been expecting? The Prime Minister wearing riding boots and a black motorcycle helmet? The American Secretary of fucking State? The tax boys to do another audit on Dr. Rosner?

'It's Mr. Slaughter!' She would smile her phoney recognition, and always there would be that blood smear of lipstick on her upper front teeth.

Good tropical afternoon to you, Miss Simmons, scratching crotch lice under your hanging Boston Fern, in front of that four-foot fan palm by the window, crouched behind your potty jungle.

'Please – '

'Ooops! Forgive me!' Didn't mean to slam my helmet down right on top of your lovely purple African violet. Not really. Blame it on my impaired ego; it isn't functioning so well this afternoon. Primitive id contents of my consciousness have come to a full boil today. Seems to happen every Monday and Wednesday and Friday just before I have my go at Dr. Rosner. Makes it so difficult for us to track down the reason for the non-metabolized persistence of my pathological, internalized object relationships. More simply and clearly put for your limited understanding, Miss Simmons, I cannot stand the sight of you! Or your African violets! Or my kike-iatrist! Again, please forgive me and ask your African violet to forgive me, too, because if you don't, Miss Simmons, this here woodman ain't going to spare that palm tree. Next time!

'Sit down over there!'

Watch it, Monkeyface! Other times you always said politely for me to please take a chair and make myself comfortable while you went in to tell the doctor that Mr. Slaughter was here.

Three to one odds, after you've knocked on his door and waited for him to respond, you'll get no answer. Then you'll push the door open and go inside and come right back out again and tell me you thought the doctor was in his office but that he must have just stepped out for a moment while you went over to records or took your afternoon coffee break or gone down the hall to . . . then you will ask me to wait because you are quite sure that Doctor Rosner will be back momentarily. Bet you he won't be.

I win!

That had been a Wednesday one. The next Friday he kicked the bike into life, threw his leg over the saddle, revved her three times, and took off almost an hour early. He made one stop: Food Vale for the bananas for Monkeyface. After he had leaned the bike against the cottonwood and camouflaged it, he circled wide around the parking lot, and came out into the open on the east side of the clinic buildings. He took the bag of bananas with him under the weeping birch tree that would shield him and give him a clear view of the ground-floor window to Dr. Rosner's office.

He checked his watch: three-ten. Twenty minutes till appointment time. He was certain he'd figured it out right. He knew. He just knew. Sure enough! The lower half of the window began to rise. Rosner's face appeared, then Rosner's leg, then all of Dr. Rosner, to drop to the flower bed below. The doctor got up off his hands and knees. For several moments he stood flattened against the bricks; looked first to the left, then to the right, then straight out. Then he beetled off across the grounds towards the parking lot.

So, Rosner! Can't take it any more? Really getting to you? Well, Doc, you ain't seen nothing yet!

Next! Monkeyface.

He made it to the front of her desk right on the dot of three-thirty. The wounded purple African violet was gone.

'You may tell Dr. Rosner that I am here.'

When she came back and said that the Doctor must have stepped out for a moment, he corrected her. '*Jumped* out, Miss Simmons.'

'Pardon!'

'The window. I really think you should open your window. Fresh air is good for all your plants, too, you know. They need it just as much as we humans do.'

It was written all over her face: she had asked him to wait and told him the doctor would be back soon, knowing that the bastard had smoked through the window. Every single time!

'I'll just make myself comfortable until he comes back.' He sat down. He took the bananas out of the bag. He pried one off. He replaced the cluster in the bag, set it on the floor by the side of the chair. He cupped his hand around the head of the banana, set the other end into his crotch and held it erect there. He knew he had her undivided attention from behind the plants as he stroked the banana three times before he began to peel it back.

He grinned at her. She looked down.

'Missed my lunch. I hope you don't mind?'

She said she didn't.

'Would you like one?'

She said she wouldn't.

'Rich in potassium, bananas. Great, quick energy food. Perhaps that's why they constitute the main diet of anthropoids.'

He took a long time eating it and when he had finished, he dropped the skin into the bag and broke off another banana. Still grinning, he held it out towards her. 'Miss Simmons. Sure you won't – ?'

'No.'

'You aren't sure?'

'I *am*.'

'I don't suppose they eat bananas because of the potassium content, though. Possibly because the banana plant – it's a plant, not a tree, Miss Simmons – is the most common food source their jungle environment affords them.' He put the banana back into the bag. 'Anthropoids.' He stood up. 'Quite a varied family. Apes. Gibbons. Chimpanzees.' He began to walk towards her desk. 'Orangutangs.'

He lifted the bag over her plants and set it down in front of her. 'And the monkey, of course. You've been so kind to me on my visits to Dr. Rosner. I didn't miss my lunch. Not really. I brought these bananas as a gift just for you, Miss *Simian*. I knew you'd enjoy them.'

The next session the doctor was in. Halfway through the same old horseshit about his mother and their interpersonal relationship after his father had blown AA the second time and finally died with a liver like a bath sponge when Slaughter was ten, he said to Rosner, 'Look, you keep asking me all the questions. How about I ask you a couple?'

'Go ahead.'

'There's one main question I've been wanting to ask you ever since we started all this silliness.' He had definitely done a dye job on it since their last session. Histrionic. Specific manifestation of ego weakness.

'Ask your question, Charles.'

Escaping through windows unmistakably a regressive manoeuvre of low infantile order.

'I would like to hear your question, Charles.'

Not really, Larry. Brace yourself, because I have come to a nosological diagnosis on your case. 'How would you like me – to suck your cock?'

One and two and three.

'Not really.'

'Surprise, surprise.'

One and two and three.

'Not at all.'

'Oh. Then give me an answer – to – my question – to – you.'

'The answer is: I would not like that.'

'Wait a minute, Doctor. I want an honest answer.'

'Why do you think I might – '

'Hold it! I got the hammer now. Remember? I ask the questions. Not you. I should explain something to you. Even though you'd like me to, did it not occur to you that I might not *want* to do such a disgusting thing?'

'Are you sure you don't, Charles?'

'Quite. It's just that I'm a warm and loving-hearted guy and I'd like to show my gratitude to someone trying to help me. No matter how stupid and inefficient he may be at it. You know. To show gratitude to you – for *trying* to help me. How come you don't wear your yarmulke?'

'I am not orthodox.'

'Ah hah. But you do have an orthodox prick.'

'That's right.'

'Then I must withdraw my grateful offer to you. Tell you what I'll do, though, I'll let you suck mine.'

'No, thank you.'

'Come on, Doctor. You've admitted you're not orthodox and I believe that. No foreskin on your head. But you are definitely loose in the wrist. You have been sending me signals ever since we first met. Possibly without even knowing it. You are attracted to me, aren't you.'

'On the contrary. I find you a pain in the ass.'

'Whoops! Buggery is definitely out. You want to do a blow job on me, then be my guest.'

'All right, Charles, let's not – '

'Ah-hah! You have just said – '

' – waste any more of our sess – '

'You said – *"all right."* I clearly and unmistakably heard you say it.' He laughed his short explosive laugh.

'You find that funny, Charles?'

'Nope. I was remembering a definition I heard going around about guys like you. Therapists. Psychiatrists. Analysts. "The odd treating the id." '

'I've heard it before.'

'Just a lay definition, of course. But id does fit – '

'When you're through punning – '

' – you shit shamans. You wizardly, gizzardly asshole pokers!'

'That's it for today, Slaughter.'

'No, it isn't it for today!'

'Yes!'

'So *you* say, Rosner. I say it isn't. I have not finished with you yet!'

'I have! With you!'

'Sit down!'

Dr. Rosner quick-stepped it over to the door. He jerked it open, stood to one side and gave a side toss of that charcoal head.

Grinning, he leaned back in the chair. 'That mean I'm dismissed?'

'Out!'

He widened his grin. He stretched out his legs.

'We're through for today!'

'You're wrong there, Rosner.' He got up. 'We are through for good.'

'You're right!'

He started toward Rosner. Halfway there, he stopped. Then he turned and walked to the open window. He threw one leg over the sill, and sat there for several moments, still grinning. 'What a lovely and rewarding breakthrough we've accomplished today, Doctor.' He threw the inside leg over and dropped from sight.

One and two and three. He let his head rise slowly above the sill. 'A bit of advice, Larry. Either get yourself a pro to do it for you – dye your hair, that is – or use Grecian Formula.'

End of therapy.

In the Pink Paradise that evening, he let the tubby, middle-aged queer buy him three double martinis with a lemon twist, that he said he also preferred way ahead of olives or onions. He could not agree more with him that this noisy chaos was no place in which to carry on a serious conversation about Reagan and the contras, Jerry Falwell, anti-nuclear summits, Save the Whales, and cabbages and kings. With a reassuring squeeze he answered the hand that happened to end up on his lower thigh, and before they had finished their last drink, had agreed to a hundred-and-fifty-dollar honorarium.

As soon as they reached the orange Trans Am at the far end of the parking lot, he gave the son of a bitch a good shit kicking. Even though the wallet had almost three fifty in it, he took only the hundred and fifty – he wasn't a goddam thief – but when he got into the light and saw that the bastard had bled all over the ultra suede jacket and his tulip-stitched kangaroo riding boots, he went back and took another fifty. Cleaning costs. The gold necklace, that would probably go eighteen carat, was pretty damn nice, and the fat bastard hardly moved when he ripped it off his neck. In the bathroom at home, he disengaged the lambda charm and flushed it down the toilet.

Too late he regretted that impulse. He should have gift-wrapped it and delivered it by hand for monkey-face to carry in to Larry Boy. He did, however, a week later send away a money order with the PLAYGIRL subscription form he'd filled out in Rosner's name, Foothills Clinic address.

———

Much as he hated to, he had to give Rosner some credit. The guy had improved his memory aim for him, clarified the target: his mother. Before and after his father had left them, she had never given him a chance to become himself. Good or bad. Just to be her, and one of her in this world was more than enough. What trespass damage she had done inside him, draining his battery so the will-power motor could not turn over for him. Another term paper late, another nine o'clock missed, another final blown to bits. Her fault!

How had she done it to him? Through unfair denials: no second helpings of wobbly cherry jello, lovely maple-walnut ice cream. With broken promises, made just to ignite his anticipation so that she could later destroy delight. And with *did not* time: you did not do your homework; you did not pick up your room; you did not flush the toilet after. *Next time* time. Next time you forget to say your prayers. Next time you slam the door. Next time you go in over your rubber boots. *I told you never* time. I told you never to lie to me ever again. *Guilt questions* time. What do you think your father would do if he were not up in Heaven, Charles? You've got his whereabouts wrong again, Mama. If he were still with us, what do you think he would have to do to you now?

To start with, one thing he would not do, drunk or sober: make me take down my pants and bend over his knee so he could slap that strap just as hard and as often as he could across my bare ass! And when I refused to cry for him, he sure as hell – where he is now – would not use the piano on me.

Nor would he all of a sudden in the middle of Saturday have a headache so he had to go to bed and lie on his back with the curtains drawn and get me to ferry the wash cloth again and again between the cold water tap and his forehead, after he had promised me he'd take me to Kiddy Playland so I could go on the Devil Drop and the Corkscrew and the Tilt-A-Whirl and the Octopus and the Crazy Mouse just as many times as I wanted to.

Don't you think Daddy knows just as well as you do and I do that you lied when you said you did not climb up on the chair by the living-room fireplace and did not stand on the arm so you could reach up and open the bevel glass door and find my purse in the new place? A stolen dime is just as sinful and wicked as a quarter or a dollar. Our Father Who art in Heaven knows too when you break His Commandments.

Take down your pants!

Praise God, praise His Holy Name for leading him to the black triangle!

So far he hadn't been able to figure one out, but there had to be a pattern of some kind; during their sessions Dr. Rosner had told him that. Often. Precisely what pattern, Doctor? What sort of warning signs should I look out for? That's for you to discover, Charles. All I can do is help you to help yourself. Thanks a million, you helpful son of a bitch. One thing we do know for certain, Charles, those headaches are a bad signal. OK, but everybody suffers headaches, and how in hell can you tell whether or not it's just another normal headache that will go away in time, or one that says things are getting out of control? In time you will come to know and recognize the difference, Charles. Do you still find yourself talking out loud to yourself a great deal? So who doesn't? Join the Ebenezer Victory Temple if they'll baptize buggers; listen to them gobbling like a flock of idiot turkeys, then claiming it's not them but Him. I'm sure you'll find Elijah . . .

Sure. Maybe he did talk out loud to himself more than most people. When he was a kid up there in the black triangle, he'd done plenty of it. He'd got pretty good at mimicking her voice. Didn't even have to try; it just went on and on by itself, bitching and whining and scolding and screeching. Even now, just before dropping off to sleep, he could still hear her. Sometimes singing, the worst of all!

> 'I come to the garden alone,
> Where the dew is still on the roses.'

See her too! Could he ever! Those pale eyes trained on him from above, lips thin with anger and that left arm high and wide just before the swinging slap that would knock him ass over piss-pot, with at least twenty of the strap to follow.

> 'And He walks with me
> And He talks with me . . .'

Pull up your pants. Lie down on that couch.

> 'And He tells me I am His own . . .'

Piano-punishment time has come, with that black back rigid and unforgiving, regular as a human metronome, her talon fingers crooked over the ivory keys.

> 'And the Voice we share
> As we tarry there . . .'

With his ass still on fire he was forced to listen as she dirged away, knowing that sooner or later the sad chords would make him lose control and break into tears. She wanted him to cry, of course – that was the point of piano punishment –

99

and the best way to get even with her was *not* to cry for her. Or so he'd thought, until he realized that her arms and fingers would never give out.

Even though he hated himself for crying, he decided he must cry for her benefit, or rather, *pretend* to. Start off with a couple of short whimpers as though he were trying to hold it in, hiccup a while then build till he was sobbing as heart-broken as she wanted him to be.

With practice he'd got pretty good at it, would even make requests. 'Abide With Me' was a great help. So was 'The Ninety and Nine.' If she hadn't already played it. She would almost always end up with 'Blest Be the Tie that Binds.'

> 'And the Voice I hear
> Falling on my ear
> The Son of God discloses.'

What really worked best for her were her withdrawals, silences no question could ever break. Not a nod, not a shake, not a flick of an eye or a quirk of the mouth would indicate she'd heard him. Or that she was even *seeing* him. Once she had pulled down that blind on the window of herself there could be no seeing in or seeing out. I am here; you are not. In this room or in this world. This neither saddens me, nor angers me, nor pleases me.

When his father had been alive, it hadn't been much better, because he'd be away for weeks at a time: Texas or Oklahoma, Alaska, Mexico, South America, Iran, Saudi Arabia. When it came to oil, his old man was a big shot; the hammer was his all right, except with booze and probably with women. He never forgot to bring home presents: the sombrero rimmed with scarlet balls, the black walrus carved out of soapstone. Not that he could remember him all that well any more, except for the few times he'd come to his defence against her. Before he died and left him all on his own.

Then he had just the black triangle to fall back on when he needed it. It worked most of the time.

He had found it by accident in the storage room on the third floor when he'd moved the cardboard cartons and shoved the clothes hangers over on the closet rod. A big patch of plaster was missing, so there was a hole ragged round the edges with broken lath; some past plumber or electrician must have left it that way when the job was done. He had crawled through, then bumped his head when he tried to stand up in the dark. Next time, and every time after that, he took a candle and matches in with him.

Even now he could close his eyes and still see that teardrop of flame flickering and revealing skeleton joists and slanting rafters. Here he could really feel sorry for himself, relish his hate, and construct Tinker-Toy revenges against her. It had been in here that he had first imagined suicide to punish her. Right after Elijah.

———— ·

With his gaunt and suffering face, black beard and shoulder-long hair, the Reverend Elijah Matthews could have stepped right out from under the gold halo and down from the stained-glass window in Ebenezer Victory Temple, to preach and to pray and to heal the sick and the deaf and the halt and the blind. He'd been eight and a half when the new pastor with the long hair came to them from almost as far away as Heaven: Long Beach, California. Very soon most of the congregation had made up their minds: Elijah *was* Jesus.

The very first change he made was to segregate the Bible Classes; girls, for Mrs. Valentine; the boys, under himself.

This willingness to devote personal time to the little ones testified to the loving-hearted unselfishness of their new pastor. Right away Bible Class became interesting. Elijah's really was the Voice of Jesus, as though a pipe organ had learned to talk. He and the other children looked forward to their basement meetings, eager to find out exactly how the Holy Spirit could enter them, could ignite them with glory as easy as scratching a kitchen match. He wanted to be able to talk in tongues, too, and he tried it out at home, up in the black triangle, but all he could ever get was his mother's voice after him again, though it was in there that he figured out ways to get even with her. When he remembered how Elijah had warned them that Satan could get inside there too, he quit for a while.

Elijah told them all about divine healing done by Jesus in the New Testament and by himself in almost every state in the Union. It was near the end of their third Bible Class that he went over to Aubrey Buller, in his little red Bible Class chair, knelt before him and looked right into his eyes, which wasn't all that easy to do, because the right one was crossed. He cupped Aub's head in his hands, thumbs against both eyeballs, and closed his own and looked upwards and pressed. Real hard, Aub said afterwards.

He talked in tongues and he yelled, 'Heal! Heal! Heal!' Then he jumped up and stepped back and threw his arms up and yelled, 'Open! Open! Open!'

Aub did that. His crossed eye was straightened right out. It stayed so for just a second or so, but it had been a real miracle. No mistake about that. Elijah did it again next Bible Class, but it didn't work that time so he changed the ritual. This time he placed his hands one on top of the other on the back of Aub's head, pulled it face down into his crotch and kept pushing it again and again, then sat back and you could hear the Holy Spirit leave him in one long sigh.

Aub was still cross-eyed, though.

Next Bible Class, Elijah took a white oval eye-patch with a gold cross on it out of his own fat white Bible with a gold cross on it. With cotton batten underneath, he put it over Aub's good eye and told Aub he could take it off only at night when he closed his eyes, and that he must replace it in the morning as soon as he opened his eyes. He said Aub must do this for one hundred and fifty days and nights, and that he had explained this to Aub's mother and father. Then he shoved Aub's face into his lap.

After one hundred and fifty days and nights Aub's parents brought him up to the mercy seat, blindfolded. Elijah talked in tongues and ripped off the blindfold, and this time the miracle lasted; according to Elijah the eye would stay straight for the rest of Aub's life. Praise God! Praise His Holy Name!

Everybody felt sorry for Elijah because he seemed to suffer a lot. He explained this to both the congregation and the Bible Class. In Long Beach, he told them, he had thrown himself into the path of a Budweiser Beer truck to save the life of a little golden-haired three-year-old girl, who had run out into the middle of Ocean Boulevard to retrieve her red balloon. He had snatched her from death, but a back wheel had rolled over his stomach.

It was nice that Aub's eye stayed true, for now Elijah turned to Charles. Whenever the pain from his old injury became acute, it was Charles he would ask to sit on his lap. As his suffering increased he would tighten his arms around Charles's waist, pulling him tighter and tighter against the almost unendurable agony.

Then came the afternoon that Elijah asked him to stay after

the others had left, and took him into the supply room with all the cardboard cartons and one dim overhead light bulb. He turned that off. Charles had been nine by then, and it had hurt, and he had told his father.

The next Sunday Elijah informed the Ebenezer Victory Temple congregation that the Lord had called him away to another flock in another pasture. Indianapolis. His announcement was almost like talking-in-tongues, for most of his upper front teeth were missing. Both his eyes were swelled up red and black and purple. His right arm was in a wrist-to-shoulder cast, and up there at the mercy seat he was propped on one crutch, and he seemed in great pain from the old injury inflicted on him by the truck, when he had saved the little Long Beach child.

———

A year later, when his father died and left him at her mercy, he spent much more of his time alone up in the dark triangle. It was in there that he decided to join his Dad. He almost had, after he'd got the King Cutter razor out of the bathroom cabinet, filled the bathtub to the top, then managed to do his left wrist. He should have done both because the water hadn't yet turned real red when she found him and hauled him out.

6

WE'RE COMING ALONG JUST GREAT, AREN'T WE, SAM. GOT
to give Nadya credit; this house, this office, all my notes and
papers have never before been so neat and tidy since Sarah . . .
And that isn't all; she's the best researcher I've ever had,
tracking down my correspondence, going out to the university almost every week for me. Been doing that for over a
month now. I didn't ask her to; it was her idea, said she'd like
to help.

Thanks to her I've made it through your early Mississippi
and California years. Last week that Calaveras bullfrog

jumped you right into the Eastern limelight – *Harpers* – *Atlantic Monthly*. Hell, now you're looking irresistible to all those British and Canadian theives – oops, Sam – 'i' before 'e' except after 'c' – thieves. Still doesn't look right, damn it.

Now – something I have to find out: just what was the final tally on your honorary doctorates? Pretty high, I suspect. Must have been a great day for you when you hung that Oxford scalp on your coup stick. Long time coming, that one, Bret and Howells scoring ahead of you by several years. Sweet victory all the same, with Livy and the girls cheering, though I do wonder how they felt when you started wearing the scarlet and gold gown and pancake tam all over the house, in place of your bathrobe.

What brought this to mind was the square envelope under the mail slot this morning. From Livingstone University. The Chancellor's office. It seems they want to give me a degree at Spring Convocation coming up next month. Not only that, I am to deliver the Convocation address.

Nadya's face lit up when I told her. She had to blow it, of course, by suggesting for the twenty-third time that now I was doing a Convocation address maybe I should get a hearing aid. Said I wouldn't have any trouble hearing my own goddam Convocation address; told her to save her advice for the hard of hearing in my audience. I also told her to go to hell. I don't think she's going to do that, or drop the hearing-aid matter in a hurry.

─────────

That kutya up on the wall last Christmas was really working overtime; the honorary degree and Convocation address were not all the week's good news. Three days after the Convoca-

tion letter, when he picked up the mail in the front hall, there
was a letter for Nadya, return address: Tyrone Guthrie Theatre, Minneapolis. He had a hunch it was an important one,
wondered if he shouldn't phone her at the Sock and Buskin,
decided to wait until she got home.

It was indeed an important letter.

'It's from Seth.'

'Who's Seth?'

'I knew him years ago,' she said. 'Summer I was in Stratford. Before Rosemary.'

'I didn't know you'd acted at Stratford.'

'Not really,' she said. 'I was in their summer program for
young actors. So was Seth. He's made it big – assistant artistic
director at Tyrone Guthrie in Minneapolis. In line to become
their new artistic director. I always knew he'd make it.' She
looked down at the letter. 'This went to my old address.' She
looked up to him again. 'They're going to do Shaw's *Saint
Joan*. You know the play – '

'Goddam right I do.'

'Seth thinks I'd make one hell of a Joan.'

'I do too,' he said.

'He says keep in touch. Let me know in a month or so.
What do you think of that, Doctor!'

'Just great.'

'Not a cattle call. He says I'm on the short list. Could be
my big break.'

'I hope so, dear.'

Thinking it over later, he wasn't so sure he did hope so. If
she were cast and pulled off a fine job on Joan and her acting
career caught fire, the calls that followed would most likely
be Eastern ones, and that could mean that she and little
Rosemary . . . Enough of that, Lyon. Let's not be selfish. For a

change. There's nothing firm yet; it's not for a month or so, and you've got better things to worry about. Not just Sam now; you've got a Convocation address to do as well.

Very quickly he knew the message he wanted to give them: the need, in a contemporary materialist world, for the arts and the humanities. In schools and universities, teach the young not only how to make a living but how to live. After a week of false starts he'd managed to get going on the thing. He was working on it the Sunday morning she showed up in the office.

'How's it going, Doctor?' She was standing just inside the doorway. Barefooted.

'You really know how to sneak up on a fellow, don't you?'

'Yeah. Easy if he's got a hearing problem he won't . . . I don't want to interrupt you if you're on a roll. You know, it can wait till – '

He pushed back the chair, swivelled to face her. She was wearing a towel turban, a blue terrycloth robe that almost reached her knee caps. Eye *and* leg man! 'What is it?'

'Did you know it was Rosemary's sixth birthday a week next Saturday?'

'She's mentioned it to me. Several times.'

'What you working on? Mark or the Convocation – ?'

'The address.'

She had crossed to the couch. 'Make it a good one.'

'I'll try.'

She sat down, the Greek comic and tragic masks tilting away from each other on the wall above her head.

'What about Rosemary's birthday?' he asked.

'She asked me if she could have a birthday party. All right with you?'

'Of course it is,' he said. 'Can't have a birthday without a party. You didn't have to ask me.'

'Be about twelve – fourteen of them. We'd be infested by most of the Peter Pan kids.'

'You still didn't have to ask me,' he said.

'I promised her that – if there was a party, it would be special.'

'Her age are there any other kind?'

'She wants a magic one,' she said.

'How do you think you'll manage that?'

'Oh – I don't – I couldn't pull it off by myself.' She stood up. 'She wants you to do it.'

'Do what?'

'Be a magician for them.'

'Oh.'

'You know how she loves that magic candy – '

'You want me to do that for each one of them?'

'Mmmh.' She started for the door. 'Between now and a week Saturday maybe you could work up a magic routine for them.'

'Wait a minute – '

'Just a few tricks,' she said. 'You know. The ones you're all the time telling about – the ones you did as a kid – after you got the magic set for *your* birthday – '

'Hold on. The Convocation – '

'Is over before her birthday.'

'I haven't done any magic for years,' he said.

'But it isn't something a person would forget completely, is it?'

'Have you already discussed this with – '

'What were some of the magic tricks you used to do?'

No doubt about it; the two of them had it all plotted out. 'I never did get to be very good at sleight-of-hand.' She'd probably already promised the child that he'd do it. 'I needed props – devices that came in the magic set.'

'What would you wear?' she asked.

'What the hell are you talking about?'

'When you do your magician act for them,' she said.

'I didn't say I was going to do any magician act. Damn it, Nadya. If I take time off from the biography it's hard to get going again – '

'As a magician you've got to wear a magician's costume and – '

'And this Convocation address has already robbed time from . . . what do you mean – what costume?'

'Oh – cape – black one with a scarlet lining. Top hat. White gloves. You know the things that magicians wear.'

He swivelled his chair back round. He ripped the sheet out of the typewriter. 'I do not own a black cape with or without a scarlet lining.' He began to roll in a new sheet. 'Or a top hat.'

'Dressing up for something, that's a big part of the fun for children. Or having somebody dress up for them.'

'Or white gloves.'

'No problem. Sadie at the Sock and Buskin can get them out of costumes.' She swung him round in the chair to face herself. 'Are you pissed off with me for some reason?'

'Yes!'

'Just because I asked you to . . .'

'Because I do not like to be manipulated!'

'I am not manip – '

'You sure as hell are! You had this all planned before you stepped into this office. You have already told Rosemary all about it, haven't you?' He waited for her answer. 'Spoken to whatever her name is in wardrobes at the Sock and Buskin.'

She had all right. The expression on her face was a fair match for one of the Greek masks on the wall above the couch. The left-hand one.

'Okay, Doctor. Sorry.' She turned away.

'It wasn't what you . . .'

'I got your message.'

'. . . it was the devious way . . .'

The door had closed behind her.

Now why did you do that to her? Why couldn't you have been gracious about playing a dressed-up magician at Rose-mary's birthday party? Wasn't because you were afraid of writer's block from interrupting the biography. God knew you wouldn't be where you are with it if it hadn't been for her. And it wasn't because you had to get the goddam Convocation address down either. Very simple reason you were rude to her; it is now 8:45 a.m., and until 10:00 a.m. at least you have always been one mean son of a bitch. That explains all those mute breakfasts opposite Sarah. Right up to her final silence. God knows you spilled irrelevant annoyance over her for three decades. Often enough for her to have called you a wife-batterer once. Of the worst kind! *Verbal*! She asked you if you did it to your students, too, and that made you do some serious self-examination then, didn't it? Not very comforting to realize that you almost never had with your students. Saved it for the woman you loved most. Now with Nadya. Rose-mary next?

And Henry! Come to think of it, you were pretty hard on him too, weren't you? Maybe that's the way older brothers are with younger ones. If they love them. And I did! Oh Henry, I did! What a sweet and vicious performer in criminal court you were, defending every loser but yourself! How I wish you were still around! She wants magic for Rosemary's birthday party. Wouldn't our dwarf knock them out!

Remember when we did him together on top of the folding card table before the dining-room archway's brown velvet curtains for Mother's booth of Knox Presbyterian Church?

You were the arms and hands over which I had no control, and I danced the feet and sang 'I'm a Little Teapot Short and Stout.' When I got to 'Here is my handle,' you put *your* thumb to *my* nose and fanned your fingers at the ladies of Mother's Burning Bush booth of Knox Presbyterian Church. And with: 'Here is my spout,' you reached down to the little dwarf's crotch with your thumb erect. They all laughed as one, or, rather, *except* one. Mother! You deserved the slipper. I didn't!

How they would love that dwarf! And the invisible hen. The egg that had come in the magic set had been white-enamelled and wooden, but it would be easy to blow a real one, seal the hole with candle wax and fasten black thread to it and get in some practice between now and a week Saturday. He pushed back his chair and got up.

Still in turban and robe she was sitting at the end of the kitchen table. He sat down at the opposite end. Her elbows on the table, she lifted the coffee cup in both hands. She did not look at him over the rim.

'I'm sorry if I was abrupt with you.'

She set the cup down.

'I'll do it,' he said.

'Never mind.'

'I – I would like to do it.'

'No.'

'Please. I've said I'm sorry and I mean it.'

'You've got lots more important things to do – '

'Not more important than Rosemary's birthday party,' he said. 'Take my word for it.'

'Look, Doctor. I shouldn't have laid it on you the way I did.'

'That's right. And I shouldn't have been so short with you. Now we've agreed about that, you go ahead and get the magician costume from your friend. I've been thinking about what I might do for them.'

'Like what?' Now she was looking at him over the cup.

'Oh – the invisible hen.'

'Really?'

'She's in a handkerchief,' he explained, 'keeps laying her eggs into a hat.'

'You don't have to rupture yourself for them – invisible hen – sawing a lady in half – '

'The hen's quite simple, actually. I think I can do her. I can still cluck.'

'Keep it clean for them. What other ones?'

'Breaking the matchstick in a handkerchief and then making it come back together again.'

'That sounds kind of dull.' She got up.

'I believe it was.'

When she had poured herself another cup and come back to the table, he said, 'The dime trick.'

'Yeah?'

'You put it flat on the palm of your hand and you press your wrist with the tip of your finger on your pulse and the magic dime rises and stands on its edge.'

'Really?'

'And when you release the pressure,' he explained, 'it lies back down again. Over and over. Then you hand it to the most cynical-looking one in your audience and invite him to try it and he can't do it. So you do it again.'

'How do you do that one?'

'Interesting you should ask that,' he said.

'Well?'

'Why do you want to know?'

'Anybody would. Sounds great.'

'Not anybody,' he said.

'Anyway – how do you do it?'

He got up.

'Come on.'

'I'm not telling you.'

'Because magicians never tell?'

'No.'

'Because you're still mad at me?'

'No.'

'All right, then – why won't you?'

'You asked the wrong question.' He started for the door.

'Hold on, Doctor.'

'In the first place your question indicates that you didn't believe it was a magic dime, which means it was an adult question, asked only because you hate to have someone fool you – to be smarter than you are.'

'A kid would ask the same question.'

'No. A child *wants* it to be magic. A child doesn't ask a question to *expose* the magician.'

'The kid still asks a question.'

'Not the one you asked.'

'All right. What does he ask?'

'*Will you show me how to do that?*' he said. 'The child wants to be a magician, too.'

'Now who's manipulating who?'

'Whom.'

'All right. Whom's manipulating who?'

'Whom is the objective case . . .'

She laughed. 'I know that. Got you there, Doctor. Tell me another one and I'll ask the right question this time.'

'The three-foot dwarf.'

Her mouth dropped open. It stayed that way.

'Actually he used to be just over two feet tall, but he's grown some by now.'

'You are kidding.'

'I did him with Henry, my younger brother. I found him in the magic section of *A Thousand Things a Boy Can Do*.'

'Wow!'

'I'll need you for it,' he said.

'Sure!'

'And we are getting into costumes again.'

'Like what?'

'Pair of Rosemary's slippers – shoes. Knee stockings. I have a turtleneck sweater that would work. When Henry and I did it we were nine and eleven. For formal occasions like Sunday School or birthday parties we had to wear these middy suits with the pants cut off just above the knees. They're no longer inflicting them on young males. Henry and I wished they hadn't been doing it back then.'

'How about a pair of Rosemary's slacks?' she suggested.

'Nope. With them you couldn't see the dwarf's legs. Unless you took a pair and cut them off and hemmed them – '

'I got a better idea. One of her short skirts!'

'Wouldn't work.'

'Sure!'

'At all!'

'The girls are going to outnumber the boys four to one,' she explained. 'They'd rather have a girl dwarf.'

'I wouldn't! I'm the torso and the legs, from the knees down, so it's my face and my body from the shoulders down. You'll be hidden behind me with your arms under my arms and into and through the sweater sleeves rolled up. If it were a girl dwarf then the whole arrangement would have to be reversed. My big arms wouldn't go under your – around your – ah – wouldn't work.'

'It would if you were in drag,' she said.

'What?'

'Make-up. Eye liner and rouge – lipstick – a wig. Blonde.'
'No!'
'Twice as funny!'
'I certainly would be! You just get a pair of Rosemary's – '
'Ah-ah.' She shook her head. '*Girl* dwarf.'
'Nadya – '
'Real dingly dangly earrings! The wig – '
'Goddammit, Nadya – '
' – has to be red! Flaming red!'
'If you don't pay attention to me there is not going to be any flaming dwarf – male or female – at all!'
'Aw!'
'Or magician!'
'Okay,' she said. 'Sounds like a great act. Now – I've broken off a big chunk of your morning.' She pointed up with her thumb. 'Go pick up your shovel.'
'There might be a couple of card tricks I can still manage – '
He felt her arms go round him and tighten. 'Aw – you are one dear guy!'

7

TODAY WAS THE DAY, AND WAS HE EVER READY FOR IT! HE'D rolled up the gym mat and sleeping bag, stashed them with his other stuff behind the furnace in Wapta Tower basement. He'd showered and shaved in the Kinetics department locker-room off the basketball court, had bacon and eggs and coffee in SUB cafeteria. Thanks to Clyde.

Last night after he'd helped the guy with his janitor chores, he'd told him how he was broke, couldn't even pay the rental fee for a mortarboard and gown, and Clyde had got them for him. He promised him he'd return them right after Convocation. What the hell, he wasn't going to need them after he got his M.A. – the bastards should have given it to him eight months ago at fall Convocation. He'd almost cried after Clyde slipped him the ten-dollar bill.

But getting that parchment in his hand was not going to be the end of it. He had some evening up to do. That was life, wasn't it? Plain and simple: war!

Vengeance is mine, sayeth Charles Slaughter.

———

Putting the final polish on his Convocation address, he had worked in the office till after two last night, then wakened late and reluctantly at ten-thirty by the clock on the night table. Must have slept right through the alarm. But when he checked, he found the white button on the back pushed to 'OFF'. He was sure he'd pulled it out before climbing into bed. Ah well.

He sat up, lowered his feet, waited till the giddiness had subsided. Thank God his was an afternoon Convocation. Beginning this morning at 10:00 a.m. Education, Business Administration and Agriculture were being herded through. Arts and Fine Arts, Science and the Pseudo-Sciences of Sociology, Psychology, Political Economy, and Human Kinetics were at 2:00 p.m. Engineering, Architecture, and Medicine would do their costume parade tomorrow afternoon.

Now why had he thought 'parade,' he asked himself in the middle of shaving. They were for the young and the innocent, easily excited by bands and balloons and floats and painted Indians. There would be colourful academic robes and hoods and bonnets at the Convocation, of course, and a procession, but not cowboys and cowgirls, the R.C.M.P. Musical Ride, or a beauty queen in virginal white, throwing kisses right and left from her chuck-wagon throne, followed by a democrat loaded with wrinkled oldtimers. Nor would there be marching bands this afternoon, led by majorettes spinning batons high, catching them behind their backs, then shoving them through their crotches to toss and twirl them again. No clowns on flagpole stilts or unicycles, or tasselled Shriners on scooters. But at his Convocation this afternoon the processional would be led by a bagpiper; the high thrill of the pibroch had all the marching bands of North America skinned a mile.

When three hundred gowned and mortarboarded graduands filed past the Chancellor to receive congratulations and parchments, he predicted as he went down the stairs, they would be outnumbered by watchers about three to one. He could not recall a Convocation that he had not been moved almost to tears as he looked out over fathers, mothers, sisters, brothers, uncles, aunts, grandfathers, and grandmothers, all gathered to cheer for their winning young. On upturned faces this afternoon he would read pride, delight, love, and on some, surprise. No doubt about it, a Convocation *was* a victory parade.

So much of his life had been parade, or rather performance, up at the lectern, in seminar and class with young watchers and, he hoped, listeners, doing his best to excite them with wit and with drama and with passion real or pretended. Age had made him only a listener and a spectator now; with hearing and sight impairment, not a very good one at that. More than he wanted it to be, the parade now was interior and of the past. In time, there would be only street cleaners left, coming along behind to sweep up road apples and all the other parade garbage. Poor self-pitying old bastard. Young or old, how clear and trustworthy a view did anyone ever have of the parade? Outside or inside.

At lunch Nadya confessed she had sneaked in early this morning and turned off the alarm button. Thank God for Nadya!

Thank God for Irma! What a research champion she was, flushing up enough honorary-degree and Convocation detail for half a dozen chancellor introductions. No twice telling needed, just ask once and it's done; a two-and-a-half-page speech that came in at the allotted five minutes first time he tried it out – right down to the second. And, boy, could she ever capture his voice on paper for him, just the way he'd have written it himself. Not exactly an Oklahoma voice though, after fifty years up here.

Been a Canada fan right from the start. Seventeen when the old man booted him out. Rode the rails all the way north to Havre, Montana, where he heard they'd struck crude at a new record depth of six thousand feet in Paradise Valley north of the border. Canadians were having a depression, too, but roughnecks cashed in forty dollars a week, which wasn't peanuts. Hauled off the freight by the Royal Canadian Mounted Police, but only one night in the Medicine Hat bucket thanks to that ten-dollar bill he'd always kept in his left sock to cancel vagrancy charges.

Sure, they were all for crowning their Prince of Wales that year so they could kiss a new royal ass, but they didn't go in for Lords and Dukes and Earls. Didn't even talk like Englishmen, almost like Americans, though they did say 'zed' for 'zee', 'eh?' for 'huh?' But they didn't hold it against the prince when he threw away the crown to make an honest woman out of American Wally.

He owed this country, he truly did; hadn't drifted north,

he'd never have found Rachel, one beautiful redhead, sprinkled all over with freckles like nutmeg, though her temper tantrums were pure cayenne. Born in Sweet Clover, Utah, brought up to Canada at the age of sixteen when her parents migrated. Her Daddy, Jake Card, was a cattle buyer and one shrewd Mormon. During the American beef-quota-by-weight-restriction period old Jake bought a section just over the Montana border, had it declared a customs hold-up field, then used it as a feed lot so he could truck down light spring-weaned calves and hold them till they came out of bond as heavy two- or three-year-olds to be sold duty-free at high post-war American prices. That clever whizzer was probably the reason the tabernacle boys anointed Jake Card bishop years later. Two months after Rachel mislaid her period, then told him he was just a Jack Methodist anyway and ought to turn, he'd compromised: their kid and any others happened along could be brought up Mormon, but he'd have to keep running south with Wesley. The Cards agreed to that. He'd married the hole card of his life.

Hey there, Harley boy, there you go doodling again; never broke that habit since you started it as a kid. Longhorn steer – chuck wagon, right down to the pie drawer – oil rig – little black bug. No wonder Rachel called you a real doodle bugger. The doodle bug! What a fluke that had been, running across Willy Plucker, with his doctorates from universities all over Europe: Amsterdam in his native Holland, Düsseldorf, Heidelberg, Hamburg, Bologna, Turin. Found Dr. Willy Wooden Shoes and his doodle wonder bug in a machine shop on the edge of Shelby, forty miles south of here. Willy had prospered there doing metal castings during the war and when it was over had made a fortune buying crated airplane engines in mass quantities from war surplus, then selling them in Brazil and Argentina. Sucked his gin straight through sugar cubes, bred gigantic St. Bernards, correcting the breed's gentle nature and turning them into vicious guard dogs. Claimed he'd invented a perpetual-motion machine, but that was bullshit, too, like all the phoney degrees listed on his letterhead.

That doodle bug for finding oil clear down to the Devonian was no bullshit, though. Hadn't been for Willy, Harley Alcock might have gone on the rest of his life as a landman with long sessions in hotel rooms, steeping ranchers and farmers in scotch, rye, rum, bourbon, gin, whatever it took, softening them up till they signed their mineral rights over to Brown Oil. Thanks to Rachel's persuasion, Jake Card staked him to the ten thousand Willy wanted, and what a royal flush they'd been dealt after the doodle bug smelled sour gas way over to the east of Paradise Valley in the Honker Hills everybody had ignored! Kept it quiet until the blow-out so they could nail down rights on a territory the size of Wales. Had to bring old Red and his fire crew in asbestos overalls up from Texas to snuff the blowtorch and cap the well. Made millionaire before his twenty-ninth birthday. Professor Plucker ginned himself to death in Amsterdam ten years later. You were alive today, Willy boy, this here chancellor of Livingstone University would confer on you a *genuine* doctorate, honoris causa!

Convocations belonged to the chancellor really, and God only knew, he'd spent time enough in meetings planning this one. It was an important one, Livingstone University's twentieth anniversary, and the big question was how to make it special. Not a single one of the academia nuts could come up with anything fresh, but Irma sure could: a time capsule to be buried at the foot of Wapta Tower and to be opened centennial year 2068. At first it was to be just an alumni time capsule, but as it got going, everybody had to jump into the skipping rope. Main capsule would be an earth-coloured urn

turned by that long-haired art professor Fournier, would hold
a current copy of the *Western Post* and the student newspaper,
The Advance, and a black and gold seventeen-mile-marathon-
run alumni T-shirt.

'We want the contents of the alumni time capsule to repre-
sent the farm and ranch agricultural and the energy-resource
bases of our province,' President Donaldson had said at one of
the meetings, 'as well as aboriginal.' A great meeting man,
the president. Never forgot to dot his 't's and cross his 'i's.

So: in must go the goddam seeds from the Faculty of Agriculture, including malting barley, tetra-clone day lily, saffire
safflower, and sugar beet. Irma had suggested the miniature
oil derrick to him; they bought that. When it came to Native
Studies, Whyte wanted hand-beaded moccasins, shaman and
chief headdresses, and a medicine bag donated by the Paradise
Valley Stony Reserve, as well as a blond scalp lock given out
of their large collection by the Foothills Museum. Rumour
said it had been sliced off the old Indian fighter, Sam Livingstone, after whom the University had been named, but unless
he had been sporting a toupee at the time, he died a quite
natural death in Spokane. Also in the capsule would go letters
from the prime minister and the provincial premier along
with their photos. It was Irma who had suggested Reagan,
though only to him, and he had thought why the hell not give
it a try. The good old boy came across in record time. Himself, not Bush. Student council wanted a Michael Jackson
glove in there too, but he hadn't complied, thank God.

Fifty years in Canada come next month, and they'd been
good ones. Canadians could truly teach Americans a few
things: take that smart political wrinkle of theirs, vote of
confidence in the government. Nixon would have been out on
his smart ass way before Watergate. What a heartbreaker
that had been, all that dirty laundry showing that the U.S.A.

123

was as corruptible as any banana republic. Looked like the death of the presidency, and he'd been *this* close to taking out the Canadian citizenship. Damned if he hadn't. But Rachel said she'd leave him if he did. Meant it just as much as she had when she found out about Becky down in Apple Valley and he'd said to her what the hell's wrong with polygamy? Shouldn't have said that. End of Apple Valley Becky.

He owed this country a hell of a lot, not just the hundred and twenty million, give or take a few. Canadians weren't as warm as Americans and they weren't risk-takers, but one thing for sure, they were not innocent. When Nixon cuddled his little cocker spaniel, Checkers, and gave his mea culpa speech, there wasn't a dry eye from Anchorage to Key West. In front of their television sets most Canadians were throwing up.

He leaned back in the chair, looked around the den, where he had spudded in so many great deal ideas over the years.

He picked the speech off the desk. Good job, Irma girl. When I bow out of the chancellorship after Convocation you're coming with me. You should never have ended up in the university toolies, covering academic asses for the President, the Board of Governors, and the Senate. What an executive secretary you'll make for me. You'll board the jet whenever I go mulleting in New York, Washington, San Francisco, London, Paris, Tokyo, Dallas. You're in your late forties at least. Washboard chest. Sandpiper legs. No problem with Rachel.

Funny. She had never really cottoned to Canada, Rachel. Eskimo and beaver country. Hated the oil patch, she said. Look at who's all the time calling people 'noovo reesh.' Scarlett O'Hara was no cattle-buyer's daughter raised in the short-grass country. Hadn't been for Canada, Rachel girl, you wouldn't have Picassos and Monets on your walls and a rosewood concert grand that nobody can play 'Chopsticks' on, even if it were in tune.

Anyway.

Maybe she'll listen to the speech one more time if she's finished her crossword puzzle. On his way to the family room to try it on her one last time, it hit him: life was a crap game. Truly was. Either you were born lucky or you weren't. Either you were a wheeler dealer or you weren't. Jake Card was. Willie Plucker was. He was.

She hadn't finished her goddam crossword puzzle!

———

This job of being Convocation chairman had to be the biggest challenge he'd faced since making English Department Head three years ago. He'd welcomed it as one more rung on the ladder to becoming Dean Tait, but he'd never anticipated what a tricky one it would turn out to be. Very early there had been the bagpipe problem. Duncan McBain of Agriculture wanted them to lead the processional. Dempster of Music did not, protesting that his new composition, which would première at the Convocation, was intended to be a Convocation salute, '. . . both fanfare-like and concerto-like. I wrote it with some of our local talent in mind. It's scored for brass, string, wind and percussion instruments. The Chinook Symphony Association – '

'I'm perfectly aware,' Duncan had said, 'that the Chinook Symphony Association does not do pipe concertos. I'm not suggesting for a moment that – '

'My composition is supposed to open the Convocation.'

'The piper's role is simply to pipe in the procession,' Tait had explained.

'In which case my composition does *not* open the Convocation. It is no longer a salute or a fanfare. Also – I don't care to have my music introduced by squealing bagpipes!'

'The bagpipes do not squeal!' Duncan squealed.

'All right – caterwaul!'

'Gentlemen – gentlemen,' Tait said. 'This musical – '

'When bagpipes are blown the result is not music!'

'It is the *oldest* music,' Duncan protested, 'the pentatonic scale of Damascus!'

'Now – wait a minute,' Tait said.

'We've had bagpipes for all nineteen convocations – '

'And it's time for a change – '

'Come on, you fellows. I am the chairman of this Convocation.'

'No argument, Tait,' Dempster said. 'So – you make the decision. One way or the other – bagpipes or music.'

'They are not mutually exclusive – do not have to be. I suggest that the faculty be piped in, take their places on the platform, and that's the end of the pipes. Then the graduands – there are over three hundred of them – fill in the six front rows. This involves several minutes. Then the chancellor declares the Convocation opened. *Then* – we have your salute – your fanfare, Dempster.'

He'd handled that one well. Whyte of Native Studies had been even easier. When he found out the guy intended showing up on stage in Indian regalia, he told him moccasins were all right and he could wear the doe-skin, fringed, and bugle-beaded jacket if it were *under* his academic gown and topped off with a mortarboard, but for the Great Spirit's sake no harness bells, bear claws, weasel tails or porcupine quills. The president and the chancellor had unselfishly promised not to do the Chief Dance, so the least Whyte could do was to save the eagle-feather war bonnet for the reception afterwards.

Unlike Sitting Bull, Whyte had been born and raised in posh Rosedale, Toronto.

But the biggest problem of them all had been Lyon. It was one of his own making, he reminded himself. He'd been the one to pull the rug out from under Lyon. At the time he'd had no choice.

'Gross shortage of office space,' he'd written in his report to the President and the Dean of Arts and the Academic Vice-President. 'We find ourselves faced with the situation pertaining to four professors returning from sabbatical leave, five newly hired professors and no offices for any of them. At this point in time it is not a small budget item, cost and finance-wise. Besides the office there is the involvement of a T.A.'s time and salary for a research assistant to Dr. Lyon, xeroxing, typing and other costly support benefits at a time when all universities are suffering cuts and a shortage of funds. This decision is the most painfully necessary one I have been faced with since becoming Chairman of the English Department. I am the first to recognize Dr. Lyon's great contribution in the past to Livingstone University ever since its founding, indeed. But all good things must come to an end and I am extremely sorry that this umbrella afforded to Dr. Lyon has to be folded up.'

They'd gone along with him in the end, and in a way he had come to wish they hadn't. The move had probably inter-rupted Lyon's momentum badly on the Mark Twain biogra-phy. Herbie Stibbard and Colin Dobbs and a few others in the department would probably never forgive him. Maybe some would after today, though they'd probably never appreciate how hard he'd worked to get Lyon the honorary professorship and the privilege of delivering the Convocation address.

It hadn't been easy. From the start Environmental Design

had wanted it to go to Spivak of Zoology. So did the Biology Department, pointing out that Spivak had discovered that bighorn mountain sheep belched, and that this flatulence was characteristically shared with *Ovis aries* or domesticated sheep. Once he had found that sheep wild and tame shared this same ruminant gastric phenomenon, Spivak had established a direct correlation between belching and a decline in wool and meat production for *Ovis aries*, a discovery which had changed feeding techniques for domesticated sheep first in Australia and New Zealand, then all over the world. The honorary Professorship should be conferred on Dr. Spivak.

However.

Environmental Design had been helped by Spivak in their fight with the provincial government and the Winter Olympics Committee, who wanted to use Paradise Valley as the venue for ski events. Spivak's report, saying that such wilderness rape would destroy the last great grazing ground for bighorn mountain sheep, and the subsequent stink raised by Environmental Design, wrecked Human Kinetics' plan to take over the area for their winter sports program after the Olympics. Large provincial and federal operational grants to the university also went down the drain. That brought the president and the chancellor on side with Human Kinetics to finish off Spivak's candidacy.

Political Economy, Sociology, History, and Business Administration had nearly pulled off Armand Hammer, but he had good reasons for declining: he was recovering from surgery, and he had already accepted an LL.D. from Trent University, to be awarded in absentia. Psychology had recommended their Dr. Harbottle on two counts: (a) he was the father of the Norwegian albino research rat and (b) he had received wide acclaim for his Phallometric Study of Erotic Preferences of Deviate and Non-deviate Males through Measurement of Changes in Penis Volume. Harbottle had not even made the short list. Dr. Lyon would be the recipient of the honorary degree.

Next decision: who delivers the Convocation address? This time round the adversaries had been formidable: President Donaldson versus Chancellor Alcock. Their pick of the four recipients: Carl Schlitgen, c.e.o. of Muhlerberg Beer, whose generosity had made possible the construction of Livingstone's Olympic-size Muhlerberg Beer swimming pool. If three hundred and seventy-five big ones wasn't worth the honour of delivering the Convocation address, inflation had really got out of hand.

But he'd won that one too for Lyon. The head of Muhlerberg Beer would not give the Convocation address, but he would be the main speaker later at the Chancellor's dinner honouring the recipients of honorary degrees. Perhaps Lyon and others might forgive him some day, though he doubted that. They'd never know the lengths to which he'd been driven by contrition.

No end to problems. As soon as he'd got up this morning and seen those dark clouds to the west, he'd known he shouldn't have gone along with the Master of Kathleen MacNair on the retractable-plastic-roof-over-the-close question.

'Open,' said the Master. 'Let God's bright sunshine shine through – '

'But – '

'We've always had an *open* Convocation. Traditionally sunny – we've always been jolly lucky. Never a drop in nineteen years.'

'Could be this time.'

'I rather doubt it,' the Master said. 'Besides, my dear Tait, it's not as simple a matter covering and uncovering the close as you might think.'

'Then maybe we better play it safe and do it the day before.'

'People can always bring umbrellas, you know.'

'I know they can. I also know that as Convocation chairman, I have a responsibility to deliver a dry one.'

'We shall see.'

'Let's play it – '

'Professor Tait, I am the Master of Kathleen MacNair. I have the responsibility of deciding whether or not we shall have, so to speak, a condom pulled over the close.'

So. An *open* convocation. He turned on the television; 'Sat. morning . . . prob. precip. 40 percent . . . clearing evening . . . prob. precip. . . . 20 . . . percent . . .' Damn it all! When you came right down to it that was life – in or out of Parliament or Academe: politics.

Looking good, Harley boy, no dark cloud threatening any more. Moved out of the west and right on by, and the sun had come out just as the last of the graduands made it to the seats. So there wasn't going to be a goddam two-hour delay while the plastic lid was pulled over the close. Or the quad. Or whatever they called it. Hadn't realized how much this Convocation and chancellor's swan song meant to him. After they bury that time capsule – good bye, Livingstone University.

Going to be a great Convocation. Right on time. Fanfare starting up now. Processing each graduand should take between fifteen and twenty seconds, at least three per minute, or a hundred and eighty per hour. Left a good hour for his and the president's speeches, delivery of the Convocation address, awarding of the honorary degrees. All went well this Convocation should come in under the wire in record time.

Hey, not bad! Short and sweet. Better congratulate that composer at the wine and cheese after. Get his name from somebody. Now Tait's heading for the lectern to introduce you, and it's your turn to come out of the chute number one in the bareback event. Give 'em hell, Harley boy, and stay on till the horn blows!

———

'I want to welcome you all here today for the twendieth birthday convocation of Livingstone University. Also want to congradulate everybody helped make this birthday pardy happen. Hasn't been easy. Just ask your president. Or me. Lot of barrels of midnight oil burned in planning meedings this past year. You should have seen the Chairman of the Convocation Committee, Charles Tait, University Secretary, Irma Sawyer, Executive Officer, Ralph Norton, and many others, fussing over this affair. Looks as though we might pull it off. We'll know that for sure tomorrow afternoon when we bury the time capsule. Understand they spudded in the hole under Wapta Tower early this morning . . .'

'So much for preliminary engineering madders . . .'

———

Because Slaughter began with an S, he was fourth from the tail end of the English Department Graduate Degree line. Altogether there were twelve of them, which made him number nine. Three times three makes nine. Three left over. Good sign. He'd dropped out of line, headed for the faculty washroom in Kathleen MacNair, but he realized he'd left it too late when he heard the bagpipes starting up just as he went inside. When he came out, the fanfare had started. He'd run down the two flights of steps and out into the close.

'Hold up,' the commissionaire said. 'You can't go – '

'I sure as hell can!'

'No-one admitted after the processional.'

'I had to get to the can!'

'Our orders – '

'I had orders from vicious stomach flu – cramps – '

'Sorry, but – '

'. . . not to shit myself up on stage in the middle of Convocation!'

'I can't help that.'

'Yes. You can. Let me past!'

———

Sorry, Chancellor, wasn't easy wrestling myself free from that officious old bastard and at the same time keep my gown from flying apart. Took a knee in the nuts to make him let go.

———

'. . . whole thing started out in Europe, maybe Germany. Being awarded by Cambridge and Oxford in the fifteenth century. When they were fed up with Old World oppression, scholars and teachers packed the custom in their suitcases and brought it to the New World.

'First honorary degree was awarded in 1692 by Harvard Universidy to Increase Mather – "Doctor of Sacred Theology." Not sure whether or not Harvard ever did confer a "Doctorate of *Profane* Theology" on anybody, though that's the same year in Salem Village that nineteen alleged witches were hanged, and one pressed to death . . .'

———

'Can I have a look at your program, Nancy? Thanks.'

Ah. Right after the chancellor the honorary degrees, then Dr. Lyon doing the Convocation address. Then the president. Then the English B.A.s. Then . . . oh, God. Very last, the graduate degrees. Cool it, Slaughter.

———

'Conferring of honorary degrees spread to many, though not all, American universidies, spilled over into Canada. Can't think of a single Canadian universidy today doesn't confer honorary degrees. Old and New World, those with honorary degrees make up the Who's Who of prominent cidizens. The Iron Chancellor, name of Bismarck, got at least one; Sir Winston Churchill bagged them by the dozens. Universidy of Alberta brags it has conferred an LL.D. on every Prince of Wales since 1905. George Washington picked up two LL.D.s, one from Yale and one from Harvard. Doctorates of Law seem to be your most popular honorary degree, which leads me to the conclusion most people wish they were lawyers. Can't understand why.'

———

'Here's your program back, Nancy. Thanks. I mislaid mine.' In the faculty washroom.

They'd all been in the run-through last night. As each

department's turn came up, graduands were to leave their seats and form a line in alphabetical order in the aisle below right stage corner. One by one Professor Holroyd would announce a name; that person would mount the steps, turn left, and walk to centre stage. That might be the time to do it. No. Too soon. Not then.

'I think I know why honorary degrees are so popular. They make fine substitutes for hereditary titles. Russians have their orders: "Hero of the Soviet Union" – "Order of Lenin" – "Order of the Red Banner of Toil." France has its "Legion of Honour"; in that country it's been said it's inconceivable a Frenchman can reach middle age without picking up a Legion of Honour. As well as syphilis.'

That one had got her to look up from her crossword puzzle.

Come on, Slaughter. Let's get it exactly right. When you reach centre stage, you turn right, stop before the chancellor and that scarlet and gold footstool at his feet. How about then? Maybe.

'Now in case our four people might get swelled heads, I have to point out that in the same honourable company of the World Record Holder, the late Herbert Hoover, who was granted eighty-two of them, and the runner-up – Dwight Eisenhower – just fifty – there is also Bongo, the seeing-eye dog, who received a D.C.F. (Doctorate of Canine Fidelity) from Newark University a few years ago . . .'

'. . . we have, however, taken great care in selecting candidates for degrees honoris causa, which are, as the Oxford Dictionary explains, ". . . a recognition of distinction, or a tribute of honour." I wanna salute our graduands this afternoon and the four people who have merited the highest honour this universidy can bestow – Doctorate Honoris Causa.'

————

'I wish to present Dr. Kenneth Lyon for the degree of Honorary Professor,' Tait began after he had bowed to the Chancellor. 'He is only the second in the lifetime of Livingstone University to be named Honorary Professor, the other recipient being Dr. Arnold Johnston, who was a member of the international team which pioneered the ice-box approach to open-heart surgery. Dr. Johnston did his great work in the laboratory of Livingstone University's Medical Faculty, and in due course shared with his American colleagues a nomination for the Nobel Prize.

'In conferring this degree we recognize Livingstone's great debt to Dr. Lyon, internationally respected Mark Twain scholar, a creative and caring human being who despises the arcane, the vain, the hypocritical, the pompous and the pretentious as much as Sam Clemens ever did . . .'

————

Well, Sam and I can't say the same for you, Tait. I appreciate the honorary degree, but it doesn't make up for pulling the emeritus chair out from under me without warning. Hadn't been for Nadya and Rosemary, I'd still be in intensive care.

———

'. . . a decade he held the Mark Twain chair at New York State University in Buffalo; he initiated the first Canadian Studies program – ever – anywhere – at Michigan State University. Twenty years ago he came back to the land of his birth and to Livingstone to serve as chairman of the English Department he created, and to give that department the finest creative-writing dimension of any university on this continent.'

———

Hopeless trying to pick out their faces in that crowd out there, especially Rosemary's, so small and so dear. Ah – there! In the very back row. Centre. She's got her beloved Wrinkles with her.

'. . . today writers are still discharging their debts to Dr. Lyon in their poems and plays, short stories and novels, and there are English teachers in schools and universities on both sides of the border, carrying his Mission Band Message to others. Mr. Chancellor, may I present for honorary professorship – Dr. Kenneth Lyon.'

———

All right. All right, Tait. You're forgiven. Almost. My turn now, Sam. Oh dear, both of them were waving to him! Now Rosemary was holding up Wrinkles so he could see too!

'Mr. Chancellor, Mr. President, graduands, honorary doctoral candidates, mothers, fathers, sisters, brothers, aunts and uncles, grandmothers and grandfathers. The novelist and historian and teacher, Wallace Stegner – who was a prairie boy once in Eastend, Saskatchewan – has said in his book *Wolf Willow* that the prairie and the foothills West should create poets. I agree with him. It certainly teaches early that to be human means to be conscious of self and of being separate from all the rest of the living whole. Human therefore equals lonely. The cost of being aware of a unique inner self, which mirrors the outer remainder of the whole, has an outrageously high price in loneliness. It is impossible to rejoin the living whole to ease the human pain of loneliness except by dying. That does work. In the end.'

Oh, God, how I wish you were out there this afternoon, Momma! What a lovely surprise it would be for you. Yes, Momma, I'll take down my pants, yes, Momma, it's my naughty fault you've got another headache and can't take me to Kiddy Playland so I can go on the Devil Drop and the Corkscrew and the Tilt-a-Whirl and the Octopus and the Crazy Mouse. Too bad you're not here, Dr. Rosner and the Reverend Elijah Matthews, oh, what glorious hard-ons you'd get this holy Convocation day!

'I wonder, since we on this continent are New World humans, if we do not have to pay a higher price because we have such a shallow and recent past and because our part of the earth's skin is still both wild and tame. We have no medieval cathedrals with soaring Gothic arches to awe and comfort us with ancestor echo; we do not unearth Roman baths and walls and roads. In the Canadian West we are the newest of the New World. My own generation was newest of all, the first white children to be born and stained in childhood by the prairie or the foothill or the mountain West. It is difficult to be much newer than that, and, therefore, it is historically lonelier. Because of an earlier appointment, seventy-eight years ago, with a mysterious stranger, Samuel Clemens, wherever he may be, cannot take part in our Convocation ceremony this afternoon. But I assure you that, because of his own frontier boyhood, he would agree with me.

'My early years were not along the Mississippi, but as a child I wandered over the foothills a great deal, the wind urging me, dirging for me through the foothills harp of telephone wires; they hummed and they twanged and they sang, and they seemed to endlessly adjust themselves against the wilderness stillness. In my young world, at a very early age, I learned I was mortal; I could die. End of Kenny Lyon. The humming, living, foothills did not give a hoot about that; Ikey did, and Mate and Hodder, my brother Henry, my mother, my grandma. My Aunt Myrtle maybe. When you learn you are going to die, you truly understand you are human; you have then been given a new perspective, which is very helpful in deciding what is important and what is unimportant.

'Socrates observed that the unexamined life is not worth living; there is a foothills expression that says much the same thing: "Don't you eat that there stuff, Elmer, it's horse . . ." I'm sure most of you out there know the finish of that wise warning. I have a corollary. Man also does not live by reason alone; the simply *intellectual* life is not worth living. It is for this reason that humans build their bridges from lonely human self to lonely human self. This human need to bridge explains wives, mothers, brothers, sisters, regions, nations; these bridges cannot be built out of money, power, prestige – just love. We are the only animals who paint, sing, sculpt, compose, worship – all bridges. There has never in the time of man and woman been a truly great nation whose people did not construct such bridges, and there never will be.'

You kneel on the footstool – as rehearsed – then – after you've risen . . . Nope. Won't do either. You'd have your back to the audience. Have to be *after* you've shaken hands with the chancellor and you turn around and face out . . . Wait a minute. Wait one minute. First you've got to march left stage – no – right – and get that rolled-up M.A. from Doctor Swann. This is what six years is all about, isn't it?

'Artists, philosophers, historians know that a human is a finite, warm sack of vulnerability. Because they do, they have an unfair advantage over politicians and generals and quarterbacks, the heads of United Fruit, Dow, or Hooker Chemical. Art is the only thing humans do for its own sake that does not involve an adversary relationship. Religion, unfortunately, cannot be included in this category; the Crusades, the Spanish Inquisition, the Covenanter wars, the Ayatollah Khomeini, Jerry Falwell, Oral Roberts, all confirm that. In the arts, there are no winners over losers, victors over vanquished, Soviet over American, toreador over bull. Creative partners to artists, who look with wonder and delight at a painting or a play or a ballet, who listen to a symphony, or even an opera, do not take anything from the artist. A novel, a poem, a play remain their makers': through shared pity and terror, compassion and empathy, laughter and tears, *both* the writer and the creative partner win.

'Death and solitude justify art, which draws human aliens together in the mortal family, uniting them against the heart of darkness. Humans must comfort each other, defend each other against the terror of being human. There must be civilized accountability to others. The coyote, the jack rabbit, the badger, the killdeer, the dragonfly do not experience alien terror; they are not accountable to each other.

'We lift bridges between ourselves and others so that we may walk from our own and into others' hearts. Our schools and universities, through the Arts and Humanities, must teach the young not just how to make a living but how to live, must keep humans from destroying bridges and returning to the heart of darkness. The bridges are fragile and they can be destroyed, for they are only man-made. We also make patterns, which are not divine or absolute; they are life patterns, which grow and change in a living manner. We have grown them generation after generation to defeat the heart of darkness. The good guardians of the Arts and the Humanities reveal such bridges and patterns to our young. Our vulnerable young.'

———

No parchment's going to be handed out to you if you've already done it. So leave the Chancellor. Go to Swann, take the thing. Shake hands with Swann, then march back to centre stage and let them have it. First the Chancellor and all those faculty bastards sleeping in their seats, then turn and face down stage to do the audience. Yeah! Yeah! Hang in, Slaughter, your turn will come. Praise God. Praise His

Holy Name, the time for retribution will come; in its good time!

———

'Over a hundred and fifty years ago, Shelley said, "We have more moral, political, and historical wisdom, than we know how to reduce into practice . . . . There is no want of knowledge respecting what is wise and best in morals, government, and political economy . . . . We want the poetry of life; our calculations have outrun conception; we have eaten more than we can digest. . . . Poets are the unacknowledged legislators of the world." '

———

Holroyd had called out his name. Been a long long wait, but now the time of revelation is at hand! He mounted the steps. He turned left, marched centre stage. He turned right. Took six steps and stopped underneath the Livingstone coat of arms banner with its wheat sheaves and its recumbent and cross-eyed black Angus bull. Before him sat the fat toad robed in crimson and gold, with his academic tam hanging over his left ear like a tired pizza. He knelt. As rehearsed. Both knees on the footstool.

'Congradulations, Mr. Slaughduh.' Didn't even look up from the list on your lap, did you?

'Up yours too, Mr. Chancellor.' He stayed on the footstool. Now the guy was looking left toward Nancy Thompson prancing toward them. Didn't even hear what I just said did you, Mr. Chancellor? Well, brace yourself, because in a moment or two I think I am going to get your undivided attention.

'Please move along now.'

'A flash in time saves nine, sir.'

'I said move it, boy!'

He rose. He turned. He bowed to the audience. Flipped up the back of his gown. He held it for a count of three. Though she had only a side view, Nancy squealed. The Chancellor's jaw dropped. He rose halfway up from his throne, fell back, his mouth still ajar.

He dropped the gown. He turned right, walked to Swann, grabbed the parchment that Swann was still holding out to him. He turned left, marched back to centre stage, lifted the corners of his gown and spread them high and wide in black bat-wings to pirouette. Slowly. Three times round. Look, Momma. No jock strap.

Exit. Stage right.

The Chancellor, the President, Vice Presidents, Deans, and Faculty members stared after the departing M.A. graduate, naked but for his gown, socks, and shoes. Heads of all the Convocation spectators turned as he ran with black gown flying from Kathleen MacNair close.

Still in shock the Chancellor looked down at the program in his lap. Been doodling again. A pair of dice this time: Snake eyes!

———

Convocation Chairman Tait felt the first drops of rain spatter against his sweating forehead. Umbrellas were mushrooming all over Kathleen MacNair close.

———

That made two scores evened up. Kick me out of Psychology,

Harbottle, then see what happens to your Duke of Downs-view. And that's no bull. Hah! Good only for bologna now! What is the current Chicago livestock market price on no-balls bulls? And how did you and the president and the chancellor and all the vice presidents and deans and department heads and graduands enjoy that flashy Convocation? And I did get my M.A. first.

Didn't expect me to show up after for the wine and cheese, I bet, but I couldn't resist. Gratifying to accept a few grinning congratulations here and there. Mostly from engineers. Great stroke of luck, spotting her and the kid with old Lyon. Special connection there. Must check that out.

Two down, and one to go. She's next. She should have been first maybe, but there's nothing wrong with saving the worst for the last. By God, she's going to get it.

He was pretty sure she hadn't seen him in all that crowd. His hunch had paid off; she and the kid had left with Lyon. To stay on the safe side he left early and headed for the Triumph. He spotted them leaving Kathleen MacNair together, trailed them at a careful distance all the way to the house across the street from Livingstone Park. He had finally run her to ground!

They were living with the old man all right. Next stop: move out of the groves of Academe and into those of Livingstone Park.

———

After supper, during which Rosemary had worn the mortarboard he'd stuffed with rolled newspaper so that it wouldn't slip off, Nadya came down.

'She's had her bath now. Wants you to tuck her in, read to her.'

'Sure.'

'But this time something not quite so long as *War and Peace*, eh?'

'Okay.'

'Better take this with you.' She handed him the mortarboard.

'Mmmmh.'

'Congratulations, Honorary Professor, Doctor.'

'Thanks.'

'One hell of a Convocation address. I was proud of you.'

Just as he reached the foot of the stairs, she called out something to him.

'For God's sake, Nadya, do not try to tell me something from any distance over a hundred goddam feet away and from another goddam room!'

She had come to the doorway. 'I just said I hoped you'd perform as well at the birthday party next week as you did at the Conv – '

'Oh, shit!'

'Ah-ah, you've got to watch your foul language with the little ones.'

'I will! I promise. I'll save it just for you!'

Rosemary was in bed with Wrinkles. He laid the mortarboard down on the dresser, picked up *Through the Looking-Glass*. As he sat down on the edge of the bed, she said, 'You make me feel good inside.'

'Do I?'

'Uh-huh. Just being with you.'

He stopped looking for their place in the book. 'Same here.'

'But you don't brush your hair very much, do you?'

'I guess not.'

'It's always sticking up over your ears. Makes you look like a owl.'

Oh yes. Here it was: 'The Walrus and The Carpenter.'

'Out at the zoo there was two of them. They were Horny Owls.'

'Horned owls.'

'Yeah. Pointy feathers sticking up over their ears just like horns. Like you got.'

'Rosemary, you want me to read to you or don't you?'

'Sure I do. I love you to – '

'Then shut up and start listening.'

But the lobster quadrille ending saddened her and she didn't want him to read any more. 'Let's just talk, Professor.'

'Sure.'

'About this afternoon at the – the – '

'Convocation.'

'Yeah. Everybody all dressed funny up there. Why did that guy open up his black nightgown wide and he didn't have anything on underneath it?'

'He's sick.'

'Huh?'

'Mentally. You know.'

'Crazy guy?'

'Getting there,' he said.

'But – in front of all those people – why would he want to show them – '

'End of discussion.'

'You said we'd talk.'

'Simple, choose another subject,' he said.

'But why did he – '

'He just wanted to spoil it for everybody.'

'Wrinkles didn't like what that guy did.'

'Good for Wrinkles.'

'Hey!' She sat up. 'Let's put that mortal board on Wrinkles and then he'll be real happy.'

They did, and conferred upon him a Doctor of Laws, Doctor of Letters, Doctor of Philosophy. Honoris Causa.

'Are there any other ones?'

'Lots. Doctor of Education – Sociology – Medicine – Psychology – Economics – Business Administration – Science – Horoscope, Teacup, and Crystal Ball Reading – '

'Let's give him those ones too.'

'Not tonight.'

Both agreed that Wrinkles bore a striking resemblance to the chancellor. After he had straightened up from kissing her goodnight, she said, 'I think birthday parties are way more fun than con . . . conger . . .'

'Convocations. I do too, dear.'

———

Tonight she had seemed distracted all through supper; he took the first game by twenty-three points. When he broke for the next one, but didn't sink a red, he had to speak to her twice before she got up from the couch and came to the table.

He said, 'Something's really bothering you.'

'Mmmmh.'

'Care to tell me?'

She put down the chalk, went over to the rack and put up her cue. 'Come on over to the couch with me, will you?'

He leaned his cue up against the scoreboard.

'Better put it in the rack, Doctor. I don't feel like playing any more tonight.'

When he was beside her, she said, 'The Convocation this afternoon – that fellow showing off his crown jewels.'

146

'*That's* what's bothering you?'

'No. Not seeing him do that,' she said, 'Seeing *him*.'

'Yes?'

'Uh – I know him. He's the one I told you about – Charles Slaughter. He saw us, too. In Kathleen MacNair at the wine and cheese. Uh . . . This isn't going to be easy for me, Doctor.'

'Anyway.'

'He – uh – he is the reason I answered your ad. We were on the run. From him. Maybe I should have told you about this sooner than now, but I figured – uh – we'd – we were – safe now. I changed my mind this afternoon. We're not.'

'What changed it?'

He saw that the knuckles of both hands, clasped on her lap, were white.

'He was looking at us – several times. At the reception after. Have you ever seen pure *hate* on a person's face?'

'Probably.'

'It was there on his.' She shuddered. 'You know about the fellow sniped all those people from the bell tower at Stanford?'

'Yes.'

'The one that did in all the Florida sorority girls?'

'Yes.'

'And the Vancouver guy – ten – eleven – fifteen young – '

'You trying to tell me this fellow's a serial . . .?'

'I'm just trying to say that he is the kind of person, who is quite capable of – of – oh God!' She turned and put her head down in her arms on the back of the couch.

There was no sound, but her shoulders were moving convulsively. He put his arm around her; she turned to him, buried her head in his chest. 'I – huh – I duh-don't cry – uhuh-easy, Doct-tuh-her.'

147

'All right. All right now.'

When she had got a grip on herself and straightened up and wiped her eyes, she said, 'Brace yourself and I'll tell you the whole goddam story – I should have given you it right at the first.'

She had known, she told him, that Slaughter lived in the same apartment building as she did; she'd seen him several times in the lobby, twice on the elevator. She also knew that he rode a black motorcycle; their acquaintanceship had been that casual until last fall. Her friend Debbie had taken in Rosemary to be with Kimberly for a week in their apartment three floors down so that Nadya could swamp out her own place and catch up on all her accumulated laundry, from slipcovers to curtains to sheets and pillow slips to socks and shirts and jeans.

She had been alone in the basement laundry until Slaughter had come out of the storage room, where tenants' trunks and cartons were kept. She felt that the encounter had startled both of them. They had told each other their names. He was out of cigarettes. They had lit up. It was funny they hadn't run into each other at Livingstone University, where he had finished his M.A. with a creative dissertation which would some day be recognized as the great Canadian novel. He was still at the university, but now in Psychology as an assistant researcher.

'He was a real charmer and I guess I'll never learn. I don't know what it is that draws guys like him to me. Like Rosemary's father. I shouldn't be acting at all. Wrong line of work. Should have been a snake charmer.'

'You charmed me.'

'Yeah. You're a pretty nice old snake.'

Slaughter had helped her load the washer and the dryer, and she put in all the quarters they would need for the next forty minutes, and why didn't he come up to the apartment and have a cup of coffee during the wait. He had washed and dried a week's worth of dishes for her, then took down curtains and helped her move the hide-a-bed couch to the other living-room wall. When they returned to the basement he lugged three bags of garbage down. After he had helped her unload and load, he had gone back into the storage room. He came out carrying a sleeping bag and suitcase; he returned to come out again wearing a backpack and a long canvas carryall slung over his shoulder. When she had asked him if he was vacating his apartment, he said he had done that ten days ago. He had been sleeping ever since in the storage room.

'He said he'd been in hospital, hadn't been working in Psychology long enough to qualify for sick benefit, was behind in his rent, and they'd kicked him out. He said it was a return spell of his old malaria. He called it quartan ague. I looked it up. I believed him – God, how could I be that stupid! Most Canadian mosquitoes can't give a person malaria, you know.'

'I know.'

'Let's finish this upstairs.'

She had felt so sorry for him when he had told her he was broke and had no idea of where he could find shelter, that she had told him he could move in and use the hide-a-bed.

'At first it was all right. No misunderstandings. One of the things that really made me buy the malaria was the way a couple of times, when he had one of his spells, his face flushed scarlet, right up to the roots of his hair. The second time, he cried. He made me cry once when he told me he'd never given up trying to find his mother, who'd had to abandon him as a baby. How he'd spent years searching for her, putting ads in the paper, going to Vital Statistics people, who wouldn't tell him who his own mother was, how he'd been shuffled and dealt from foster home to foster home, where they beat him. Tragic bunch of shit. I know that now. You want a cup of tea?'

'No. I'm going to have a good stiff Scotch.'

'Me too.'

She brought their glasses to the coffee table, sat down beside him, took care of half her drink in one long swallow. 'This isn't going to be easy, Doctor. The third night – ah – I woke up out of a sound sleep. Pitch-dark. Two – three o'clock. He'd wakened me. What a sneaky bastard! He'd climbed in – he was there beside me before I woke – he . . .'

She finished her drink.

'He – did he . . .?'

'Not really. You want another?'

'I do.'

When she came back to him, she said, 'You asked me a question.'

'Did I?'

'Did he rape me. Don't you want to know the answer to that?'

'No!'

'I think you better hear it anyway. I offered to do a blow-job on him. What else was a defenceless girl to do?'

'I said I didn't want to . . .'

'I went down on him.'

'I told you I . . .'

'I bit it – sank my teeth right in. Hard as I could.'

'Oh, God!'

'He was lucky. Been my Kiev great-gramma, it would have been right off.' She stood up. 'You just going to keep on shaking your head?'

'Thank you for your – candour.'

She sat down. 'I got away, made it down to Debbie's. Next

morning she went up to the apartment for me. He was gone. I moved in with her.'

'Did you get in touch with the police?'

'I wanted to but Debbie said if I did I was just asking for it. She knew what she was talking about. Her cousin was raped once and she went to the cops and there was a big hassle and when it went to court the guy's lawyer got her on the stand and she ended up having to prove she didn't ask for it – and what was unusual about going from a bar to his apartment for some fun? Debbie said if her cousin hadn't been able to prove it wasn't a willing one-night stand, what chance did I have when I'd invited him in with me for almost a week. I still went to the cops.'

'Did you charge him?'

'No. They said I could if I insisted, and I said yes, I did insist. I asked them how come they weren't very goddam enthusiastic about the whole idea. They said it was my decision to make, and then I realized they were trying to give me some kind of important message. You know what it was?'

'No.'

'That I could go ahead and lay a charge against him even though I didn't stand a snowball's chance of making it stick, and what was more important, if I did, I'd better keep looking over my shoulder, because now he'd have double reason for getting me. Debbie had been right. They were a bunch of irresponsible male bastards that were not at all fervent about seeing justice done for a female!'

'I see.'

'About a week later a very frightening thing happened. Addressed to me – Debbie's apartment number – two dozen yellow sweetheart roses. That's when I made up my mind to answer your ad. Up until yesterday I'd figured we were home free. No more, though. And the awful thing about it is – that was the first time he'd ever laid eyes on Rosemary!'

He tried to reassure her. And himself. 'Ever occur to you that when he sent those roses – might have been an act of contrition – '

'There was a card! It said, "*Vengeance is not His!*" I guess I haven't given you a clear picture of this guy. He's inside four walls.'

'What?'

'You know. On stage. The way you have to project all the way to the back row. Come on broad with every move – gesture – facial expression. This guy is not responsible to any audience. He'd never make a move *through* even if it was only a quarter turn . . . Am I making him clear to you, Doctor?'

'It's not a bad stage analogy.'

'Try a squash court. If he wasn't born with a fourth wall, his mommy or daddy sure nailed one up for him. He does only one-handers and he doesn't give a damn whether the house behind that wall is full or empty. Laughing or crying.'

'Socio-psychopath,' he said.

'If you want to understate it. Yes.' She got up. 'Goodnight Doctor.'

'Goodnight, dear.'

———

Both of them still sleeping in, and it was damn near noon. Call them, or wait for them to wake up and come down, *then* turn on the heat under the frying pan he'd loaded over an hour ago with bacon, start cracking eggs and doing the toast? Better wait; it *was* Sunday, so sleeping in was justifiable. How could she do it, though, after going over for him the dreadful affair that had caused them to come to him for sanctuary. She had been in full flight then, and last night he had read fright on her face – no, terror – when she told him more than he cared to hear.

Turned out to be the same fellow as the one who'd given that disgusting performance at Convocation yesterday. Been considerate of her not to tell him before now. How times and morals and sexual vocabulary had changed, though blow-job was a much softer term than cock-sucking. Wonder what they call muff-diving when they take that pleasure now. Don't care to know.

Maybe he ought to wake them; he could hardly wait till they'd come down and see him. Table was all laid, plates stacked and ready by the stove. He'd get them to sit down; he would dish out and they would be the world's first people to be served by a waiter wearing a black velvet mortarboard with gold bullion tassel, D. LITT. hood of scarlet superfine cloth lined with French grey (large cape with well-rounded semi-circular cut). Oxford style, by God. Call them down. Right now.

———

Well, Sam, we both knew that sooner or later this life of yours was going to turn dark; all of us can be dealt rotten cards. The loss of your beloved Suzie and Livy, Clara's nervous breakdown, Jeanie drowned in her bath, were dreadful ones, but you shouldn't have stained your bereavement with regret and guilt so that it would keep right on hurting. You should have mourned them more and yourself less. You held some pretty nice cards in a long run of luck: affluence, fame, friends, three daughters, and a loving and supportive wife, the best wild card of them all. You should have played them better.

Your mysterious stranger visits all of us, but he can't per-

suade us all to say no to humans. Not by a long shot. Bishop
Berkeley called him. So did Socrates and Shakespeare, Chau-
cer and Donne and Blake. Never sit down with a fellow like
Nietzsche, who will go mad and kiss a horse in Turin. Ten to
one it was not the velvet nose but the horse's ass. By choice.

You should have been ready for the mysterious stranger, for
he made many visits to you early in life. He called on me
when ants and undertaker beetles worked over my first dead
gopher, and when cream maggots brought to life again the
guts of a lump-jaw steer carcass, and when shrikes impaled
caterpillars or grasshoppers or field mice or dragonflies on the
barbs of prairie fence lines. If I didn't clearly recognize him
then, I sure as hell did the January afternoon in Knox Presbyterian church when Henry and I wore our blue middy suits
with their velvet collars and all the mourners sang 'Rock of
Ages' and 'Blest Be the Tie that Binds' at the open-coffin
horror of our Dad's funeral. When I was twelve he stole the
use of my right arm from me for five years, then took away
the only child Sarah and I were given, for ever. Three years
was not enough time for my Susan to make it to Radcliffe and
run crying tears of humiliation from the auditorium where
you began the Golden Arm story, the one you had promised
you would not tell in front of her classmates. And while we're
on the subject of despair, my brother, Henry, blew away his
head with a twelve-gauge Winchester. Special goose load.

I have cried for my Susan, Sam, and for my Sarah and for
Henry. I have cried for many mortals in my time. I cried for
the starving little Armenian children, who had only cakes of
mud and grass to eat. I cried for the little Belgiums, too,
without their severed hands. Years later I found out that the
pictures of their wrist stumps were First World War propa-
ganda touched out for horror's sake. It was pickled pigs' feet,

not child hands, that littered the street around their feet. The sadness and fright upon their faces were real.

The tubes to Sarah's throat were real. They made her breathe, but would not let her talk. Only her eyes could plead with me to pull them loose for her all those days she suffered in Western General before the last night of her life. Would you have done the same for Livy, whose face you could not recall two days after her death? Sarah's still comes back to me, Sam. Often. For Christ's sake wear your lonely old age as gracefully as you do your white Palm Beach suit.

My God, was he buried in it? Check it out, and while you're at it, see if the licensed embalmer and funeral director used blueing rinse when he washed Sam's hair for him!

———

He'd taken great care to find the right spot. Near the play area – with all the yipping young and their nannies and grannies – wouldn't do; had to be away from the benches and tables and the laughing lunchers from stores and offices across the river, the joggers and the touch-footballers and the cyclists and the frisbee nuts sailing their dishes and making their smart-ass ankle snatches. Once the spring chinooks had breathed grass and trees and bushes to life again and the sun was high and warm, it brought out damn near as many humans as it did mosquitoes.

Who needed spring to flaunt everyone's idiot delight at getting rid of scarves and overcoats and snow boots, the season conning people into thinking the world was simply wonderful. Take a look at those losers sleeping on newspaper, with their McGoof bottles in paper bags, their topcoats buttoned up at the neck, dogs cavorting and pissing and squatting, or the faggots with bush or washroom assignations. Spring or no spring it was the same old garbage pile alive with human maggots.

What a lucky find it had been, the clearing under the overhanging rock half-way up the park escarpment. Next step on the agenda, getting the trench shovel at war surplus, then half a day's digging and scooping and camouflaging with brush to turn it into a new residence. If he were to scare up seventy-nine fifty he could get a Lee Enfield. With the clear view of the house from the top of the rock, he could touch her off easy as a rabbit in a shooting gallery, as soon as she stepped out onto the front porch. Then up to the flats above, past the convent house and on to the empty shed in the cemetery, where he'd pried loose the door and stashed the Triumph.

Too simple. Too easy. Too good for her. Even strangling, or clubbing her to death with a tire iron, the way that big shot in the oil patch had evened it up with his ex, would be too good for her, almost the same as forgiving her. She must really suffer, for the rest of her life. Her child had to be the target.

8

<hr>

'NADYA, LAST COUPLE OF DAYS – EVER SINCE YOU TOLD ME about . . . I haven't been able to get that fellow, Slaughter, out of my mind.'

'Me, either.'

'I think he's a serious – problem,' he said.

'I know it. Look at how he got even with everybody at that Convocation. At the reception after, I saw him looking at me – his face – he intends to settle the score with me, too. I *know* it!'

'We've got to do something about him,' he said.

'What?'

'To begin with – find out more about him.'

'How?'

'I thought I might go out to the university, talk with some people in the English department. You said he'd been involved with the Psychology Department. Didn't he tell you he'd been a research assistant?'

'Could have been.'

'What do you mean could have . . .?'

'He's such a goddam liar. If it served his purpose he'd tell you Freud was his uncle,' she said.

'All the same, I'll check him out with the head, Dr. Harbottle.'

'Then what?'

'Maybe before that, I'll check with Counselling. Probably got a record with them. The head – I think her name's Cogswell. Might be a good idea to talk with her first.'

'You've got lots better things to do with your time . . .'

'No. I haven't. He keeps clouding up the biography on me. I have a personal interest in clearing up . . . Look, just let me handle it. You've got enough on your hands with running this house and Peter Pan and the Sock and Buskin and that birthday party of Rosemary's – Jesus, the day after tomorrow!'

'I got the magician outfit.'

'We get Slaughter taken care of – and the birthday party – maybe I can get back on track with Mark Twain.'

He did not tell her that depending on what he turned up, he might go to the police – maybe a lawyer – and to the court for a restraining order.

———

'Nice of you to see me, Miss Cogswell.'

'Dr. Lyon. I'd rather hoped to meet you one day. I've heard so many good things about you.'

'Oh.'

'During my years here there have been a number of your students come to me, and from what they've told me, I gather you're a pretty wise guardian.'

She couldn't be all bad if she had read William Blake. 'Was,' he said.

'Oh, yes. You're retired. What can I do for you?'

'I don't want to impose . . .'

'No problem,' she said. 'You've picked a good time. Inter-session. See that calendar?'

'Yes.'

'I don't need it to tell me what month or what week it is. Just have to look at my appointment book and right away I know it's, say, September and registration confusion time. First of December – mid-term test time. Month of May – lights on all night-time in a last desperate and hopeless attempt to make up for all the year's homecoming and grass and bridge and beer and fraternity and sorority parties – overdue theses and papers, mid-term and final failures. Right now, my work – it's a lark. So what can I do for you?'

'I'd like to know if you know a student – former student – he just received his M.A. in English – was a research assistant in Psychology.'

'I'm not a priest or a lawyer, Doctor,' she said, 'but you do understand there's – ah – a principle of confidentiality involved in my work.'

'Yes, I do.'

'So – now I've mentioned that, what would you like to know about Charles Slaughter?'

That was a surprise twist! 'How did you know?'

'Take your place in line. Since Convocation I've had

enquiries from the president – the chancellor – Dr. Harbottle in Psychology, and now you. I imagine there will be others.'

'So you do know him?'

'Of course. Haven't seen him for almost a year, but for a couple of years before that he checked in with me for one reason or another – with some regularity. Not always for help or guidance. He's quite a charmer. Articulate. Smart. And . . .' She looked away. She sighed. '. . . sad.' She sighed again. 'You know something, Doctor? Being young isn't all it's cracked up to be.'

'I can agree with you on that.'

'Or being a counsellor. Be nice if a person could skip youth altogether – or at least get it over much quicker.'

'You said you found him sad?' he asked.

'Oh yes. He never had a real father or mother. Abandoned in infancy. Foster homes. Abused. I felt quite sorry for him. He needed much more than we could give him. I advised professional help. I believe he got it.'

———

Harbottle had been at Livingstone almost as long as he had, and head of the Psychology Department for the past ten years. Though he'd only a passing acquaintance with him, it was hard not to be very much aware of Harbottle, for he was one of the most salient of Livingstone faculty members. He found him in the basement lab section of the Biology Building, and asked him if he could give him any information on Charles Slaughter.

'I understand he was a research assistant here for some time.'

Harbottle's face tightened. 'He was. He isn't now.'

'I gathered that.'

'Came to me almost a year ago – very well recommended. First by Whyte of Native Studies. Evidently he was one of Slaughter's supervisors for his M.A. dissertation – a novel dealing with native people. He said it was a very fine creative-writing thesis. You know Tait, of course.'

'I do.'

'His was the other glowing report I got on Slaughter. If you can't trust faculty references what can you trust?' Harbottle laughed ruefully. 'I know better now. Should have examined that word more closely.'

'What word?'

'Faculty. Leave out just one letter – "c" – and what have you got?'

'You may have a good point.'

'After Slaughter, I'm sure of it. Would you come with me – I have to look in on my rats. Just down the hall, and we can carry on in there.'

The room had a glass wall through which he could see a raised carousel platform. 'Be back with you in a minute,' Harbottle said.

Through the window he watched him in there, as he lifted a door out of which a rat appeared.

'I interviewed Slaughter,' Harbottle said when he came back into the observation room. 'Most impressive. Charming, in fact. Articulate. I was quite surprised that a young man who'd majored in English had considerable knowledge of Psychology. He said it had been his minor, that now he'd like to try for a degree in it as well, using some of his English credits and taking make-up courses in Psychology. He won me.'

Harbottle had not taken his attention from the carousel beyond the glass. The rat, which had been trying one path after another, examining each and retracing to explore

161

another, had come to stay and to sip at the end of the one
where Harbottle had hung a syrup tube. On a chart, Harbottle was making notations. 'In its laboratory aspect,' he
explained, 'the Livingstone Psychology Department deals
mainly in animal-learning measurement.

'Pigeons and rats. Dogs are expensive, and monkeys are
right out of sight. We breed our own rats. We found the
albinos not all that satisfactory, and we came up with a Norwegian wild rat and albino cross of our own. That's why
they're black and white – skin as well as hair. Most
researchers all over the world are using our hybrids now.
Much higher I.Q. They learn and they retain rules much
better.'

Harbottle's enthusiastic dedication to his rats was infectious, almost to the point of clouding the Slaughter purpose of
the visit. In memory, it seemed, the magic number had been
seven – two times either way, whatever that meant, but Harbottle and his assistants had discovered that by grouping
related memory bits into chunks, they could move the number
as high as twenty-one. Area was the important factor in the
wheel, with the reward of sugar water at the end of one of the
spoke tracks. The real breakthrough had come when he had
hit on the use of wire-mesh surfaces laid down to set out
perimeters with similars in each pie-shaped grouping.

'Gestalt,' Lyon said.

'Hard to admit for a fellow who started out Skinnerian,'
Harbottle said, 'but you could be right.'

'This man, Slaughter, became a research assistant.'

'Unfortunately.'

'In what way?'

'Several,' Harbottle said. 'Why?'

'I don't know just how to begin.'

'Just a minute. I'm through here. I think it would be nicer

if we carried on in my office.' Evidently it was the last rat for the day that had just finished its syrup reward and left the carousel.

Before reaching Harbottle's office down the hall, they stopped. 'This is our nursery. Just take a minute.' Inside, Harbottle began an examination of the four-row line of cages with glass fronts. 'We breed, gestate and deliver our hybrid infants in here. I probably check them out much more often than needed. I'll tell you something about Slaughter and those babies later.'

When they had settled down in Harbottle's office, he said, 'Coffee?'

'No thanks. I'm one of the tea minority.'

'Hey – me too.'

'Dr. Harbottle – '

'I don't like last names or titles. Please call me Stan.'

'I'm Ken. You said – regarding this man, Slaughter, your association with him was unfortunate – in *several* ways.'

'That's right. How about you?'

'I'm not sure. Yet,' he said, 'that's why I've – I'm – '

'Would you like me to go first?'

'Please.'

'Okay. Slaughter was just briefly involved in the rat learning program. He seemed a natural for another project of ours. "A Phallometric Study of Erotic Preferences of Deviate and Non-deviate Males through Measurement of Changes in Penis Volume". Ah, Ken, cream and sugar?'

'Clear and weak.'

When he had handed him a cup of tea, Harbottle said, 'This may turn out to be more than you care to hear.'

'I have not led a sheltered life.'

Harbottle explained that the sexual response study had been going on for two years before Slaughter showed up. It had taken over a year to set up the project; acceptance by the University itself had been difficult, to be followed by initial resistance from the National Research Council. Since there was no intention of treatment to follow, Harbottle had not even approached Health and Welfare. As it had turned out, the Review Committee had approved the study, but only to the tune of thirty-five thousand dollars, which was not nearly enough for space, payment to research assistants, computer technicians, grad students, and subjects.

'Once we had the up-front funding cleared, there were real problems. The Heisenberg Principle: does the operation for measuring the phenomenon destroy the phenomenon? Must the subjects be naive? No. Not really. No question – there'd have to be a dry run to acquaint each of them with what it was all about, to make them familiar with it so it would cease to be unusual.'

He had to agree with Harbottle that it *was* unusual from the subject's point of view: to be invited into what seemed an ordinary family or living room, to sit in a chintz-covered easy chair, to be paid the hourly minimum wage rate for looking at a series of images on a screen of home movie size, after you had unzipped your trousers and pulled on a water-filled condom with cream-coloured, plastic, spaghetti tubes winging out not from the base or the glans but from the trunk of your penis.

'The context had to be natural,' Harbottle went on, 'so we got a stage designer from Drama. Broadloom on the floor, drapes and sheers for the picture window. Wasn't really a window – one-way glass. Subjects were never allowed to see beyond to the projector, or the computer panel for measuring time of exposure of the stimulant images. Hidden overhead television cameras. We correlated with other measurements, a whole subjective scale handled through checks and balances, but this was an on-line test with penile blood turgidity and tumescence as *the* measure. Excited all of the team. Measurement under pure, scientific and objective conditions of sexual variations – sodomist, pederast, cunnilinguist, pedophile, sado-masochist. And we thought that maybe, just maybe, we might even shut the West Germans up on the question of hereditary print from conception for homosexuality.'

Once through a maze of questions and suggestions which handicapped and took attention away from *the* measure of changes in penis volume, the human sexual-response study had taken off. It had attracted international attention after *Eros Democratic* had done an outraged article with a full front-page illustration, a drawing of an erect penis in scientific harness of condom and tubes. Queries were promptly received from prestigious publications; *The Physiological Psychology Quarterly, The American Journal of Psychiatry,* as well as British, French, Italian and West German journals and *Hustler*. This interest had served as an effective lever; their grant had been renewed; this time for $90,000.

God Almighty, when was the man ever going to find his way through all this research underbrush to Slaughter!

'We thought we had it made. Then Slaughter joined us. He was great at first. For one thing, within a month our deviate subjects tripled. This guy knew where to find them and how to persuade them, though at the time I didn't realize the nature of his persuasion. I assumed these male subjects were coming to us for the usual reasons: monetary reward or vanity. Slaughter really understood a pretty complicated matter, the cluster that constitutes sexual arousal; adrenalin, blood sugar, body temperature, respiration rate, nerve energy flow indicated by galvanic skin response, and of course the most important of all – penis volume change. He was a natural at all the tests.'

The honeymoon period had lasted for almost four months, during which time Harbottle had turned over more and more responsibility to Slaughter for monitoring sessions and supervising records.

'It freed me – more time for my rats – and for an extracurricular project of mine. I have a hobby ranch – eighty acres west of town. Pure-bred cattle. Charolais. I was able to use Slaughter out there, too.'

It seemed that Charolais calves could be delivered only through caesarean section, so that the birth limit for cows was three offspring. By taking measurements of the width and length of bovine vaginae and pelvic baskets, Harbottle was seeking correlation and recurrence in sires and cows for a solution to this genetic problem.

'I guess you're thinking I'm pussy- as well as prick-struck.'

'Possibly.'

'Goes with the Freudian territory,' Harbottle said.

'I hadn't known he analysed Charolais cows.'

'Not bad, Ken. Another cup?'

'No thanks.'

'I should have twigged to Slaughter much sooner than I did. I missed lots of signals – inexplicable contradictions showing up in our data, change in the moral tone of the whole research team, all kinds of nasty sharps and flats I should have caught. I can't blame the others for not warning me. They knew how he was getting all those subjects – saunas, dark theatres, public washrooms, shopping malls, gay bars, parks – where he accosted and threatened and frightened them into taking part. Later, when I smartened up, I found out he was just as good at promising violence to non-deviates if they didn't keep their mouths shut about how he'd failed to show up for sessions when it was his shift, pushed wrong switches, failed to record results accurately or at all, and got stimulant

images out of sequence. He covered his error tracks well; he is
one clever, tricky son of a bitch.

'Slaughter wasn't content with doctoring reports to protect himself,' Harbottle went on; 'he got carried away with
the delight of deliberate damage. He not only faked responses;
by substitution, he changed the stimulant images as well. It
seems that for quite some time before he came to me, cour-
tesy of those two jokers in the English Department and
Native Studies, he'd been a regular life model in Visual Arts.
I found that out after I began to ask around about him. He
hadn't included it in his *cv*. I understand it pays very well. It
was in Fine Arts he got the slides. Still lifes of bananas – of
peaches. One of them was a bowl of anthuriums.' Harbottle
leaned back in his chair, was silent for a moment. He sighed.
'Rather wish I'd thought of that one myself. You know the
anthurium flower?'

'Yes.'

'Very suggestive. Scarlet spathe generously vaginal – the
yellow curved, erect stamen – '

'I know.'

'. . . phallic . . .'

'Tumescence, Dr. Harbottle, also is in the eye of the
beholder.'

Harbottle laughed. 'Not bad, Ken. Not bad at all.'

'Had better be – for the purposes of your study.'

Harbottle straightened up in his chair. 'Altogether, there
were thirteen substitute slides. Michelangelo's David.
Should have thought of him, too. Whistler's Mother. Two of
them I think he found in *Sunshine Magazine* or some other
nudist publication. One was of seaside skinny-dippers, the
other a volleyball game. Got them made into slides. He num-
bered his own, slid them into the files for proper ones, on
which we had based two years of research. He mixed up the

old and the new research so expertly that bang went the whole hundred-and-fifty-thousand-dollar project!'

'Back a way I believe you said *several* unfortunate – '

'I'm getting to the others,' Harbottle promised. 'I confronted him with what he'd done and failed to have done. He denied it. I told him he was fired. He threatened me. Here in this office. I said be my guest, but he stormed out. God, how I wished he hadn't.'

'Really!'

'I'm a pretty active fellow. I ride, I rope. He knew that from being out at the ranch. Seen me swing a fence-post maul, ear a horse. I didn't have to tell him I had my orange belt.'

'Do you?'

'Oh yes. It was quite reassuring to me at the time. This is a disturbed and very dangerous man. I recognized that then, and there were two more things that happened in the next ten days that confirmed it. The Sunday after I fired him, I went down to the lab with my little girl. Weekends she often comes with me. She was five – six now – and she loves those baby rats. It was only when we walked into that shambles that I remembered I hadn't got the keys from Slaughter. He must have brought a baseball bat into the nursery with him, or a crowbar. All the cages were smashed. There was not a single rat – mother or infant – left living! Noreen still has nightmares!' Harbottle looked away, towards the window. 'Now then, I've gone on at much too great a length.'

'No – that's all right. I think I'm going to need everything I can find out about this man. I'm here about another six-year-old girl and her mother.'

Harbottle proved to be as good a listener as he was a talker. Only when he'd finished the story of the attempted rape of Nadya did the psychologist interrupt him.

'Hey! That's about the time I fired him. The woman he was living with – off – got caught in the crossfire of his rage. She left him after he beat her up.'

He told Harbottle about the two dozen yellow sweetheart roses, how Nadya and Rosemary had sought sanctuary with him, and about the Convocation flashing.

'I wasn't there, but the news got around quickly,' Harbottle said. 'I thought of Slaughter right away. I'm going to level with you, Ken – you people are in deep trouble with him. After the research foul-up and something else I haven't told you about yet, as soon as I'd let Tait and Whyte know what I thought of them, I did some checking. Found out he'd had sessions with a psychiatrist, Dr. Laurence Rosner. He finally had to kick Slaughter out of his office. Don't bother with him. Ethics wouldn't permit him to say anything. . . it was only because I was a – ah – fellow psychologist . . . Look, take my advice. Make sure you've got security locks – guard dog – take up karate – '

'Little late for me.'

'Yeah. Yeah. You know – I haven't given you everything about this guy. Remember I was telling you he worked for me out at the ranch?'

'Yes.'

'I have a Charolais bull, the Duke of Downsview. Royal Winter Fair auction in Toronto, they'd knock him down for fifty thousand – would have until the middle of last March. No more. Slaughter castrated him!'

———

Was that goddam coyote going to bark and yipe the whole goddam Götterdämmerung all by himself high in the park out there? Must be close to the escarpment edge, maybe in Holy

Cross cemetery itself or lifting a leg against the corner of Marywood Convent. Last week the *Western Post* had done a feature on it. Had no business being an urban citizen. How could anybody get any sleep if it kept it up till daylight, which it had done the last two nights? He'd be lucky if he got in three hours tonight.

It wasn't all the coyote's fault of course. Pretty unsettling, what Harbottle had told him about Slaughter. And Dr. Rosner hadn't been as professional and discreet as Harbottle had promised.

'The man is probably one of the most dangerous patients I've ever had – he is capable of ultimate violence. I'm not so sure he hasn't already gone over the cliff. Eventually I would expect a serial pattern. He's a classic case.'

Thanks a lot, Doctor. I feel so much better now. If only there were someone to share his apprehension with. The police, perhaps, but what the hell did he have to go on that they'd take seriously? Look at the dead end Nadya ran into with them. One thing was certain; there was no point in upsetting her further by telling her the disturbing results of his investigation.

Shut the bedroom window now that Brünnhilde and the Valkyries had joined the son of a bitch. No. One coyote could always sound like a whole pack. All the same, better give the police another try. In a day or two. After the birthday party tomorrow.

Even more than usual, Rosemary had been reluctant to go up to her bath and storytelling and bed tonight. 'Why can't I stay up? It's my birthday – '

'Tomorrow,' Nadya said.

'But it's almost tomorrow now.'

'You were born,' Nadya explained to her, 'June the second, 1982 – 3:21 a.m. I ought to know.'

'Just a little bit long – '

'I was there and you didn't whine or pout,' her mother said, 'at that time.'

'But – '

'March!'

'I'll help with the dishes.'

'Not tonight.'

'Do I get a story, Professor?'

'Yes,' her mother answered for him. 'After you've had your bath and climbed into bed.'

She wanted *Alice* again. Had to be the fifth or sixth time round, but that was all right; when he was a child it had been a high favourite with him too. Still was. So much fun at six, or seventy-six, to doubt axioms, fall down a rabbit hole, step through a looking-glass. For all the distrust in their pockets, senior citizens still had a lot to learn from the other side.

One chair only to one person? Don't be silly; that would mean that according to the last Gallup count there was just one chair in homes inhabited by one; two if two; four if four. If visitors come, do you then insist they must bring with them the one chair each is entitled to? B.Y.O.C. Smarten up and have another cup of tea. Oh? You've not had a first cup of tea, so it is impossible for you to have *another* cup of tea? Don't try to tell me you've never had a cup of tea in your life before now. Yes, you have? All right then. Have another cup of tea.

No, you cute son of a sophist, I'm going downstairs to have another Scotch and soda with Nadya.

He had to put it off, for she was well into complicated baking preparations for tomorrow's birthday party, and needed him to crack eggs for her, sift flour, grease pans, take over the eggbeater a couple of times. When cookies came out of the oven and birthday cake went in, she joined him for a drink on the couch in the family room.

171

'Thanks, Doctor. It's going to be one hell of a party. Six is a very important birthday, isn't it?'

'Well . . . there are others.'

'Of course,' she said, 'but six is special. Was for me. You too?'

'I found seventy special. In a different way. I'm not sure about six. I think ten was more important to me.' He finished his drink, set the glass down on the coffee table. Sighed. 'How I ached to be ten.'

'I've often wondered why they set so much store by twenty-one.'

'Age to vote,' he pointed out. 'Drink. Legal age of – '

'Yeah – but why not twenty? Why pick twenty-one?'

'It is odd.'

'I hope that wasn't a – '

'It wasn't,' he said. 'I could hardly wait till I'd get to be thirty.'

'Thank God I won't see that one for another three years. Why would you want to be thirty?'

'I guess I wanted to be taken seriously,' he explained. 'I always looked four or five years younger than I was.'

'You still have that problem.'

The kitchen stove began to buzz.

'Cake's done.' She got up and headed for the kitchen area.

When she came back, he said, 'I'll tell you something about birthdays. Between thirty and seventy there's no great difference – but after that, look out.'

'Don't you worry, Doctor, you've got a long ways to go before you ever hit thirty.'

It took a moment till he could handle that one. 'That's very dear of you, Nadya. How about a game of snooker?'

'I'm sorry, Doctor. Icing the cake – '

'Got to cool first, doesn't it?'

'And presents to wrap – aw – what the hell.'

'I meant it,' she said as they started down the stairs. 'Sometimes you act as young as Rosemary. When it comes to getting your own way, you can be just as stubborn as she is.'

'Does come in handy,' he admitted.

'For both of you.' She turned back to him at the foot of the stairs. 'Either one of you were to drown we'd have to search for your bodies upstream.'

'You're plagiarizing me again.'

'So – what's wrong with plagiarizing a plagiarist?' She switched on the light. 'You break.'

'You.'

'For once,' she insisted, 'you.'

'Your turn. You won the last game.'

'We haven't played a game yet.'

'Last night we did,' he said, 'you won the first. I won the second, then you . . .'

'See what I mean – about you and Rosemary? We'll lag.'

She won. He broke. And scratched as usual. The game went right down to the eight ball. He sank it on a bank to the side pocket.

He stayed behind after she turned down a chance to get even, and went upstairs to do all the things she said she must. Sarah had often accused him of being stubborn too. Childishly so. She'd probably been right then. Nadya now. And how often Livy must have brought it to Sam's attention. Not in the billiard room, though; he wouldn't have let her chalk a cue. Quite unwomanly. Sam would have told her that the great pool shark in the sky couldn't abide the sight of a rump-sprung female stooping over a table any more than He could abide young ladies in the Louvre looking at Titian's disgusting nude. Livy likely gave Sam no argument there.

What was it that Nadya had said that was still nudging, he

asked himself as he lay back in bed. About six being an important birthday, and you said ten meant much more to you. That hadn't been quite right. You did look forward to being ten, but you're underrating six. First year in school, first time for paste that smelled lovely as clover or wolf willow, and Plasticine that seduced. Miss Penny had smelled nice, too, and no matter how many times she sent you to the cloakroom, her arms and soft cheek could win you back again.

It wasn't Miss Penny, though; it hadn't anything to do with school, because it was summer holidays and it was with his father. July. His Dad had taken him to the fair. God! Six and twelve. 1918, with three more months left in the trenches. There'd been a bearded lady, and a fat one, and a giant, and a dwarf right out of the Black Forest. There had been the yellow balloon they blew up in the middle of the race track. The woman in khaki breeches and knee boots, with a hairnet on her, stooped and went through the rail and climbed into the basket and they let loose the ropes so she lifted higher and higher and the balloon got smaller and smaller and then she turned into a falling ant and the scarlet parachute blossomed and she swung gently all the way down to earth, and . . .

———

All right, old man, take your time; wait until your legs clearly understand you're awake now. Warn both knees in case they've forgotten that this is the time the unfriendly sorcerer plays his inertia trick on you. Your body has not really become heavier; beds and upholstered chairs and couches have not without exception been lowered all over the world. The true reason you must, after two or three aborted efforts, try for extra lift with the help of your own or someone else's hand is that the age magician simply increased the pull of the earth mass. He did this about five of your birthdays ago, and the way to spoil his act is to get your much heavier feet further back and precisely under the anal centre of that changed gravity. Maybe a little behind it.

Ah! Made it – another day to be sliced off the life cake. Hey – hey! There's a brand-new dime in this one: Rosemary's birthday party! Today we are six. Both of us, Sweetheart . . .

He moved the saucepan with its porridge cargo off the burner and turned the button to medium low. Bumping sounds came from overhead. Rosemary's room. What did she do up there as soon as her feet hit the floor? Exercise a pet elephant! How in hell could a five-year old Tinker Bell or Batwoman shake an entire two-storey house! And this early – not yet seven o'clock.

He slid the porridge back onto the burner. No longer five. Six today.

She showed up barefooted and in her yellow nightgown.

'Right back upstairs and get dressed.'

'You going to be grumpy for my birthday?'

'Not if you don't – if I can help it.'

'Okay then.' She went over to the table by the window and sat down.

'Look – the porridge won't be ready for another ten minutes. Plenty of time for you to go up and get – '

'I don't want porridge – *this* morning.' She really meant it.

'Do we have to have this same argument every bloody morning?'

'It's my birthday all day today and you're supposed to get what you want on your birthday and I want toast and peanut butter and strawberry jam . . .'

'Damn it – '

'Damn is a bad word and I don't see why it's all right for you to say bad words all the time but it's awful for me to . . .'

'Because God intended blasphemy and obscenity solely for the use of adults,' he explained.

'Why did He do that?'

'He knows we need them a hell of a lot more than children do. Happy birthday, Rosemary darling.'

'It will be if I get toast and peanut butter and straw . . .'

'You got it,' he promised.

'And don't have to go upstairs to get . . .?'

'That, too. Be nice to eat my porridge with a little buttercup.'

'Did they make you eat porridge when you were little?' she asked.

'Yes.'

'Did you like it?'

'Not at the time,' he admitted.

'Now?'

'You must have noticed I eat mine every morning,' he said.

'Because you like it?'

'Not really.'

'Then why do you eat it?' she said. 'You're old – isn't anybody left to make *you* eat it.'

'It's good for you, as well as being a very dull topic for early morning conversation – '

'But *why* is it supposed to be good for you?' she persisted.

'It is rich in carbohydrates, proteins, vitamins and minerals. Like rice or bread or potatoes, it's what's called the staff of life, which means it has everything necessary for human survival. Orientals went for rice, the Irish for potatoes, Americans for McDonalds. It was oats that nourished all the Scots as well as their cattle.'

'Well, I'm a Canadian and I like peanut . . .'

'Just take my word for it, peanut butter and strawberry

jam are not in it with porridge. And for a bonus value, Prairie Maid has flax . . .'

'Bird seed!' Distaste was written all over her face.

'True,' he agreed. 'But it does guarantee regularity at both ends – of the human life span. White or brown?'

'White.'

'I thought so.'

Halfway through her first slice she said, 'You're old, aren't you.'

'Yes. I am.'

'Real old.'

'Uh-huh.'

She took another bite. 'I wish you weren't.'

'Not with your mouth full, dear. Me too.'

She swallowed. 'How old are you?'

'Quite a bit.'

'How many?'

'What do you think?' he said.

'I don't know. Isn't me.' She picked up the second slice of toast and peanut butter and strawberry jam.

'I am seven and eight which should make fifteen but they don't. In my case they make seventy-eight.'

'That's real old.'

'That's right.'

'But that doesn't mean you're going to die soon. Does it, Professor?'

'Not the day after tomorrow,' he said.

'Or next week?'

'I don't think so.'

'Next year?'

'Maybe not,' he said.

'I want you to come to my birthday party next year too.'

'I'll hang around long enough for that one,' he promised her.

'Good. Can I have some more toast and . . .'

'Another slice.'

'*Two* more – please.'

When she had finished her fourth, drained the second glass of milk, and sat back in her chair, he said, 'When I was six do you know what my Dad said to me?'

'Nope.'

'And I'm going to say it to you. "You may be little, but you sure are well dug out." '

'Was your Dad funny a lot?'

'Yes.'

'Was your Mom?'

'Sometimes.'

'You are,' she said.

'Thanks.'

'Mom is too. I just got her – and you.'

'Thanks again.'

She was over at the swinging door to the dining room. 'That's the cake on the sideboard under that tea towel, isn't it?'

'Could be,' he agreed.

'I hope it's chocolate. Is it?'

'Aah . . .'

'You helped her last night.'

'I did,' he admitted.

'So you ought to know,' she said.

'I guess I do but I wouldn't like to spoil the . . .'

'That's for presents.' She turned back to him. 'The birthday cake doesn't count.'

'You're probably right.'

'So?'

He got up. 'Let's do the dishes.'

'So?'

'I think it might be,' he said.

As she kneeled on the stool beside him at the counter, she said, 'We're supposed to blow up two hundred balloons.'

'*Whaaat?*'

'Mom said.'

'Not to me she didn't.'

'She did to me. Last night after my bath she said, "You and the Professor – I want you to blow up all the birthday-party balloons first thing in the morning so we get that done."'

He handed her the last plate. 'Two hundred balloons is a lot of balloons.'

'Not if we got to hang them up all over the ceiling after we rub them so they stick up there and in the living room and the dining room and the hallway and in here too and outside on the lilac bushes and the birch tree . . .'

'Two hundred of them would pretty well do the whole park, too. Where are they?'

'The second drawer down on the left of the sink.'

'All right.'

'You want me to get them?'

'Later.'

When he had wiped out the sink and she had hung up her dish towel, she said, 'I sure wish Duane Cooper wasn't coming. I didn't want him to come. I wish he didn't come to Peter Pan, too. I wish he didn't live at the end of our street either.'

'I take it you don't like Duane Cooper very much.'

'He's got red hair!'

'Is that the reason you hate . . . ?'

'He punches people and he kicks people and he pushes them down and he takes your turn on the swing when it isn't his turn on it. He bit Sadie. Then he lied to Miss Harper and said Sadie bit him first and she didn't.'

'Bite Duane.'

'Bite him *first*.'

'I see what you mean,' he said.

'He's fat, too.'

'Is he?'

'And he'll just wreck my whole birthday party,' she predicted.

'Maybe he won't. Which drawer did your mother say those balloons . . .?'

'Second one down. He will. He spoils everything he can.'

There *were* two hundred of them! 'Shouldn't have invited him then.'

'That's what I told Mom but she said we couldn't invite his sister, Lucy, if we didn't invite him. I want Lucy to come.'

'So you're stuck with Duane and you'll just have to – '

'I like Lucy a lot.'

' – make the best of it. Maybe if you were extra nice to him . . .'

'That's what Mom said, and it doesn't work with him at all. I'll point him out to you. You watch. You'll see. He'll burst the balloons, too.'

'We'll blow them up anyway.'

'I sort of wish Sadie wasn't coming to my birthday party either.'

'Look on the bright side,' he said. 'She may bite Duane again.'

'Yeah! Can we blow the balloons up outside?'

'Wind might give us some trouble,' he said.

'Look.' She pointed. 'Out the window. The leaves aren't moving at all. The trees . . .'

'I see. They aren't bowing down their heads. We'll do the balloons outside.'

The cedar lawn chairs and table glistened in full sun; the

mock orange, the lilacs, the birch, the grass were full of diamonds.

'Yike!' She had sat down, then jumped up out of a chair, was pulling the yellow nightgown away from her bum. 'It must've rained!'

'Dew,' he said.

'It's just as wet as rain is!'

'Sure it is. But it could have been worse.'

'How?'

'There are three kinds of wet,' he said. 'Rain wet and dew wet and . . . Go on in the house and bring back some paper towelling, and we'll wipe off a couple of the chairs.'

When she came back, she said, 'I figured out what the third one is.'

'I thought you would.'

'And it hasn't happened since way before we came to live with you. And I'm six and it won't happen ever again.'

'I'm sure it won't.' He wished he could guarantee it for himself with such certainty.

Now she was looking up at the robin's nest. Three weeks ago he had moved the Boston fern outside, hanging it up under the deck canopy. He and Rosemary had agreed that it had been inconsiderate of the robins to build their nest in it, but since it was almost finished before they had discovered it there wasn't anything they could do about it. He promised Rosemary that he'd be very careful about watering the plant. Just on the side away from the nest. It had meant that he couldn't use the hose, had to get up on the stool and pour very carefully out of the enamel coffeepot. The morning he had found the five eggs in the nest, he had lifted Rosemary up to see them.

'They're blue.'

'Robin's eggs usually are. We'd better get down and let the

mother come back. That's her over there on the fence,' he said.

'How do you know it is?'

'Because she's cussing us.'

'Maybe it's the father,' she said.

'No. I think that's him in the weeping birch.'

'Where?'

'To the left,' he pointed out, 'over your swing – on the branch that . . .'

'I see him! Real red. Why is he red and she's just rusty?'

'Because she's the mother and he's the father,' he explained. 'Way it is with birds. Mallard drakes, peacocks, orioles . . .'

'Not with us, though – is it?'

'I guess not. Let's go out on the lawn chairs – give her a chance to get back to her eggs.'

'Or the guys would be using lipstick and rouge and wearing red dresses,' she said as they went down the deck stairs. 'And the Red Queen wouldn't be red. Hey! Maybe she was really the father and that's why she threw that baby boy at Alice . . .'

'That was the Duchess, Rosemary.'

'Oh yeah. And he turned into a pig. Like Duane Cooper is.'

'So were most of Lewis Carroll's Oxford students.'

'I didn't really like that pig part,' she said.

'Neither did I.'

Now there were five unsteady and gawping mouths in the nest.

'Let's get some sort of system going for us with these balloons, Rosemary.'

'There's banana ones too!'

'Or we won't get them done before your guests show up. I'll start each one and hand it to you and you blow and hand it back to me to finish. I'll twist the knot in the neck.'

It went rather well, except that at first several got away

from her, and he had to tell her to quit it when he realized she was deliberately freeing them into mad, spiral flight. As he and Rosemary blew up balloons, the robin parents ferried worms to their young. In full blossom now, the mock orange had turned the back yard into a citrus grove, and the scent carried him back to his Florida childhood.

'Hey – look Professor,' she whispered. She was pointing to the eave of the deck canopy and the hummingbird at the plastic red-apple feeder.

'There's another one,' she said. 'And another one.'

Emerald or ruby, they thrummed and they darted, punctuating flight by hanging at attention to sip or to beak duel at the nectar feeder. Such vicious and greedy and dear little airborne jewels!

Wasps, too, were coming for syrup, and he reminded himself he must look for their grey paper nests under the house eaves and the plank deck. He was getting pretty bloody short of breath and they'd blown up only a dozen or so balloons.

'Let's ease off for a minute.'

In spite of the wasps and the balloons, it was one hell of a lovely way to start a birthday morning.

––––––

Debbie and Kimberly showed up an hour before the first of the other guests would arrive. While Rosemary and Kimberly were out in the back yard, the two mothers did their last-minute preparations and worked out the agenda. The party would start out in the back yard, would come inside for the performance part and the birthday-cake event, then move outside again. He would do the magic dime for them first, then the invisible hen would cluck and lay her eggs, dropping them out of the bandanna and into the hat on the card table set up in front of the swinging door to the dining room. Seven eggs would give Nadya time behind the door to get ready with Rosemary's slippers, the long stockings, his turtleneck sweater, the shorts, and the mortarboard for the dwarf act. After the hen, Debbie would get the card table into the dining room and drape it with a sheet to hang down the back and hide his and Nadya's legs. Debbie would open the swinging door for them.

At the last moment Nadya added a complication: after he sang 'I'm a Little Teapot,' Debbie would give the dwarf a slice of birthday cake, and also a chocolate-chip cookie. So far so good, but then she said, 'I got a better idea. Let's have him smoke a cigar.'

'Yeah,' Debbie said. 'I give it to him and your hand takes it – '

'Wait a minute,' he said.

' – and puts it in the Doctor's mouth . . .'

'You light it first,' Nadya said. 'Then you hand it to me.'

'No – after,' Debbie said.

'Not at all,' he said.

Debbie said, 'I light the cigar before you take it, and put it in his mouth . . .'

'We have not had a rehearsal for this bit of business!' he protested.

Debbie said, 'He puffs away on it.'

'Then my hand takes it out of his mouth so he can exhale,' Nadya said, 'and then I put it back in his mouth so he can puff some more . . .'

'Just the cake and the cookie!'

'Aw – come on, Doctor,' Nadya said.

'You try for my mouth – blind – where you think it might be – you could get me with the lighted end. I did not agree to do a flame-swallower act for you.'

'I'll just lift the thing,' Nadya said, 'and you put your mouth around it.'

In the end they compromised: no cake, no cookie, just the lighted cigar. Some compromise!

Through the binoculars he had seen the first car drive up to the front of the house, then a woman and a child get out. The little girl was embracing a bright parcel. The place ended up with five cars parked over there. All those gifts, it had to be a birthday party; Rosemary's! Now then – how might this fit in with his plans for her? Definitely a plus, because there'd be plenty of confusion and there just might come the chance he'd been waiting for.

Duane Cooper did have red hair, or more precisely orange – Rosemary was right; he was fat as well. His mother had to be the genetic reason for it. In her red Chautauqua-tent dress she was massively imperious, turning her garden chair into a cedar throne, which she would not leave throughout the whole afternoon, no matter what her son might do. He ran; he climbed; he pushed; he tripped and he punched and he wrestled; he threw cookies and dirt and jelly beans; he interrupted; he shouted; he did burst balloons, and when sent to the house for shoving Kimberly into the lily pond, he tore open three of Rosemary's birthday presents before it was birthday-present opening time. He didn't fart, but again and again, by undoing their neck knots, he was able to make the balloons do that for him.

In cape and top hat Lyon had opened his act with the magic

rise and fall of the dime on his palm. Before the magic hen
had laid her third egg, Duane had grabbed the hat nest and
dumped out the blown egg hanging by the thread, but even
Duane had been riveted by the cigar-smoking dwarf.

The yellow two-wheeler bike he had got for Rosemary was
the jewel in the birthday-present crown. He promised he
would teach her to ride it without the training wheels, and
that he would get her a handlebar basket so that Wrinkles
could ride it, too.

For his closing act Duane had got to the garden hose, which
should have been unscrewed from the foundation tap and put
safely away in the garage. No one could get near the volun-
teer fireman, or out of range of the hose, before he had
accomplished great dress and hairdo damage. He scored first
on his mother, the largest and the easiest of all possible
targets, getting her with full pressure right in the face –
initially. He didn't miss a single mother, child (male or
female), balloon, or birthday package. Kimberly ended up in
the lily pond again, accompanied by three other guests, one of
them adult. The birthday cake was an early casualty (possibly
unintended).

In the end it had been Nadya who ran him down under the
lilacs at the back of the yard. She was successful only because
his back was to her, and he seemed to have found a new target
beyond the bushes. She had missed a wonderful opportunity to
strangle him slowly with the hose after she had wrested it
from him.

When he had asked Nadya what the little bastard had been
aiming at out in the alley, she just shook her head and changed
the subject. Whatever it was, she did not care to share it with
him.

Damn it! Soaked to the skin, and what was worse, the fat little porker had spooked him out into the open, and she'd got a good look at him! But that wasn't all bad. In fact, come to think of it, he couldn't have planned it better. She wouldn't sleep well tonight.

She had no way of knowing he was holed up here right across the street and under the convent house, just waiting for his chance to get at her kid. At first he'd been sure he'd made a right choice in picking this end of the park for his escarpment cave. He could keep them under surveillance; and it wouldn't be a long trek down to the river for water. Now he wasn't so certain about that decision; the nun on her son-of-a-bitching bells morning, noon, and evening, and that coyote going at it till daybreak, were really getting on his nerves.

One dollar and eighty-seven cents, and it was going to stay that way no matter how many times he counted it. Fine Arts summer session didn't begin for another week yet and the bastards wouldn't pay for jock-strap sessions in advance. Half a stale loaf left, but no butter or jam for it. Out of coffee, too, and milk and beer, so it's had to be boiled water from the river the past three days. Down to six wieners, which had been a mistake in the first place – five and three-quarters, actually, because this morning he'd bitten the end off one of them raw and instant nausea had made him spit it out.

Gas was low in the Triumph tank too, but that was the least of his problems; after dark into a self-serve, fill her up, and away without pay. Trust in Him. Maybe Livingstone Medical Faculty anatomy department might have use for the finest body in the land. Enough of that stuff, Slaughter; you learned your lesson your last try. Death is not the answer. Not yet. Not yours.

He watched her as she rolled the cigar on the deck table, bit the end off it, sucked the other, then puffed till it was glowing.

'You're getting pretty good at that, aren't you?'

'Had a good teacher.'

'For a filthy habit,' he said. 'According to Doctor Gallstone.'

'What's his real name anyway?'

'Gold – ah – Good – Gladstone.'

'You were one hell of a magician for them. Just how does that magic dime work?'

'Good magicians never tell, Nadya.'

'Okay. Glad it's over for another year. Did you ever see anything to tie that Duane Cooper?'

'I don't think I have. Or ever will.'

'Did he ever get his mother!'

'Pretty hard for him to miss her,' he said.

'Why in hell didn't somebody think of grabbing any part of that hose and kinking it? Would have saved a lot of dresses and hairdos.'

'Easy for you to say with hindsight,' he said.

'Yeah.'

'We should have listened to Rosemary.'

'Rosemary! She loved it. Said it was the best part of the best party she's ever been to. She says all the other children thought so, too.'

'You know, that doesn't surprise me as much as it should,' he said. 'Nobody got hurt. Really. This time. But how often the comic is prelude to the . . .' He stopped as he saw that her face had saddened. 'Did I say something that . . . ?'

'Yes, Doctor. You did. You know when I grabbed that little bugger it was under the lilacs at the back.'

'Yes?'

'And he was aiming at something out in the alley?'

'Uh-huh.'

'There was somebody out there – behind the lilac bushes. I didn't get all that good a look but . . .'

'You think it was . . .?'

'Don't say his name! Please! I didn't get a good – just a glimpse through the bushes before he took off.'

'All right, Nadya. Relax. Relax.'

Just before they turned in, the sound of the carillon bells began to roll across from the park to them. Now why hadn't he thought of it? He should have asked that nun if she'd do 'Happy Birthday' for Rosemary.

Oh Jesus, joy of man's despairing, she's at her bloody hell bells again! Lay off! All that risk last night to discover they haven't even got a poor box there. Lay off, you tight-assed brides of Christ! Lay off before my headaches begin to flame again. If you don't, sister, thou art going to get the holy shit-kicking of thy life! Thy devil's instrument shall be destroyed as well!

Rosemary loved her yellow bike, and he was grateful to the salesman, who had assured him that six was not too young for a two-wheeler.

'Not at all. These are designed for riders as young as even four – those training wheels are detachable, come off when the child has learned to steer and balance.'

How thoughtful of them. Ingenious. He remembered he hadn't got a bike for a good two years after all the other kids in the neighbourhood had been given theirs. He had ridden, though, with his right leg under and through the crossbar of older boys' bikes. His birthday was the eleventh of February, so the bike had to live in the basement for a whole snowy month, during which time it leaned against the wall, and all he could do was mount and wobble half a dozen indoor yards and dismount.

As soon as she'd had her breakfast and until her mother took her to Peter Pan, and as soon as he picked her up and brought her home, she headed straight for the back yard to ride the bike with the training wheels supporting her.

'Professor.'

'Yes?'

'You know what I'd like?'

'Not until you tell me, I won't.'

'It's a whole week now,' she said.

'What is?'

'Since I got the bike.'

'And?'

'And I figure it's time to take those baby wheels off of it,' she said.

'Oh.'

'Don't you think it's a good idea?'

'I don't know about that, Rosemary.'

'I been riding it with them on it for a whole week now and I'd like to learn to ride it really.'

'They're called training wheels, Rosemary, and that's why – '

'The only thing they train you to do is ride a three-wheeler and I already knew how to ride a three-wheeler before you gave me a two-wheeler for my birthday. What's the use of having a two-wheeler if it's going to be a three-wheeler?'

'Not much,' he admitted.

'So – will you take them off for me? It takes a wrench to get the nuts off.'

'All right. I'll nut it for you and we'll see how you . . .'

'I'll need you to hold the back of the seat at first until I . . .'

'Yes, dear.'

She watched as he worked with the wrench, and when the training wheels were off they wheeled the bike round to the front of the house. But as she put her foot on the pedal he said, 'I don't think the sidewalk is a good place to start. Concrete's hard. Let's go across into the park so you can have grass to fall on.'

Once there, he grabbed the back of the saddle, walked behind as she wobbled along. He told her to turn the wheel in the direction – always – that she tilted. After two sessions she was managing to restore her balance with the handlebars herself. He explained that the slower she pedalled the harder it was to balance. That had been a mistake; by the end of their second session, she had him up to a trot. He was able more and more to let her determine her balance for herself, just letting his hand rest lightly on the saddle, ready to support her if she threatened to fall to one side or the other.

He began to take his hand off the saddle for longer and longer stretches. Then, without his intending it, but because she had gained speed, she got away on him. By the time he got his breath back, she had travelled on her own a good fifteen feet. He called out to her. She kept on going. He yelled again. She looked back; the front wheel buckled and she went over. He ran up to her.

'I rode it! I rode it!'

'Your knee! It's bleeding, Rose – '

'I did, didn't I! Without you holding on!'

'Rosemary – let's see your knee!'

She looked down at the blood streaking down her leg.

He could see there was a cut, but mostly, he guessed, it was scraped. 'We'd better get some disinfectant and a Band-Aid on it.'

'It doesn't hurt much.'

As they started for the house, she said, 'Why don't I get on and ride it back?'

'I have a better idea. You get on but don't pedal it. I'll push you.'

'Aaw!'

'That's best – until we get a better look at that cut.'

'Then after the stuff's on it and the Band . . .'

'I think we've done enough for today.'

———

All that I did need, Pal, in the depths of my despair, was one good sign that Thou hast not forsaken me, and Thou hast given me a dandy one! Praise Thee forever more! I shall praise Thy name throughout the valleys green, upon the hills and to the snowcapped mountain-tops beyond! Hear me! Hear me now! Hallelujah! Hallelujah! Yaaaaaah-hah-hooooo and yip-pee! Which is the colloquial thereof!

I was hungry and I was broke, and Thou didst deliver the faggot into my hands and now my cup runneth five thousand times over. The lisping son of a bitch said he was vice president with an international oil consortium, which was foolishly indiscreet of him. He said this was the first time since his marriage break-up two years ago that he had done anything this spontaneously casual, for he found promiscuity simply gross. I told him I found it so too. I also told him that checking in separately at the hotel would be quite tacky, that I was dying to see his Art Deco, and why didn't we go to his place instead.

The bugger hemmed and hawed but finally agreed, for his lust was great within him. He drove us in his Porsche, let me out half a block before Pine-Aire Towers, told me to wait a good fifteen minutes, then press the button to 714 and he would let me in. Which I did. The seventh-floor condominium must have set him back at least half a million, and the paintings and crystal and Persian rugs of the infidels must have cost another fifty big ones. Even as Thou bade me do, I left him unconscious, probably with broken ribs, a fractured jaw, and crushed balls, if he had them to begin with, and considerably less well-to-do, if he had no insurance.

Thou ledst me then to E for Economics in the *Encyclopaedia Britannica*, where I found the wad of money and tore up the uncashed American Express traveller's cheques before I finished trashing the place. I could hardly believe it when I counted up the take: almost five thousand! This time for Thee, have I really pulled off the hat trick against Sodom and Gomorrah!

Easy, Slaughter, easy; up can be just as bad as down. You got some heavy planning to do.

9

AFTER HE HAD GONE TO THE FRONT DOOR AND SIGNED FOR the special-delivery letter from Minneapolis, he phoned her at the Sock and Buskin.

'Open it!'

They wanted her for *Saint Joan*!

'I'm catching a taxi!'

Delight was bright on her face as she read the letter. She looked up to him.

'I'm so glad for you, dear.' But even as he said it he saw the sun go under cloud. 'What's wrong?'

'I don't think I can – '

'What the hell are you talking about? This is your big break.'

'I know,' she said.

'Then why . . .?'

'Didn't you read it?'

'I always read other people's mail,' he said. 'Especially when they ask me to.'

'Next Tuesday.'

'What about it?'

'First read-through,' she said.

'So – you'd better start packing.'

'What about Rosemary? I can't – she can't – hotel room – rehearsals . . .'

'How long do rehearsals . . .?'

'Two weeks usually.'

'The run?'

'Four.'

'Six weeks. What's the big problem? You head for Minneapolis. Rosemary stays with me.'

'Oh, Doctor, that isn't fair to . . .'

'Of course it is. Keep it simple and sensible. Rosemary and I will make out just fine while you're down there knocking them out.'

'But . . .'

'I'll get her to Wendy and Peter every morning, back home in the afternoon.'

'Do you really . . .?'

'Yes, I do. Matter of fact, it'll probably be the best six weeks of my entire life, having her all to myself.'

———

Now then, you're really loaded, т-bone and french fries and half a pecan pie for supper, four and a half six-packs to the good, in the river, out of the current, weighted with rocks and hidden so well no thirsty son-of-a-bitch can ever find them. Aaaaah, wouldn't a little dinner music be nice. Where are you, Sister, now that my spirit and my stomach runneth over and I could enjoy your vesper bells? No. No. Only kidding. Stay off the bloody things, and if you do I shall deliver unto you and all the other nuns for their enjoyment daily a six-pack of Miller Light.

———

She had cried at the airport when her mother had left them to go through security, hiccupped all the way home, and was inconsolable through supper, not touching her spaghetti and meatballs. A frozen raspberry slurpy did help some. After an hour of 'Dallas' in his arms, she said she was maybe hungry now, and he heated up the spaghetti for her. She had another slurpy for dessert; his own took most of the taste of 'Dallas' out of his mouth. He read her two chapters of *The Wind in the Willows* before he kissed her good night.

———

Well, well, well! That had certainly simplified matters. As soon as he had caught them in the binoculars, loading those suitcases into the car trunk, he'd known something was up. All three of them had taken off, but just two had returned: the old man and the kid.

Thanks a million, Good Old Buddy!

———

Just as he had known they would, they had settled within a few days into an effective and comfortable routine. As soon as he got up he would call her on his way to the bathroom, then again from the head of the stairs after he'd dressed, one final time when he had the tea kettle on, had started the oatmeal in the double boiler, had accomplished the stairs and pulled the covers off her. Saturday and Sunday she could sleep in if she wanted to. She did.

After breakfast, teeth and hairbrushing, they would drive to Wendy and Peter's Day Kare and Kiddygarten across the river. Wrinkles came along with them. Always. Rosemary said he liked it at Wendy and Peter's because there were five Cabbage Patch babies and seven Barbie and Ken couples enrolled. Nearly all the guys over three had transformers.

Under the full day program she would be given a hot nutritious lunch, mid-afternoon cookies and milk, and a lie-down period. At three she would be waiting for him with the others by the fence of the play area with its slides and swings, sand-boxes and teeter-totters. On their way home they must stop at the Dairy Girl for soft ice-cream cones. Medium size.

———

He set the porridge bowl and the milk glass in front of her.

'Minneapolis. It's quite a ways away. Isn't it?' she said.

'Fair distance.'

She pushed her porridge aside. 'Is it where apples come from?'

'I don't think so.' He slid the bowl back into place. 'Mainly from the Okanagan or Ontario or Quebec.'

'Apples are very good for you.'

'So is porridge.'

'Apples – I like.'

He went back to the stove, returned with his tea.

She had made no move on that porridge yet. 'Where is Minneapolis anyway?'

He lowered his cup. 'The States. What they call the Midwest.'

'Where's the States?'

'You know where it is, Rosemary. I showed you on the map last night. After the phone call. Eat your porridge.'

'Yeah. Under us.'

'That's right.'

'On the map it was anyway.'

'Maps are generally right,' he assured her.

She gave her porridge a couple more stirs with the tip of the tablespoon. 'Can we go over in the park this morning?'

'Only if you eat your porridge.'

'Then?'

'Yes,' he promised.

She laid down the tablespoon, took a drink from her milk glass. 'And you'll lift me up on the monkey bars?'

'Yes.'

She finished her milk. 'And push me on the swing?'

'I generally do, don't I?'

'Can I have another glass of milk?'

He got it for her.

'And around on the roundabout?'

'Just as soon as you eat that . . .' But she had already picked up her spoon and started her attack.

How many bargains they seemed to strike. What wheeler-dealers the young could be. The old, too, of course; since she and Nadya had come to live with him, he had probably initiated negotiation just as often as she had. No going to arbitration now that her mother had left to pick apples in Minneapolis.

'It may slow you down a bit, but keep your mouth shut when you chew.'

'Sorry,' she said.

'All right,' he said.

'I forgot,' she said.

'Okay.'

'Like you did in the bathroom this morning when you got up and you . . .'

'Okay, Rosemary!'

'. . . real loud one . . .'

'I guess I forgot too,' he said.

'It's snowing!' She was right.

It was as though an absent-minded morning had forgotten it was June. The air was bewildered with white down freed from the cottonwood trees in the park to float and to fall and to drift against curbs and parked cars and house foundations, skiffing sidewalks, lawns, and hedges. But cottonwood fluff was not the morning's only surprise magic, for the sound of carillon bells began suddenly to tumble over the edge of the park escarpment.

'Boy, would I ever like to go up there and see her banging her bells!'

'It's electric. No bells,' he said.

'Sounds just like bells.'

'I agree. But it isn't.' He straightened up from locking the front door.

'What's she playing?'

'I told you – electric carillon.'

'Uh-huh. I mean – is it a song?'

'Yes. "Immaculate Mary." '

At the bottom of the steps she turned to face him. 'You know the words to it?'

' "Immaculate Mary, Your praises we sing. You reign now in Heaven with Jesus, Our King." It's a traditional Lourdes hymn.'

'What's that?'

'Religious song people sing at a place in the Pyrenees mountains, in France, where they go to be healed.'

'Will you show me that place on the map too?'

'Sure.'

She was in the gutter now, kicking up clouds of the cotton fluff ahead of herself. 'Who's "mackerel Mary?" '

'Immaculate. Mother of Christ.'

'Guy up there.'

'One of them. Take my hand across the street.'

'I'm all right. In Heaven?'

'Mmmmh.'

She ducked under the low pipe rail of the park fence, then waited for him to get over it. 'Can He hear her? God?'

'She hopes He can.'

———

Oh, no! She's been turned loose against me! Again! Over and down and under and up all over again! Pleasepleasepleaseplease! Stop her tumbelling dumbelling above and below and around outside of me numbelling crumbelling inside of me!

———

'Hey! She's playing a different one now, isn't she?'

' "Come Holy Ghost," ' he said.

'Ghosts are scary.'

200

'Not this one, Rosemary.'

As they neared the play area she said, 'Is God ever funny?'

That one stopped him dead in his tracks.

It had taken over three-quarters of a century and a six-year-old child to bring up that question for him! 'Some pretty funny things go on in this world of His. Whether He wants them to or not, I guess He has to take responsibility for them. Can't blame everything on humans.'

'Does He laugh a lot?'

'Hardly any one-liners in the Old or the New Testament. In earlier myths the gods seemed to enjoy quite a few belly laughs.'

'You know something, Professor? Half the time I can't tell whether you're talking to me.'

'Sorry.'

'Or yourself.' She started up the slide ladder. 'You don't have to catch me.'

After he had picked her up and helped her dust off her knees and her slacks and the whole front of her shirt, she said, 'I don't mind.'

'Coming like a bat out of hell down that chute on your stomach so you land flat on your . . .?'

'No. You talking to yourself instead of to me. It's still interesting.'

'That's nice,' he said.

'Sometimes. Even when you don't really mean what you're saying.'

'I'm glad to hear that.'

'You do that a lot, you know. Hey! She's quit. Ever since we left the swings.'

———

Aaaaah! There. There now. Bless you. Bless you. This headache none other has ever known! Still throbbing, but if she
stays off her hell bells it may go right away. Don't let her get
at them ever again. This is my warning: if she does not mend
her wicked ways the Lord of Smite and the God of Smash
shall punish her, and there shall be nun blood and broken bone
and torn flesh all over Mary Wood! He will so direct me, and
I will obey Him and see thereto.

You have a nice day up there, Mamma Superior.

———

On their way over from the monkey bars to the roundabout
she said, 'So does He?'

'Does who – what?'

'God. Laugh.'

Stubborn little thing. 'Never.'

'Why not?'

'Because He wants to be taken seriously,' he said. 'At all
times.'

'Grown-ups don't laugh as much as kids do, do they?'

'I agree. Just five times round on this thing, Rosemary.'

'And God is real grown-up, isn't He.'

'Right again,' he said.

'He's so grown-up He doesn't laugh at all.'

'Q.E.D.'

'See what I was telling you. Back there at the slide?'

'Sorry. Q.E.D. means you have just proved beyond the
shadow of a doubt that God does not laugh.'

'I wish He did.'

'So do I, Rosemary. More and more, so do I.'

On their park visits she always left the roundabout till the last. It was, and it was not her favourite; it delighted, and it frightened her. She would crawl up the shallow tin cone, spread flat out on her stomach and clutch the centre post, which would also revolve as he crouched and shoved on the outer edge, faster and faster till she had to let go and be sucked down the slippery sides and off into the sand. This amusement apparatus made about equally masochistic demands upon both of them.

Funny up there, no; ironic, often.

After the roundabout she said how about another go on the swing, and he said perhaps, but let's just sit here on the park bench for a while. Again and again they heard an oriole which they decided must be high in the blue spruce over towards the river, though they couldn't be certain about that, and he agreed with her that orioles were very good hiders. Just in front of them a black squirrel spiralled down a tree trunk, then bannered over the open ground toward the park fence.

'How come some are grey and some are black ones, Professor?'

He explained that the grey squirrels were foothill natives; the black ones, Eastern immigrants.

'So how come they came out here?'

'There's a story going round,' he said. 'Seems a Toronto family moved out West and they brought a couple of black squirrels with them. Pets of their children. Somebody forgot and left the cage door open. One of the parents, I suspect. The squirrels got loose and the black ones are great, great, great, great, great-grandchildren of that pair.'

'Is that really true?'

'Could be.'

'I like the black ones better,' she said. 'They're not so greedy and pushy as the grey ones are.'

'You are very observant, Rosemary. I've noticed that too.'

'Those grey ones are always putting the run on the black ones. They're real mean and bossy to the black ones.'

'I agree with you.'

She was leaning sideways and seemed to be examining the ground by her end of the bench. 'It's always a grey one that's chasing a black one.'

'Mm-hmh.'

She had straightened up and was tucking something into her jeans side pocket. 'I bet a black one wouldn't bite you.'

'Don't you bank too much on that, Rosemary.'

'She was a grey one . . .'

'She was *one* grey one,' he said.

'. . . that bit me!'

On this bench, almost a month ago. He would never forget her scream and the wriggling image of that squirrel dangling for long, long seconds from the thumb of her right hand. 'She didn't bite you because she happened to be grey, Rosemary. There could be a black squirrel or two that might bite.'

'Human people?'

'Sure. You know you and she were pretty close chums . . .'

'Not any more!' she said.

'Long enough for her to climb up on your knee.'

'Just for the peanuts I'd give her.'

'That's right,' he agreed. 'And you teased her once too often.'

'I did not!'

'Come on, Rosemary. You hung tight onto that peanut she already had in her mouth and between her paws.'

'No excuse for her to bite me!'

'Maybe she thought it was,' he said.

'Whose side are you on anyway?' she said.

'Yours.'

'She's still around here, you know. I've seen her lots of times since then,' she said.

'Have you?'

'Last week I heaved a rock at her. I picked it up by the swings just in case she showed up, and she did later over by the fence but I missed her.'

'Better luck next time.'

She was holding her right thumb up to him. 'See?'

He could indeed. The tiny hole scar was still there.

'Just like a long needle right through to my thumb bone! It hurt!'

'I know it did, dear.'

'Next time I won't miss her!' she promised.

'You wouldn't want to clobber an innocent squirrel, would you?'

'No way!'

'But there are lots of grey . . .'

'I know *her* when I see *her*!'

'How can you tell her from other grey ones?'

'More of her hair has fallen off of her back and there isn't any left at all on her skinny tail. You can't see her tits any more though.'

'That's probably because her babies no longer need her to feed them.'

She stood up and was reaching down into her jeans pocket. 'She bites them, too.'

'I doubt it.'

'Let's go look for some arrowheads,' she said.

'You go. When I've recovered from the roundabout I'll join you later. Good luck.'

She held out her fist to him, then opened it to show him the pebble cradled in her palm, roughly the size of a bubble-gum ball. 'Oh, I'll get her all right.'

There it was again: that oriole repeating himself, this time from high in the cut-leaf birch on the other side of the street. Could be another, though, answering the blue-spruce one. Next to the chickadees they had been Sarah's favourite. Each year in late May she would phone him out at the university to tell him they were back again. They stayed all too briefly, would be gone before the end of June, hardly long enough to build or repair a nest, have young, and care for them till flight age.

He felt a sharp one in his left hip and another one high between his shoulder blades as he shifted to turn his head. There she was beyond the swings, head down as she made her slow search along the base of the escarpment. He saw her stop, stoop, pick up and examine a flint chipping, or if she were really lucky, an unflawed arrowhead. Maybe a fragment of buffalo bone. He must remember to get a roll of cotton batten and spread it inside that picture frame for her collection! Couldn't have been an arrowhead or flint chipping or bone; she'd thrown it away. Another stone maybe, but not quite right for braining a grey squirrel. I *am* on your side, darling; I hope you get even with her too. Short of capital punishment.

Hey! That gave her a start, bounding out of the bushes just ahead of her, a few pogo-stick jumps over open ground before diving for cover again. Not all that many jack rabbits living inside northwestern cities over five hundred thousand population last census.

Or coyotes. What a surprise when he'd read about the grey interloper reported by the *Foothills Post*. According to the piece in the second section just before Births and Obituaries, the prairie wolf must have trotted in from the hills west of the city's rim, sneaked his way through the Crowfoot Golf and Country Club, taken the path threading the wild margin preserved along the Spray River bank by City Planning, Parks and Recreation, past the Municipal Hazardous Spills, Solid Wastes and Pollution Control Plant, three oil refineries, indeed an entire industrial district, then the Livingstone University complex, avoiding joggers and hikers and cyclists all the way, to take up residence in Livingstone Park. No small accomplishment. Even for a coyote.

How about that for a wild anachronism, Lyon? And there goes the neighbourhood, you urban squirrels and field mice, mallard ducklings in river-bank nests, gophers and garter snakes, rabbits and Chinese ring-necked pheasants. Rather reassuring, though, that wilderness could still contradict civilization now and again, and in what more likely place than Livingstone Park? Little wonder a child could still find arrowheads at the foot of a cliff that until half a century before his own birth had been a buffalo jumping pound. Up there where the nun played her carillon in Mary Wood House, beside Holy Cross Cemetery with its dead forest of granite and marble, had once been prairie flats, where Blackfoot built clever willow and saskatoon and cottonwood funnels, then with swings riding out to either side, drags whooping behind, gathered and herded thousands of buffalo to stampede over the edge to death below.

———

Caught sight of them almost as soon as they'd come out of the front door, lost them because of the bloody nun on her bells, then found them again at the swings and watched them at the slide, the monkey bars, and the roundabout. Great way to get a stroke, old man. You have a nice long rest on that bench.

Now she's left him and is walking along the foot of the cliff. Just what the hell is she looking for down there? She's moving to the right. Her left. Make sure now. She might change her mind and her direction. Nope. She's headed for the river all right. Now get down to the path near the river. Then start walking to *your* left, and you could meet her at the end of the cliff where it hits the river. Looking good. Looking very damn good!

———

Maybe he ought to join her now. No. This time the roundabout had really taken it out of him, and it was lovely here with that spring sun so kind on his eyelids. He'd warned her not to go too far away. Be with you in a few more minutes, Rosemary.

———

Couldn't have been better. Timing just perfect. They'd come face to face precisely on the path corner, where it turned to leave the river bank.

'Well, well, well. If it isn't Little Miss Red Hiding Rood – uh – Ride Heading Rood – I mean, Hood Riding Red. Darn it! I never can seem to get it right!'

'Red Riding Hood.'

'You are!?' Little copy of her bitch mother!

'No. I was just helping you to say her name right.' Now she was looking back over her shoulder.

'Thanks,' he said.

'And you're not supposed to talk to strangers,' she said.

'Good for you, Rosemary.'

She turned back toward him. 'How did you know my name was Rosemary?'

'Oh, I'm an old friend of your mother's.' Pig chops!

'I don't remember you.'

'I'd love to see her again.' Dead!

'She's in Minneapolis. I never met you before.' She was starting to back away.

'You were pretty young when we first met. Just a baby, but later on – about a year ago – I even stayed at your place once.'

Any moment now she was going to take off.

'I don't remember that.'

'Of course you don't, Rosemary. You weren't in the apartment. You were visiting with your best friend, Kimberly.'

That stopped her. 'She still is. What's your name?'

Careful, careful, Slaughter, 'Charlie.'

'Charlie who?'

'Piper. Not the pie-eyed Piper. Charlie Piper. What you got there?'

She held her hand up to him and opened it. The black triangle! What a sign! What a great sign! 'Hey! Hey! That's a dandy one!'

'The Professor and I found a lot of them. I think this one is the best one I found yet.'

'It's a perfect one,' he said.

'There's a little bit broken off it – not the tip – that corner of it on that side. See?'

'I do now. Sure is tiny, isn't it?'

'Yeah,' she agreed. 'I never found one this small before.'

'You know why it's so little?'

'Maybe he made it for his kid to play with.'

'No. It's a special kind of arrowhead,' he explained.

'What kind?'

'For birds. It's a *bird* arrowhead.'

'Really!' She stared at it, then looked up to him. 'Squirrels too? I hope so! One bit me. See?'

'Aw, Rosemary!'

'And some day I'm going to get her for it.'

He knew just how she felt. 'I hope you do.'

'Grey. Her hair is falling off of her back and her sides and her tail.'

'Wait a minute. Where you go . . .?'

'To show the Professor. Over there on the bench.'

'Oh. Well, see you next time.'

'Sure.'

'And if I see her around you want me to?'

'Yeah! Give it to her good!'

'I will, Rosemary.' And to you too!

―――――

'Hey, wake up, Professor.'

'Oh. How long was I . . .?'

'Take a look at this one.' She was holding her hand out to him.

'Huh?'

'It's a bird arrowhead. Charlie told me.'

He yawned and straightened up. 'Who's Charlie?'

'For squirrels, too, Charlie said.'

He yawned again. 'Who's – uh – Charlie?'

'Friend of Mom's. I just saw him and I showed it to him and he said what it was.'

'It's a very fine specimen.' He grasped the bench rail. 'Give me your shoulder.'

'Best one I found so far. I didn't see her, though.'

'Didn't you?' There. Made it.

'Charlie said if he saw her first he'd get her for me.'

'Now hold on a minute. I'm a little concerned about you and that squirrel, Rosemary. I don't like the way you're . . .'

'What if you made me a real arrow with this and feathers and everything and a bow, then I could really . . .'

'Quit it! Forget what that squirrel did to your thumb. It isn't very nice to hold grudges like that.'

'She started it!'

'For God's sake, forget her!'

'Easy for you to say.' She pulled away from him. 'Wasn't *your* thumb! I bet you Mom would make me a . . .'

'I don't think she would.'

'I do.'

'All right then. Get her to do it when she comes back from Minneapolis.'

'Okay. I will,' she said, 'and you can make me a big round thing so I can practise shooting.'

'No!'

'Will you push me round again on the round . . .'

'No. And if you don't let up on that squirrel I won't push you around on the roundabout any more at all.'

'Is that so! Then I'll just get Mom to do it for me.'

'You do that,' he said.

'She can push a lot faster than you can, and she never gets cranky every time after she's been sleeping.'

'Good for her. And for you.'

End of conversation all the way across the park and through the fence and across the street and up the front steps.

As he leaned down to unlock the front door, she said, 'And you really meant it when you said you wouldn't . . .?'

'I really did, Rosemary. I tell you what I will do, though. We'll get some cotton batten and a picture frame and we'll fix it up so you can arrange your collection and hang it up.'

'Hey! That's neat! When?'

'This afternoon.'

'Aw thanks, Professor!'

'On one condition,' he warned her.

'You don't have to tell me what it is.'

'I will anyway. Call off your vendetta against that grey squirrel.'

'Mmmmh.'

'And when you see your friend Charlie again, tell him to call it off too.'

'I love you a lot, Professor.'

'Same here, Rosemary.'

———

'Great is My love for thee and I will show unto thee the way. Mine will be thine for thou art Mine. But list thou not and continue in thy ways and I shall do unto thee even as I did unto Satan when I expelled him from Heaven and sent him down into the shit pit of Hell!'

———

As he had promised her, they had picked up the roll of cotton batten, then after Mister Rogers had changed back into his goddam shoes and the dishes were done, she went up to her room for the paper bag that held her collection, while he brought the picture frame from the basement.

'What else do we need?'

'Scissors. They're . . .'

'I know. On the peg board by the sink.'

'Which is out of your reach,' he said.

'Not if I pull out the drawer and use it for a step so I can get up on the counter.'

'So that's why it jams now. Use the stool.'

'Okay.' She headed for the stool.

'And while you're over there, the pliers. They're in the second drawer down to the left of the sink.'

When she came back to the table she said, 'What do we need the pliers for?'

'You'll see.'

She watched him as he began to pull out brad nails to release the cardboard backing on the frame. 'Can I do that?'

'Sure.'

She held up her first extraction in the plier's jaws. 'Just like the dentist does.'

She started on the next nail, then stopped and stared at him. 'He yanked out all of yours, didn't he?'

'He did.'

'Did it hurt a lot?'

'Hell of a lot more than it does that picture frame,' he said. 'When you get them all out, lift out the cardboard and set it to one side.'

'And then what?'

'You'll see.'

'There.' She laid down the pliers, picked up the frame and started to turn it over.

'Hold it! Watch the glass! Keep it upside down and take the cardboard out and set it to one side.'

'What used to be in this picture?'

'I don't remember,' he said. He had just remembered. Unfortunately.

'What do we do next?'

'Unroll the cotton – measure it on the cardboard. Then you cut it that length. Three of them, I think.'

It had been a photograph of Susan on her red trike. Sarah had snapped it and had it enlarged the week before they had left for the summer session in the Rockies.

'And now?'

'I don't think we'll need all three of them. Too thick. We'll split them. I'd better do that.'

When they had come home that summer without Susan, it had been waiting for them on the fireplace mantel.

'All right now. It's all yours. You arrange them the way you want them, and when you're done I'll put it back together.'

'I want the little one I found today right in the centre.'

'Go ahead.'

He watched as she picked them up and decided and placed them, then considered and changed her mind and picked them off and replaced them. Always the little bird arrowhead that was almost perfect stayed in the centre. Finally she was satisfied and agreed that he should reassemble it and tap in the brad nails. When he had finished, he propped it up on the table, against the wall. Both stepped back to admire.

––––––

After he had found Wrinkles for her, just under the flounce of the family-room couch, from which they had watched Transformer Titanessa disintegrate the evil hordes of the Gothardians, a compromise choice she had finally accepted in place of the three-way wrestling match between Betty Buster, Hunk Harriet, and Flying Flora, she set a new world record in the *Guinness Book of Records'* six-year-old-girls-brushing-their-teeth-before-getting-into-bed category. Then of course she simply had to give Wrinkles a good spanking for hiding on her, under the flounce of the family room couch, which made her real thirsty, but maybe a third of a glass of milk might settle that problem.

After a hummingbird sip, she asked him to leave the glass on the night stand just in case she got thirsty again. He kissed her good night and went over to switch on the blue night-light he had installed in the baseboard by her door the week after she and Nadya had moved in with him. He returned to the bed after she pointed out that he had forgotten to kiss Wrinkles good night.

As he straightened up, she said, 'He's not very smart, you know.'

'Who?'

'Wrinkles. He thinks some pretty dumb things.'

'Like what?'

'Ohhh – boys are way better than girls are.'

'Well, aren't they?'

' 'Course not. He thinks you shouldn't mix peanut butter and strawberry jam for a sandwich.'

'That's certainly dumb,' he agreed.

'Also. He hates milk.'

'That's not so dumb. Good night, dear.' He started for the door.

'And he doesn't know what goes "Oom. Oom." '

He stopped in the doorway. 'What does?'

'A cow backing up. Just close the door part ways.'

'I will,' he promised.

'He doesn't know why the boy jumped up and down after he swallowed his cough medicine.'

'I don't know that one either.'

'Well – come here and I'll tell you.'

He crossed to the foot of the bed.

'Because the cough-medicine bottle said on it to shake well.'

'I guess I should have known that,' he said.

'Sit down a minute and I'll tell you the new one I got to try on him.'

'Let's save it till morning, Rosemary.'

'Then you won't be here to see how dumb Wrinkles is.'

He sat on the corner of her bed.

'Ready?'

'Yes.'

'Not you. Wrinkles.'

Wrinkles had turned to face her on the pillow.

'What's the difference between a teacher and a train? Wait for Wrinkles.'

Wrinkles shook his head.

'Give up?'

Wrinkles nodded his head.

'He gives up. Your turn now, Professor.'

'Teachers are never late.'

'No.'

'Trains don't make you stay in after school,' he said.

'No. Do you give up?'

'Trains don't . . .'

'Give up, dammit!'

'All right,' he said, 'I give up.'

'Teachers say, "Take that gum out of your mouth." Trains say, "Chew-chew." '

'That's a good one.' He stood up. 'Good night now.'

'Kimberly gets a lot of good ones because she's in real school. You know any?'

'Oh – ah – used to.' He turned back at the doorway. 'What did the monkey say when he . . .'

'Yeah? What did he say?'

'. . . slid his hand underneath the bed and into the chamber . . .'

'Well, what did he . . .?'

'Not a very good one. What did the monkey say when he backed into the lawn . . .'

'Come on, Professor!'

'They – ah – keep coming up dirty.'

'That's the best kind!'

'You're probably right, but all the same . . . I'll need a little time to think of some, ah, proper ones.'

'Promise?'

'I promise.'

———

'. . . thou grasped her not when I delivered her unto thee. List unto me! Again and again thou listeth not when I command thee. They who are notty are an abomination in My Sight! My wrath with thee runneth over. It is hot and it is yellow and the next time thou listeth not and seize her not, it shall pour down from above upon thee, for I am mightily pist off with thee and with all those who list not unto Me!'

———

What a dear companion she had become. How she had softened the memory and ache and sadness that had never left him in all the years since the wilderness loss of the other little one. At first, when Rosemary and her mother had come to him, there had been so many explosions of remembrance, hurting with after-images and echoes. Other parks and swings and teeter-totters. Other good nights. Other story-telling. Susan! Susan! Daddy's own and darling Susan! ' 'Soozin' Van Doozin', the girl of my choozin'.'

How often had he sung Rosemary to sleep before realizing that he had been singing for *two* of them? He had heard that same belly-laugh delight decades ago when he had done for her: "There was an old man, he had an old sow. Noch-ow-eeech-ow – oink-ow – fart-ow – whistle-ow.' And how sad

217

had been the déjà vu of another child's hot, damp forehead, the remembered red thread of a past thermometer. Not nearly so often now. What a dear little inquisitor had been given him. Move over, Socrates.

Better look in on her before he went to bed. A wonder she hadn't smothered or strangled Wrinkles by now. He turned away, went into the bathroom. Mornings he must remember to be more careful in here. Before the night was over, going to have to do something more about that last cup of tea Sam talked you into. Remember to put the rim down just in case she has to get up in the dark, too. Dentures into the water glass; yourself into bed. To sleep? Not bloody likely with a goddam coyote out there in the middle of a city, to yap and howl you awake. You haven't got around yet to tightening up that goddam door, so the goddam spring wind will probably bump and rattle it again and again. Then in the night without the warm breath from Sarah's body beside you, you'll find yourself vulnerable again.

10

IT HAD BEEN SIMPLE ENOUGH DISCOVERING WHERE THE OLD man was taking her each morning by nine and picking her up each afternoon at three; he'd just had to wait till they had turned the corner of the block at the river end of the park, then follow at a careful distance on the bike. But from there on it was not going to be so easy to figure out a promising plan. In the park, last Saturday, he'd won some trust from her, but that was just a good beginning. Too risky to go into the school, tell them he was a close friend of the family, that her mother was unconscious in a Minneapolis hospital, intensive care after a five-car highway pile-up, or that the old man had suffered a massive brain haemorrhage. A recess snatch was out because whenever the children were in the play area, there was always a teacher or two supervising. Captain Hook and all his pirate buddies would have had a better chance of kidnapping a Wendy than he did.

Too many regular appearances, his bike regularly parked against the curb there, were sure in time to be noticed – or remembered afterwards. Leaving the Triumph chained and padlocked to the parking-lot fence two blocks south of the school, then walking to Luigi's Place, had been smart of him; he could have a long morning coffee or a hamburger lunch at a window seat giving him a clear view of the school across the street. Five times he had seen her skipping or teeter-tottering or swinging or playing drop-the-handkerchief. Before the week was out he decided he'd have to abandon that strategy because he got the same waitress, a flat-chested yapper who waited on him every time and would be sure to remember and identify him later on when the kid went missing. He'd settled for riding the bike slowly down the street only now and again and at opening or recess or outside game or closing times.

He never stopped, just coasted past, made a U-turn three or four blocks on and came back. He had noticed one thing; she always had that doll with her, and because she needed both hands when she took her turn on the swings or the teeter-totter, would give it to another child or lay it on the ground. If he could just get his hooks on the thing, might be able to use it for bait. No use kidding himself, the bloody school wasn't going to work out at all. Near the house would be much more promising. Some time, maybe when she was out on the street without the old man, ball-bouncing or skipping or hopscotching, or riding her yellow bike, he could just happen by, invite her to have a ride on the Triumph buddy seat. Or else the

park. He'd been lucky there once; the old man might doze off
again. If not, a good one with a rock or a wrench would easily
simplify that problem. Don't mention it, pleasure's all mine,
Professor.

He'd taken one last try at the school, but had timed it late.
The yard was empty, though he hadn't missed them by all that
much; there wasn't a breath of wind and one of the swings,
remembering some kid's ass, was still arcing gently. Hey!
Hey! Look at that! To the left over there by the base of the
swing frame, that grey bundle! Get it before she realizes she's
left it behind and comes back out for it.

Kick loose the stand, hurdle the fence, grab up on the run,
then back and over and away! Hallelujah! This time the
prune-faced puppet, next her!

As soon as he stopped in front of the school, he could tell that
something was wrong. For moments she didn't see him, was
standing sad and downcast and apart from the others waiting
to be picked up. When he called to her, she ran to him. He
got out of the car and she threw herself into his arms. She was
crying and it wasn't till they were in the car that her sobbing
had softened enough for her to tell him the reason.

'Wrinkles – is – guh-gone!'

When the bell rang, she said, she had forgotten Wrinkles
and left him alone by the swing and when she got back in
school and remembered and went out to get him he wasn't
there any more. Then Miss Carter had come with her and
they had looked all over for a long time but they couldn't find
him anywhere.

'Let's have another look, dear.'

No Wrinkles.

As he drove home he wasn't doing a very good job of comforting her. He almost told her he'd get her another Wrinkles, but decided against it, for it would only suggest that there was no hope of finding lost Wrinkles. Let her mourn a while then buy a new one and lie to her and tell her he had finally found him for her. Buried in dead leaves in the Wendy and Peter hedge perhaps.

'Tell you what we can do,' he said when they got home. 'I just remembered something.'

'What?'

'When you and your mother first came to look after me?'

'Yeah.'

'You know why you came?'

She shrugged.

'I put an ad in the paper and your mother read it and she wrote to me. How about we do the same for Wrinkles?'

'He can't read.'

'I know he can't, but if we put it in the Lost and Found –'

'What's that?' she said.

'It's a special place in the paper for people who have lost a kitten or a puppy, asking anybody who has found it to bring it back to them.'

'Yeah?'

'Yeah. We'll put in our phone number and say we'll pay them a reward to bring back Wrinkles to us.'

'What's a reward?'

'A prize.'

'Let's do it now!'

They went up to the office. He rolled in a sheet. She dictated, with slight editing help, and they came up with the ad.

'LOST: Wrinkles. He is soft and grey and has a lot of wrinkles and I lost him this afternoon by the swings at Wendy and Peter. He is my friend the Professor gave me for Christmas and there is a big reward for him if you find him for me.'

He knew it was high odds against any answers, but that hadn't been his point in placing the ad. Best thing he'd been able to think of to ease her initial deep feeling of loss. He explained that their ad would run for three days, and the first day it appeared, he showed it to her in the paper; the other two days as well, at her request. For almost a week as soon as she got up she asked him if anybody had phoned, again in the afternoon when he picked her up at the daycare centre.

'It's not going to be in the paper any more, is it?' she said.

'Afraid not, dear.'

'I knew it wasn't going to work anyway,' she said. 'Somebody stole him, you know.'

'Uh, I don't think –'

'Sure they did, and I know who did it,' she said.

'Do you?'

'I'm not saying his name, but he's fat and he's got red hair.'

'Just a minute, Rosemary –'

'Sadie thinks so too.'

'Rosemary.'

'He always wanted to hold Wrinkles and I wouldn't let him so he –'

'I don't think he did, Rosemary. Also I have a hunch that Wrinkles – sooner or later – is going to show up.'

Now the thing to do was to buy another Wrinkles and tell her that somebody had phoned in answer to the ad while she was at school. He'd leave it a couple of days before he put the plan into action.

On the phone call to her mother the evening of Wrinkles's disappearance, she had cried and Nadya had tried to comfort her, said she'd get her another Wrinkles, but Rosemary had been inconsolable.

'I want real Wrinkles!'

But since then, she'd made a remarkable recovery, hadn't even mentioned Wrinkles during the last Minneapolis call. How quickly the young could heal. They had hung up after half an hour, during which she told her mother that she hadn't missed brushing her teeth a single time or sulked, that she had done seven drawings of a baby dolphin and was sending the third one, which was the best one, to Minneapolis, that she had quit leaving stuff on the furniture and all over the floor any more and was making her bed up and helping the Professor do the dishes. Most of this was true. At the finish of the call there had been no tears. At this end of the line.

———

Hadn't been easy; whenever she was in the park, the old man was always with her. Going to have to be in front of the house. Several times he'd seen her alone out there, riding her yellow bike. Be patient, Slaughter; the right chance will come.

And it had. He'd watched her from the cliff edge, saw her ride up the sidewalk and back and down again, then dismount and wheel across the road and into the park. He headed for the shed to get the Triumph. He managed to time it just right, and, riding from the far end of the park, met her on her bike, coming from the opposite direction. He pretended he hadn't seen her, swerved out and dropped the Triumph.

'Hey, kid, watch where you're going!'

'Wasn't my fault.'

'Hey – it's Rosemary. Remember me?'

'Yeah.'

'Charlie – you found the bird –'

'I remember,' she said.

'How's your Mom doing in Minneapolis?'

'All right.'

'And Kimberly?'

'All right.'

'Nice new bike you've got there.'

'Yeah. Professor gave it to me for my birthday.'

He had lifted up the Triumph. 'I got mine for my birthday, too – last year. Want to go for a ride on it with me?'

'Nope.' Damn.

'You like to ride by yourself, don't you?' he said.

'Uh-huh.'

'Except when you have that grey doll in the carrier.'

'That was Wrinkles. I lost him.'

'No! When?'

'Last week,' she said. 'I left him by the swing at Wendy and Peter.'

'You sure?'

'Sure. We put an ad in the paper for him but nobody found him. Nobody phoned.'

'I wish I'd read it. I would have phoned.'

'What?'

'Down by the river – I found him.'

'You did?'

'I did.'

'Where?'

'Just below the bridge.'

'Really!'

'Really. Soon as I saw him lying under a bush down there I thought – oh oh – some poor little girl has lost her Wrinkles and –'

'Show me where you – '

'He isn't there now,' he said.

'Aaw!'

'I took him to my place. I live up there. Look – if you want to come take a look at him – ?'

'Yeah – I do!'

'All right then. Better leave your bike here – climb up on the buddy seat, and we'll just go get him right now.'

———

Whole goddam afternoon wasted yesterday. He'd tried the novelty store next to Ye Olde Pipe Shoppe, where he'd got Wrinkles last Christmas; he'd done four shopping malls and the toy section of three department stores without any luck. Wrinkles was no longer a hot child item, a couple of clerks told him; also it was the wrong time of the year; try next Christmas. Several said they could order one in for him, but delivery would take at least a month. He'd try again the beginning of the week.

———

So far so good. He'd helped her up, then with her arms tight around his waist and her cheek pressed against his back, he'd ridden slowly to the river end of the park without passing anybody. He'd waited till the orange pickup had gone by before he went through the opening and out onto the street. All clear down to the mouth of the alley that could take them for three blocks behind houses without anybody spotting them. He hoped.

———

Quite a shock. Almost lunch time according to his watch. He should have checked earlier, but he'd been having a fine run at

Sam and got carried away. Ah well. She'd promised him she'd
ride no further than three houses down and back, and she was
a dear little promise-keeper. All the same, better check her
out.

He'd just reached the office door when he heard it humming, had trouble spotting it, then saw it hovering just under
the skylight. No escape or nectar there, fellow. How had it
managed to get in here? Through the sliding glass to the
solarium of course; probably he hadn't closed it tight when
he'd looked down on the jungle below in his usual morning
getting-down-to-work-delay ploy.

Now it was reconnoitring high, landed on a mouth corner
of the tragic mask. He was unarmed, fly swatter downstairs.
He grabbed a folder off the corner of the desk. Too late. It
had taken off, was circling wide around the room. He swung
at it, missed, and damn near went on his ass. Now it had
begun a wavering examination of the bookshelves. It stopped
again, up there on top of *Where Angels Fear to Tread*. E.M.
Forster. Well out of reach. As many of his students had found
Forster to be.

———

He had put the Triumph in the shed. She'd pulled back when
they reached the cliff edge.

'Don't worry, Rosemary. See that slope? You just hang
onto my belt and we slide down to that overhang rock.'

'Where's your place?'

'Under there.'

'How come you live – ?'

'It's a cave. I like caves. Don't you?'

'Just to play in,' she said.

'I have nobody to play with – '

'I got to get back home. I promised the Professor – '

'Oh come on, Rosemary. Wrinkles is waiting for you.'

That did it.

Now it was bumping up and down, again and again against the solarium glass. He missed it by half a foot, and it took off. He lost sight of it, then saw it crawling on the skylight over his desk. Have to wait for it to come down from there. Maybe while he did, he ought to open the solarium window wide, then when it did take flight again, swish and wave and herd the damn thing out. Great idea, except it took its own sweet time to come down, and when it did, it headed toward the couch. It landed and began to crawl along the left arm. Got it! Finally.

He was picking it off with Kleenex when he heard another one humming somewhere behind himself, over by the opened solarium window side of the office.

'Just like coming down the slide fast and Professor catches me!' Now she had finished brushing her seat and was turning to look all around her. 'Most of the time.'

'Well – what do you think of my place?'

'Neat! Just like a little grassy yard with trees and bushes all around it!'

'I hoped you'd like it,' he said. 'But don't you tell anybody else about it, please.'

'I won't,' she promised.

'It would spoil it, you know.'

'Uh-huh. Must've been hard for you to find it.'

'Or anybody else. Come on over here.' He led her across the clearing, then through willow and bushes to the drop-off edge. 'Careful now! Hold my hand tight. It's a long way down.'

They had come to the rock shelf where he often lay with his binoculars.

'Boy, are we ever far up!' No fear of giddy heights, this kid.

'I can see the swings down there and the monkey bars . . .' Probably wouldn't need any help from anyone to fall off a steep cliff. '. . . and the teeter-totter and the roundabout – the river.' Just a little push in the middle of her back was all it would take. She turned. 'Hey – there's Professor's house.' She looked back and up to him. 'Where's yours?'

'I'll show you.'

They went back to the clearing, then to the face of the escarpment.

'I can't see – '

'Watch.' He held aside the buck brush, lifted out the door he'd camouflaged with sacking.

'In there?'

'That's right.'

She was bending down and peering into the opening. 'It's all dark.'

'Of course it is. Why would it be light with nobody in there?'

'You got lights?' she said.

'You'll see. I go first – you come in behind.'

She straightened up, stepped back. 'I'll just stay here and you bring out Wrinkles and then I better get right back home. Professor will be wondering where I – '

'Aw, come on in. Not just to get Wrinkles. I'd like you to see my house.'

'How can I see it if it's dark?' she said.
'I'll go in. I'll light it up. Then you come inside.'
She considered for a moment. 'Okay.'

———

Nowhere in sight on the street in front of the house, even though she'd promised to go no further than a couple of houses either way. He'd called and he'd called as he went from one end of the block to the other. Not a sign of her. Better go and get the car and prospect the neighbourhood. Don't blame her, you idiot, fooling around batting away at a couple of bumblebees till past lunch time, leaving a little six-year-old all by herself out here for over an hour.

———

'When I was little like you are, I used to have a secret place of my own in our house. Nobody knew about it but me.'
    'Where's Wrinkles?'
'There was a hole in the wall inside a closet on the top floor and I found it.'
    'Where's my Wrinkles, Charlie?'
'It was real dark in there too, so I'd light candles. I still like candles. Do you?'
    'Charleeee!'
'Don't you like – ?'
'They're all right,' she said. 'But where's Wrinkles?'
'Oh yeah. That's why we came here, isn't it. For Wrinkles.'
'Uh-huh.'
'Well now. Let's see. I thought he was inside this box I use for my table to eat off, but he isn't. I'm just trying to remember where else he might be. Here. You hold the candle for me,

230

please. I don't think I put him in the sleeping bag, but we'll take a look-see in there anyway. Just in case.'

Wrinkles was not in the sleeping bag.

'Over in this corner. Hold the candle up higher, will you, Rosemary? Nope. Okay – how about in this pile of blankets?'

Wrinkles was not in the pile of blankets, either.

'Now where do you suppose he could be hiding out on us?'

'Charlie.'

'Yes?'

'You know where he is, don't you?'

'Well – I – '

'Quit fooling me, Charlie. I want my Wrinkles.'

'You're not all that easy to fool, Rosemary.'

'Right now!' she said.

'Whatever you say. Let me have the candle.' He took it from her, tipped and dripped it on the box top, then held it till it was fast. 'O.K., let's go back outside.'

———

He'd driven up and down every street within a radius of five blocks, the alleys as well, in case she might be in some back yard. Nobody he'd asked had seen a little girl on a yellow bike. Could she have been invited into some home or other? No, that was out. Lunch time, and if she'd been asked to stay, she would have phoned for permission.

She had to be over in the park.

———

'This is Wrinkles's secret place. Right here behind that wild rose bush. He likes to be . . .'

She was already scrambling down and around the bush.

'Watch out for prickles.'

She came out and up with Wrinkles in her arms. 'Oh, Charlie – Charlie – thank you – thank you, Charlie!'

————

He had searched the play area first, and spoken to a young couple picnicking at one of the park tables, before he saw the bike leaning against a cottonwood down towards the river.

It was small and it was yellow. He headed for it.

It was hers.

————

'Let's go, Charlie.'

It was the third time she'd said that. 'Not right away.'

'Professor will be worried about where I am.'

Third time she'd said that, too. 'You just got here.'

'No I didn't. I bet he's looking for me right – '

'Please stay with me a little bit longer.'

'Uh-uh.'

'Wrinkles wants you to,' he said.

'No, he doesn't. He wants to get home too.'

'You don't always have to do what Wrinkles wants you to do.'

'I have to do what Mom wants me to do and teacher wants and what Professor wants and what I want and I want to go home now.'

'Suit yourself,' he said.

She turned away and went to the bottom of the slide path leading up to the top of the slope. She turned back to him. 'Come on, Charlie.'

'It's you that wants to go,' he said. 'Go ahead.'

'But I need you to help me up – ride me home on your motorcycle.'

'Okay.' He went to her, held out his hand. 'Let me have Wrinkles.'

She handed Wrinkles up to him. He went to the rock in front of the cave, sat down.

'Why aren't we – ?'

'Wrinkles doesn't want to go.'

'Charlie!'

'He says he's scared to climb up there. He says he knows a real good game we can play, and after he's played it with you and me maybe he won't be so scared and then he'll go up if I carry him.'

'Please, Charlie, I want to go.'

'I told him we'd do that after we had our lunch.'

'Charleeeeee!'

———

All right now. Don't panic. We know she's been here because she's left her bike up against that cottonwood and gone far enough away that she can't hear you calling her. And quit remembering when you lost . . . Terrible conjecture is no help at all. There is quite likely some simple and ordinary explanation, that you can laugh yourself silly over when you know it. Right now, while you dither about, she is in all probability inside one of those homes across the street. Of course she is, and right now she is sitting down in front of the TV with a new little friend she ran across here. They could be playing dolls or checkers or fish or . . . Why has she left her beloved bike behind! What if she ran out in front of a car!

Check the hospitals – certainly Western General across the river. *The river* – Jesus!

———

'Ever play Indian Princess?'
  'No.'
  'Lots of fun.'
  'I don't want to play. I want to go home!'
  'To start with, I'm the Indian Prince – '
  'Please take me home!'
  ' – the oldest son of the chief of the tribe.'
  'Please – '
  'Flaming Arrow.'
  'I won't play!'
  'Yes, you will.'
  'You can't make me.'
  'Oh, yes, I can.'
  'Hey! You're hurting my arm!'
  'Just settle down – settle – uh! You just try that again, kid, and I promise you I'll break your foot right off at the ankle! I am a promise-keeper. Stop yelling and listen to – I can't stand screechers! That's better. Now – when I take my hand off your mouth you are going to keep it shut. Understand? If you do, then nod your head. Great. Ah-ah – hold it. I don't like crying either. Now you listen to me. If you behave – do exactly as I tell you to do – no more kicking – no more yelling – crying – you'll be all right.'
  He went to the pack and came back with the clothesline rope.
  'What are you going to – ?'
  'I have to leave you for a little while. That's why I have to tie you – '

'Don't tie me up!'

'I have to, because if I don't you'll run away.'

'No – I won't.'

'Oh, yes, you will. I know you, Rosemary. I'm going to have to tie you at night, too.'

'I promise – I promise I – '

'Those blankets over there are just for you so you won't get cold at night. Wrinkles can sleep with you, but I won't have to tie him up because I know he doesn't lie and say he won't run away and then run away the way you would. I will untie you every morning when we wake up and whenever I'm here and can keep an eye on you. Understand? *Look at me!* Understand? Answer me, Rosemary! Say you understand!'

'I – I – do.'

'Do what?'

'Und – under – stuh-hand.'

Now – to the holy guidance place to give thanks to Him Who hath delivered the child into my hands.

———

The line had kept on ringing busy, but after four tries he had got through to them. They said someone would be coming as soon as possible. He went into the living room, where he could watch out the window for their arrival. In here he wouldn't miss the sound of the door chimes, though of course that meant he wouldn't be able to hear the telephone ring in the family room, so he stayed in the hall half-way between. When he could stand the interminable wait no longer, he went outside to sit on the front step.

It took at least an hour for the cruiser to show up. Two men in uniform got out. He invited them inside and into the living room. They seemed very young to be policemen, but then everyone was beginning to look young to him. The heavy-set one asked most of the questions; the other took a pen and notebook out of his jacket pocket.

The child was how old? Small – big for her age? Distinctive features? What was the child wearing when last seen? Had he checked the house thoroughly? Had there been an argument – had the child been disciplined? When had he last seen her? He told them around eleven this morning, when she'd gone out to ride her bicycle up and down the walk in front of the house. Could he give them names and addresses of her usual playmates? He explained that he had already phoned the few he'd been able to think of, but she had not been in their homes. The note-taker wrote them down anyway.

He told them how he had searched the streets and alleys of the neighbourhood and the park, where he had found her bicycle. The note-taker closed up his notebook and put it back in his jacket pocket. Would he please come with them to the park and show them where he had found her bike.

Dear God, how had he let this happen to her?

———

Keep Thy holy signals coming loud and clear. I almost missed that one Thou gavest me as I cleansed myself at break of day last week down by the river bank, when I thought it was Satan appearing unto me and I was sore afraid. I should never doubt Thee and I will no more. No more. I will doubt no more. NomorenomorenomoreThomashit no more! Forevereverevermore. He was Thine own messenger sent down to me from Heavenden above. This I knew when I saw Him at the edge of Holy Cross cemetery three days later and it was limp within His jaws. Then I knew – I truly knew that Thou dost answer all my prayers to Thee, that Thou wouldst deliver her unto me, even as Thou didst the grey squirrel unto the angel Wolf! Hallelujah!

———

He had taken them to the bicycle, still leaning against the cottonwood. He noted that both had looked away from it and toward the river. Several times. When they had finished their brief examination, the inquisitor suggested they take it back to the house with them now. Remarkable it was still here, for bicycles were a popular item with thieves, he explained, as well as VCRs and cash and cars and credit cards.

How about little girls?

At their car they said he would be hearing from them after they had talked with people in the park and houses along the street.

'I think it's likely she'll turn up, sir,' the note-taker said. 'I have a little girl too and just last month my wife and I went through what you're . . . she's probably in one of these neighbourhood homes. Children have a way of losing all track of time. If – when she comes back, please let us know.'

Just as they drove off he heard the carillon bells start up.

———

'When day is over and night is drawing nigh, go thou down to the river bank, and through the shadows of the evening walk toward the sun low upon horizon west. Beyond Spitzee bridge but before Mary Wood House above wilt thou come upon wolf willow there. From out their midst cut thou a sapling the thickness of thy thumb and exactly two and one-half cubits in its length. This shall be thy staff to comfort thee and which thou shalt use to discomfort the child. For the harlot sow and

237

for her swine daughter the time of My divine punishment is coming soon!'

He looked up at the clock over the television set: 8:10. They hadn't got back in touch with him yet, and there was no way he could reach them, because he could not remember and had mislaid the note page with the names he must ask for if he wanted them, and God did he ever want them! He couldn't put it off any longer; 9:10 Minneapolis time. Last phone call with her Nadya had said the play was going great and they were rehearsing evenings now that opening was less than a week away. Till ten. He reached for the phone.

'She's in rehearsal right now. Can I take a message?'

'Yes. To get to the phone as fast as she can!'

'I'm sorry. She's on stage. I don't know when they'll be taking a break – '

'Not during a break! Now!'

'Sir, I can't interrupt – '

'It is a critical matter – her six-year-old daughter!'

'What is the – ?'

'Please! It's a matter of life and death!'

'Yes, sir. Hold the line, sir.'

'What is it!'

'If you can, you'd better sit down there, Nadya.'

'What's happened to Rosemary!'

'She . . . she's missing.'

'Oh no!'

'I got in touch with the police. They're investigating – '

'How did it happen!'

'Oh, Nadya – I'm sorry – it's my fault. She was riding her bicycle on the walk and I – I got engrossed in working in the office and, and a couple of bumble . . . . and I went out to get her and I found her bicycle in the park but she was – gone – and and I'm – I wish I – hadn't . . . .'

'Don't, Doctor – don't. It's not your . . . . What – what do the police . . .?'

'One of them felt she would turn up – they usually did, he said.'

'When did you discover she was . . .?'

'Ah – a – couple of hours ago,' he lied.

'All right. Phone me just as soon as you know she's all right.'

'Nadya – I think perhaps you'd better catch a flight back here.'

There was a long pause. 'Doctor – how long has she been missing?'

'Since noon,' he said.

'Jesus! It's *him*!'

'What?'

'*Slaughter*! Did you tell the police about . . .?'

'I didn't think of – '

'*Tell them!* Get them to – tell them – before he can – oh God – I'm coming – the earliest – oh *God*!'

'How many times have I told it that it must obey me! That it must behave, and never again mention its mother!'

'Please – please . . . .'

'Must not whine – '

'Oh, please don't!'

'Or interrupt! Take down its pants!'

'Let me go home! I want my Mom – '

'There! Me! I! My! Three times it has referred to itself in the first person!'

'I won't.'

'Four! Drop – its – pants!'

'I promise I won't – '

'It!'

'It – it won't.'

'And it will count aloud.'

'Please don't hurt me any – '

'It! Hurt *it*!'

'Don't hurt it! I'll – it'll do anything you want but don't – '

'Right now! Good.'

'Let it go home!'

'To its Mommy?'

'Yes – yes!'

'To its wicked, sinful, evil Mommy? To its whore sow Mommy? No! It shall see her never again! For its own good, that it may learn to be good again. Bend over, for it has disobeyed me again and again when it did not say it!'

'I forgot!'

'*It* forgot!'

'Forgot what?'

'To say it when it forgot to say it instead of – '

'Watch it, it! Now – as the wolf willow descends upon it – count!'

———

It had been a redeye flight she'd managed to catch out of Minneapolis, with a six-hour holdover in Winnipeg, so that it was 10:00 a.m. by the time he picked her up at the airport. He had taken her in his arms and they had held each other long. In as much detail as he could, he went over again what had happened, told her that he had notified the police about Slaughter, that they were checking him out. He did not tell her about their other plans for this morning. As they drove over the bridge his heart sank when he caught sight of the boat barely moving in the middle of the river, with one man crouched in the stern, the other flat out over the bow and peering into the water. Several men in uniform were spotted along both banks. The boat was downstream on *his* side. Thank God her head was turned and she was staring out of her window. Upstream.

She hadn't touched her lunch; he had finally persuaded her to go up to her room and catch up on sleep. She said there was no way she could, but he insisted. He brought her up the stiffest hot rum he'd ever prepared, stayed with her till she downed it, drew the curtains and closed the bedroom door.

He had just got down to the family room when the phone rang. He recognized the young note-taker's voice. They were quite sure they could rule out the river now, were checking out on Slaughter and would report to him as soon as they turned up anything on him. The bus depot, the railroad station, the airport had been told to look out for a man of Slaughter's description accompanied by a six-year old girl. Highway Patrol had been alerted to watch for a black Triumph Bonneville motorcycle. Tomorrow morning they would comb the park again, and this time every inch of the escarpment as well.

———

'It has not two turtle doves or two pigeons. All it has is Wrinkles, which must do as its sin offering. I shall take Wrinkles and I shall wring off his head and I shall tear him by the arms but I shall not divide him asunder. I shall lay him as its burnt offering upon the altar hearth and burn the whole, that there may rise to Heaven a pleasing odour to the Lord. Thus do I make the Wrinkles guilt offering for it, and it shall receive atonement for the sins it has committed, and it shall be forgiven.'

'All night long the pleasing odour of the burnt offering has ascended to My Nostrils and it is now forgiven. Quench the embers, that no smoke may betray thee to them. No longer do they seek beneath the river waters, for it is thou they now pursue, as thou canst see them doing there below. Fear them not, for I shall protect thee. Fear not the hounds of Hell they have unleashed against thee, for I shall protect thee for now and evermore. Even as I did in Noah's time, shall I open up My Heavens, that the rain may wash away all trace and smell of footprint spoor, and they shall be confounded.'

He had not slept, had not undressed, and was lying on the bed when he heard the announcements begin, as police cars went up and down the neighbourhood streets calling for people to gather in the park to search for a little lost child. He had just got to his feet when Nadya appeared in the doorway. Fully clothed.

When they got over there they found dozens of people ahead of them, alerted either by the TV local news last night or by the Livingstone Heights Neighbourhood Watch domino-telephone committee. Before long the play area was crowded, with cars lining the whole length of the park edge.

He and Nadya sat on one of the benches, accepted hand-clasps, expressions of concern, and optimistic assurances, then watched and listened as the police organized and explained the escarpment search procedure. Form a line from one end of the park to the other – take up positions about ten to twelve feet apart – go slowly – examine every bush and gully – look for articles of clothing – any sign of earth disturbance – listen for the bullhorn.

'Nadya – maybe we ought to go back to the – '

'I'm staying.'

As the long line of police and neighbourhood volunteers had been gathering and forming along the base of the escarpment, the dark cloud bank to the west had moved closer, veined with lightning, the thunder louder and louder. The line had just begun its slow advance when the storm broke. There came a chill rush of wind, then the rain which grew in moments to torrent, but the line moved slowly upwards and did not falter, even when the downpour turned white with golf-ball hail that tore and tattered leaves and bounced off flinching heads and shoulders.

'My lightning, My thunder and My hail have not stayed them. Go! Flee even as the birds and beasts now do through bush and tree! Take flight upward and away from the horde of Satan after thee. Go straightway to Mary Wood shed and thy hidden Triumph cycle there! Get – thee – out – of – here – forthwith!

'Unbind the child. The time hath come to set her free, for

thou hast carried out my commandment as I have bade thee do. The whore mother hath been wounded well. For two long nights and days of torment hath she suffered the deepest pain and anguish a mother can ever know. Her heart is broken. This was thy purpose, and it hath been accomplished now.

'List well unto Me, my son. I have one more commandment, and it is not a new one to thee. Three times before have I so commanded thee: amongst the cardboard cartons in the Ebenezer Victory Temple storage room, where Elijah Matthews entered thee; the black triangle when thy father hadst abandoned thee to her; after thy first-year finals failure when thy mother cut thee off and all seemed lost.

'Three times didst thou heed Me not. This time thou wilt! Mount the Triumph and ride full throttle south through granite cross, winged angels, marble lambs, tombs and flower urns, thence out and over the mortal cliff!

'I am the only One Who loves thee, Charles. Come home to Me!'

———

Where, for centuries before white civilization came west, Blackfoot braves had hazed herds through the death funnel to stampede over the cliff edge of the buffalo jumping pound to their death five hundred feet below, one Triumph Bonneville 750 cc motorcycle – with dual carburetor, low-rated sprocket for faster acceleration and free-flow exhaust for high decibel level – arced high above the spruce and pine and cottonwood of Livingstone Park. Without helmet, Charles Slaughter M.A. crouched low over the handle bars.

———

When the rain and hail cloudburst happened, he and Nadya had barely made it into the park clubhouse for shelter. It had seemed only minutes before the storm had passed over and on. They had come out just in time to see the motorcycle sail off the top of the escarpment, hang high, then float down and crash in the trees and bushes just beyond the play area. Almost instantly the explosion had come, then flame, then lifting, drifting black smoke. The bullhorn had warned everyone to stay back but several had bolted toward the scene. Nadya was one of them. A policeman had stopped and held her.

Slaughter had been found dead. The child had evidently not been with him on the motorcycle. More waiting horror to come!

It had not been long. Rosemary had been found crouched behind one of the gravestones in Holy Cross cemetery, and they had taken her directly to Western General, and into Emergency.

Before he had driven with Nadya to the hospital he phoned Dr. Gladstone to meet them there.

They shared the waiting area with a young man whose face was lacerated, eyes swollen, head bandaged, his left arm in a sling.

'Broad daylight – right in front of the Clarendon Bar,' he mumbled. 'Three a the fuckers – green half-ton – baseball bat – three teeth missin' – maybe more.'

A nurse came up to him. 'Come this way.'

'Mugged an' rolled me – broad daylight – '

'Please come with me.'

'Never had a chance against the fuckers – huh?'

'They're ready for you.'

She led him through the door. Moments later Dr. Gladstone came to them, even his glasses glinting concern.

He explained that they would be keeping Rosemary in the hospital for further examination. The backs of her legs and her buttocks were bruised and welted, but the physical damage was not serious. She had not been sexually assaulted. The trauma that concerned him was psychic.

'How bad, Doctor?' Nadya asked.

'I really can't – shouldn't say. It's not my field: we want to keep her here overnight – tomorrow – day or so. For psychiatric examination.'

'When can we see her?'

'Just as soon as they have her in her room,' he said. 'The children's ward on the fourth floor. She'll be under – be asleep. I've arranged for Dr. Tracy to see her tomorrow morning. A very fine family psychiatrist. Baltimore and Menninger – a good physician too.'

The next morning, when he and Nadya got to the hospital and met Dr. Tracy, he felt a small stir of reassurance. For once, Dr. Gallstone had made a good decision; this was indeed a smart and caring psychiatrist. He could tell from her face that Nadya felt that way about her, too. Very early in their interview, Dr. Tracy asked them to call her by her first name: Grace.

'Your child has suffered an outrageous experience,' she said. 'She has taken retreat within herself. She's quite sealed off in her own world, where she hopes she cannot be hurt again. It's a world with no consensual dimension to it. Almost catatonic. That's a brutal bit of nosology, but I have to level with you. She is not going to venture out of her inner refuge in a hurry.'

'How long,' Nadya said, 'do you think it will take till . . . ?'

'Not days. Not weeks. At the very least a month before she'll be able to retrieve any trust whatever in others. I'm afraid that includes you.' What lovely empathy in Dr. Tracy's dark eyes! 'Her recovery depends a great deal on the quality of her life up to now – the love and support she's had before this happened to her. Snap judgement, Nadya, I'd say she's a lucky little girl in the warmth department.'

'Will she ever get over . . .?'

'I think so. She's only six. Yes, I think so.' She lifted a cautioning forefinger. 'You're going in to her now. She won't speak to you – or anyone else. She won't be hearing you, either. Don't embrace her – indeed don't touch her. Now or for quite some time to come. She's lost all trust in others. I know it's hard, but you mustn't touch her.'

'When will she – when can we . . .?'

'That's up to her. Don't jump into her skipping-rope until it's your turn, and remember – she is the one who will tell you it is your turn.'

'When can she come home?'

'Not right away. We'll work that out together over the next several days as we see how she progresses.'

––––––

Doctor Tracy had been very close in her prognosis; it had been a rough and painful six weeks for all three of them, especially for Rosemary, so deeply submerged within her frightened self. She was mute for one whole week; he could not recall once in that time that she had ever looked directly at him or at Nadya. She recoiled from touch. Sleep was no refuge, for then the nightmares would flare and she would waken screaming. The third time that Nadya had gone in to her, and, forgetting the doctor's warning, had taken the child in her arms to comfort her, Rosemary had kicked and scratched and bitten, driven by consuming rage that would not die.

In time, the nightmares and tantrums happened less and less often. She began to come downstairs on her own hook, then into the solarium, and then outside and onto the back deck. It was there on a sunny summer morning that she spoke for the first time. With her hand she had pointed out to them a black squirrel doing a running tightrope act along the power line to the house. Then she turned to her mother. 'Mom.'

She turned to him. 'Professor.'

Just two labels. That was all, but she had grinned when she said them.

Full sentences, however, turned out to be disturbing:

'It washed its hands after.'

'It wants to go up to its own room now.'

'It didn't forget to brush its teeth.'

'Can it watch Mr. Rogers?'

'It's sorry it didn't finish up all its Prairie Maid. It won't do it again.'

This use of the third person singular impersonal had puzzled Dr. Tracy. 'Strange. I've never run across it before – in practice or in anything I've read. More importantly, I want to tell you that she's doing remarkably well. So are you people.'

So this was doing remarkably well. Jesus!

At the end of the interview Dr. Tracy returned to the 'it' business. 'Must have something to do with the emotional shock she's been through. Right now her sense of self, or what she thinks others think of her, has been shattered. She thinks of herself only as an object. From what you've told me of her as a solid, confident little girl – before all this – I think she'll come around as she feels more secure again in your love. I think it will pass.'

She'd been right; within a week Rosemary had become 'I' again. No requests for reading at bedtime, though. And he should never have brought the yellow bicycle out of the garage; one look at her face and he simply rolled it back inside and shut the door. Stupid, stupid, stupid! He also should have known better than to suggest she come with him to the park swings and slide and monkey bars and roundabout.

There had been initial reluctance to return to Wendy and Peter, but that had faded within days. All three of them had welcomed the comfort of their old life pattern, Nadya leaving Rosemary at the school and going on to the Sock and Buskin, he picking her up in the afternoon. Short of joining the day-care teaching staff, he was making sure he kept his eye on her at all times.

———

There had been a hand-painted sign with an arrow just after he turned off the bridge on his way back from Foodvale. Halfway down the block he saw the tables and a handful of people on the front lawn, furniture and other household effects spilling over into the side driveway. At the next corner there was another sign; this Canada Day weekend, garage and yard sales must be blooming all over town. He drove by, then circled the block and came down the street again. He stopped the car and got out.

He didn't know why he'd done it; he didn't give a damn whether there might be anything of any use to him; sheer impulse. He certainly didn't want a plastic flamingo for his front lawn, mason jars, a can-opener, costume jewellery, used clothing, a kitchen chair, or that sad maroon couch, which must have served several years as a fine scratch pole for a pet cat.

'Can I be of any help to you, sir?'

Young daughter of the family, no doubt.

'I don't know . . . .' He looked around. 'That's – uh – a nice flamingo.'

'Oh that's where we always keep her. She's not for sale.'

Thank God! He was just about to say he'd like to look things over a little more when he saw it, on the card table beside the May Day tree, with the Monopoly board, the yo-yo, the coiled skipping-rope, and the set of Nurse Jane books.

Wrinkles!

11

DAMN IT ALL! A NEW JOINT HEARD FROM, THE RIGHT KNEE, inside and just under the kneecap. Over the past month, whenever he went up or down stairs, he'd probably been favouring the left too much. If he were to shift body weight back to that one, then it was sure to flare up again. No! I will not use a goddam cane to accommodate either one of you. Heat pads and ice packs, yes, and maybe see Doctor Gallstone, suggest some cortisone shots, but the answer as usual would be no, just rest and careful flex in the therapy pool and how's your balance these days and have you cut those cigars down? Are you experiencing any urinary problems? Only when you piss me off, Doctor.

Maybe he'd better ass-bump it up and down stairs, but then Nadya would notice, and he didn't care to discuss rusty knees with her. How the hell was he going to carry on? Install one of those banister elevators? Stay on one goddam floor for the rest of his goddam life?

Perhaps a cane *was* the answer. He did have his father's, an ebony one with a gold knob, that people might think he carried for swank alone. He could rap it peremptorily on the floor, point with it when he gave orders, and wave it under their noses. More weapon than cane, really. But just until both knees calmed down.

They were gone when he did make it to the kitchen; tea ready, two slices of whole wheat on the plate by the toaster, double boiler with its cargo of Prairie Maid waiting for him on the stove, marmalade, butter, and a glass of orange juice on the table. By now she'd be at the Sock and Buskin, Rosemary at Peter and Wendy. Ah, bless them both!

What a shock it had been last night when she told him. Must have saved the news deliberately, even though they'd gone over the horror script a dozen times.

'Your phone call came in the middle of rehearsal. Hadn't been for Seth, I'd have gone to pieces. Hell, I did go to pieces. He headed for the phone right away, got me a ticket, drove me to the suite and helped me pack, then out to the airport. Found I was just on standby. He came into the waiting room with me and got them to move me up to the top of the list so my name was called first. When he hugged me goodbye he said he was sure everything would turn out all right, and when I came back to bring Rosemary with me.'

'. . . when I came back to bring Rosemary with me.' He should have twigged right then when she'd said that. She'd been quite a while on that phone call to Minneapolis, telling Seth that Rosemary was safe, but that wasn't all they had talked about evidently, as he had learned just last night. It was official that Seth was to be the new artistic director for the Tyrone Guthrie; the understudy who had replaced her couldn't act her way out a paper bag; there had been some sort of crisis at Stratford and Seth had been asked to do the play there, and, well, he wanted her for Joan.

'How long a run?' he asked.

'With rehearsals, from August right through to October.'

'I'll miss you,' he said. 'Rosemary?'

'Ahh – this time I want her with me.'

'I understand.'

'One other thing, Doctor. Seth wants to hire me – two-year contract in their repertory company . . . .'

'Oh.'

———

They're leaving me, Sam, both of them. Always knew I'd lose them, one way or another; either they'd leave me or I'd leave them. With Livy and Susan already taken from you, I know just how you must have felt after that Christmas morning you found drowned Jeanie in the bathtub. Her last seizure.

I won't wear Palm Beach white for purity or for mourning; I won't hustle down and out onto the street by 10:00 a.m. every day, knocking the ash off my cigar, reminding the whole rotten, living human race I'm still around. No, I won't, because now that it's twilight time for me, too, I recognize we can no longer be important or clear to others or to ourselves, and knowing that we never were worth a pinch of coon shit, anyway, does help some.

That's it then, just one short week till the end of 'three are we'; God have mercy on this old hermit. He'd make it to her opening in Stratford this summer, and maybe to Minneapolis for Christmas with them. There'd be letters, and now and again long distance, but . . . .

All these years we've been running together, Sam, I don't think I've ever before felt so close to you as I do now. I truly understand why in your late and lonely years you started collecting your 'angel fish,' all those pretty young women you accosted and charmed. Some did not succumb; remember the redhead on one of your transatlantic crossings gave you the brush-off? The hell you don't. Years later she did. I found her account of how you bugged and bored her, about the same time as I ran across that interview with your mother.

How about your mother, Sam? I don't mean the one you wrote all those sincere letters to, telling her how you'd kicked cigars and liquor and cards, hadn't told a dirty joke in months, didn't swear any more, never missed a Sunday in Presbyterian church. I am talking about the beautiful southern belle who loved laughter and parlour games and flirting and ballrooms and lovely gowns. I am talking about the mother who said her marriage to your father was a 'spite marriage,' that 'Clemens was not my real love,' that the man she had truly loved had cast her aside . . . .

Just a minute. Why was he suddenly trying to recall something from the years he'd taught at New York State? Why should Sam's mother's indiscreet candour with that reporter pitch him back there? Something important here, but what's the link with a lover who spurned Sam's mother? Ah yes! The Mark Twain Chair in Buffalo.

The buffalo coat!

'Clemens was not my real love.'

The retired brigadier general!

'Mine was a spite marriage.'

The red and white toque.

To get even with the true love who had abandoned her. William Lyon Mackenzie, the red-wigged journalist firebrand, who set and ignited the 1837 rebellion. Two years after your birth, Sam.

Several times over the years the memory of the strange old visitor had returned to him, until Sarah's death, actually, for it had been she who had always reminded him. The evening of the general's visit he had told her about it, and she had laughed with him, but her amusement had very soon become curiosity and, later, fascination. She began to refer to it each time she gave him another shove toward the Mark Twain biography he'd promised her he'd write some day.

It had been about a week before Christmas break, his third year at New York State; the English Department secretary had phoned him to say there was a Mr. Denison to see him. Mr. Denison turned out to be a short man wearing a red and white toque and a buffalo coat; this was surprising winter attire, when even the Royal Canadian Mounted Police up in Canada had stopped wearing bison hide years ago. Cheeks red from the outside cold, he looked to be in his early seventies. The full moustache was quite white and when he took off his toque, white hair sprang free in a dead-dandelion corolla. Mid or late seventies perhaps, fit and vital-looking, with forehead and cheek skin unwrinkled, erect bearing unmarred by age stoop.

The heft of the buffalo coat surprised him as he took it from the man to hang it up.

'Have a seat, Mr. Denison.'

'Brigadier General. Retired. Thank you.' He set his briefcase down beside one of the chairs against the wall.

'What is it you wanted to see me about, General?'

'I understand you hold the Mark Twain Chair here.'

'That's right.'

'I could do with some help from a Mark Twain scholar like yourself.'

'What sort of help, General?'

'Writing a book. I'm writing one on him. My interest in Mark Twain goes back to my early childhood.'

'Most people's interest in him does.'

'Imagine you have quite a few people . . . .' He had finished lighting his cigarette, but the match refused to shake out. He blew on it. '. . . quite a few people coming in and asking you to lend them a hand writing a book on Mark Twain.'

'Not really.' The man's steady look was becoming disconcerting. 'I think you're about the first.'

'Understand you're a Canadian.'

'Yes, I am.'

'Did you know that many of Mark Twain's books were mercilessly pirated by Canadian publishers?' The pale eyes were intense and unwavering.

'I believe they were. As well as by those in a lot of other countries. During his time there were still quite a few pirates of one sort or another hanging about. Are you Canadian, General?'

'Not quite. You're an observant man, Professor. Matter of choice.'

'What is?'

'Military title, *Brigadier* General, Canadian or British rank. More often down here I'm called a One-Star General.'

Also down here damn few senior citizens were walking around in an R.C.M.P.-issue buffalo coat weighing in the neighbourhood of forty-five pounds.

The General leaned forward to stub out his cigarette in the

ash tray and as he sat back, he picked up the briefcase. 'My
grandfather was Canadian . . .' He unzipped the briefcase and
reached inside. '. . . though actually he wasn't born in Canada. Alyth, Scotland. You see, he was a bastard and his father,
my great-grandfather, left him in Scotland with his grand-
mother, *my* great-great-grandmother, when my great-grandfather came out to Canada in 1820. Year or so later she
brought him – my grandfather – with her out to Canada as a
little boy. You following me?'

'Perhaps.'

'Her name, my great-great-grandmother, was Elizabeth
Mackenzie.' He had brought out a sheaf of papers and was
leafing through them. 'That's where I get my middle name,
Mackenzie, from a long line of Mackenzies going right back
to Noah you might say. Both of my great-great-grandfather's
grandfathers fought with Bonnie Prince Charlie in 'The
Forty-Five' against King George the Second. All Highlanders.
But eventually Presbyterian.' Now he had separated two
sheets from the others. He looked up. 'My grandfather grew
up in Canada, but later on moved to the States. I am American in regard to my citizenship, but in my heart I have always
thought of myself as Canadian. In fact by blood I am first
cousin once removed – to Prime Minister William Lyon
Mackenzie King. Being Canadian, you'd know who he was,
of course.'

'Of course.'

With a sheet of paper in each hand, he stood up. 'Americans are much better informed about Mexicans or Cubans
than they are about Canadians.'

'I've noticed that, General.'

'Easier to show you what I'm driving at than it is to tell
you.' He rounded the desk and laid one of the sheets on the

corner. 'Mackenzie genealogical tree. Just look it over and you'll get a much clearer picture.' He stared down at the general's chart.

'You can see where it divides – Canadian and American. That's why I pasted the little Union Jack up there on the left and then the Stars and Stripes on the right – top of each branch. Prime Minister William Lyon Mackenzie King on the Union Jack left. I'm on the Stars and Stripes right.'

'Interesting, General, but didn't you say when you first came in that you were doing a biography of Mark Twain?'

'Yes.'

'Then why – what has all this Mackenzie genealogical information to do with – ?'

'A great deal.'

'I don't understand.'

'You will. As you can see in this chart, my great-grandfather and Prime Minister William Lyon Mackenzie King's grandfather were one and the same man. Our mutual male ancestor was the father of Prime Minister King's mother. Also the grandfather of my mother.'

'I can see that, but – '

'She was born American in Rochester to my great-grandfather's bastard son, who was my grandfather – '

'But what has all this to do with – ?'

'Just look at the chart, Professor. Elizabeth Mackenzie, my great-great-grandmother, brought Isabel Baxter across the Atlantic with the little boy to Montreal in June of 1822. Isabel and William Lyon Mackenzie were married in Dundas, Upper Canada, just three weeks later. She bore him – '

'General, you're beginning to bore – '

' – thirteen children – '

'Look, General – '

'Six of these died in childhood for one reason or another.

Explains the very close and loving relationship between William Lyon Mackenzie and his bastard son, my grandfather.'

'It very well may, but just what has all this go to do with – '

'Before and after the 1837 Rebellion, William Lyon Mackenzie, my great-grandfather, kept in constant touch with my grandfather, James, who apprenticed as a printer with his father, who published *The Colonial Advocate* from 1824 until the family went into exile in 1837. My grandfather set up his own newspaper in Lockport, New York, and later on in Rochester. Definite journalistic genetic inheritance, which I am sorry to say was not passed on to me which is why I've come to see you. Now – let's move along.'

'Please do!'

'This chart is not complete. My grandfather was not the only bastard son William Lyon Mackenzie fathered.' He laid the second sheet he had been holding, on top of the first. 'Second American branch, which explains my special interest in Mark Twain. My grandfather James and Samuel Clemens were half brothers, which makes me half second cousin to Mark Twain. William Lyon Mackenzie was Mark Twain's father. Happened in the course of Mackenzie's frequent visits to New York state. And as you know, as an adult Mark Twain came back to Buffalo for a bit. All adds up. What do you think of that, Professor?'

He really could not tell him that he had begun to think well back in all this that Brigadier General Denison's elevator was no longer making it all the way up to the top floor. 'Just how have you come by this – information?'

'My grandfather told me. Though he died when I was only seven, we were quite close. I checked it with my mother.'

'And she . . .'

'Said she didn't think there was anything to it at all.'

'I think your mother was right.'

259

'Very strict Victorian. Devout Presbyterian. Also insisted her father, my grandfather James, had not been born out of wedlock – her way of putting it. And that denial was not true either.'

He must let this old man down as easily as possible. 'Really, General Denison, all you have to go on is your grandfather's word for it – given to you when you were a little boy.'

'Believed him then. Believe him now. Always will. Ever since retirement, devoted most of my time to proving it. At night I go to sleep thinking about it. Wake up each morning thinking about it.'

'It takes much more than thinking about it, General.'

'I know. To your knowledge, Professor, has anybody else ever brought forward this fact about the parentage of Samuel Clemens?'

'I'm quite sure no one has.'

'His only surviving daughter, Clara, lives in Detroit. Married to some musician there. Sometimes I think I ought to get in touch – '

'I hardly think her father would have said anything to her about it.'

'That's what my publisher said.'

'Publisher!'

'Macmillan of Canada. In Toronto.'

This was a surprise. He had been on the point of warning the man against vanity presses, when he'd said 'publisher.' 'Did you say Macmillan?'

'I went to a number of them. Random House, Doubleday, Little Brown, Viking. You'd think Harper and Row, Twain's people, would snap at it, but they didn't. It was Macmillan finally showed interest in it, kept in touch for three years. How I got your name. John Gray.'

He had recognized the name. John Gray *was* president of

Macmillan of Canada, and John Gray of Macmillan of Canada must also be Canada's leading practical joker!

'I know I'm not a writer – like my great-grandfather, or my grandfather who set up his own newspaper in upstate New York or my half granduncle, Mark Twain. But somebody like you could take all the stuff I've gathered up and do the necessary scholarly research to back it up and write the book.'

'I'm afraid not, General. It isn't that simple.'

'And you're no ghostwriter. I see. Fair enough.' He picked the sheets off the desk corner, went to the briefcase on the chair. 'Won't take up any more of your valuable time. Or mine.' He zipped the case shut, straightened, and walked toward the buffalo coat on the wall by the door. 'When they were over Rome they should have dropped just one bomb load and they could have wiped it out.'

'What!'

'Vatican.' He had pulled the toque down over his ears. 'Cleaned out the whole works including the Pope.'

Hurray for King Billy! Hold the white horse till I get on!

The General was at the front door now. 'Another call to make before I leave Buffalo. Cardinal McNulty. Bishops, Archbishops – visited twenty-nine of them so far. Just before I leave them and when they're not looking, I drop a cigarette in their wastebaskets. Lighted. So far, no luck.' He went out.

In spite of himself, he had glanced at his own wastebasket.

———

'I hope you understand, Doctor – this is pretty sad for Rosemary and me. She – we've come to love you a lot. I told her this morning. She doesn't want us to leave you. She cried.'

'Oh!'

'I almost didn't take Seth up on his offer, you know. I gave it a lot of thought before I made up my . . .'

'Ah, you shouldn't have!'

'The hell I shouldn't! You took us in – rescued us. We'll always owe you.'

'Goes both ways, Nadya.'

'I just wish – '

'Quit wishing. You're going to be a smash at Stratford this summer. I'll be at your opening. Wouldn't miss seeing you square off against all the goddams in *Saint Joan* for anything.'

'Will you come down . . . ?'

'Of course I will. We're going to keep in touch.'

'Oh, I hope so!'

'I had an interesting – ah – shift in the biography today,' he said. 'Incidentally, I don't think you really know how much help you've been to me. Not just researching – the sort of thing Sarah used to do for me – she was a fine and encouraging listener, too. You fellows – you and Rosemary, and Seth – may have me down there with you more than you'd like.'

'Great!'

'Most of the rest of the summer. I have to admit I was pretty low this morning. Damn low. Until I started remembering something that happened over twenty-five years ago. When I was at New York State. Something I thought was too ridiculous for words. I'd like to tell you . . . Third winter I was at New York State this old fellow drifted into my office . . .'

———

'My God!'

'I told you it was ridiculous.'

'I'm not so sure about that.'

'Neither was Sarah. She kept bringing it up, and I kept telling her that the old guy was – '

'Did you check it out?'

'No.'

'But you should have. Didn't you get in touch with Macmillan?'

'No. Several times Sarah asked me why I didn't. I told her publishers already had their full quota of nuts.'

'But you said he said Macmillan had already showed interest. For three years.'

'*Pretended* to. Even publishers don't like to hurt old men unnecessarily.'

'All the same, it wouldn't have hurt to get in touch with them – find out if a mysterious stranger did visit the president of Macmillan of Canada.' She thought for a moment. 'Tell me something. Tom Sawyer – why was he being brought up by Aunt Polly? And where did that half-brother, Sid, come from?'

'Sam didn't bother to tell us.'

'Uh-huh. Look at the baby mix-up in *Pudd'nhead Wilson*. And how about the way he confused that poor reporter, told him he had an identical twin brother and at the end said he wasn't sure the interviewer was talking to him or to his doppelgänger.'

'What are you driving at, Nadya?'

'Look, for over six months I've been busting my butt doing research for you – reading all your stuff – so I do have more than a passing acquaintance with Sam Clemens, and he seems to me to have an unusual obsession with paternity, and also with ancestors. Clemens never struck me as a Scotch name, but didn't he say his family went clear back to the early kings of Scotland?'

'Yes.'

'Just as William Lyon Mackenzie's did. Hey. Your name's Lyon! Are you . . .'

'No relation at all. Thank God.'

'Doctor, I think you blew it back there. You should have got back in touch with that brigadier general. Would have been easy to track down a retired general through the army.'

'He was shot down the following summer.'

'Huh?'

'July the twelfth – by Catholic anti-aircraft guns – over the Vatican.'

'Too bad. Mackenzie – I gather he spent a lot of time south of the border?'

'He did.'

'In the 1830s?'

'Yes,' he admitted.

'And Mark Twain was born in 1835.'

'That's right.'

'Her lover let her down. For spite she married Clemens, though you tell me she's on the record as never having loved him. If she were already knocked up – '

'Impossible. Lottery odds against – '

'I know what I'm talking about, Doctor, and I'm telling you the odds *for* it are not all that low.'

'Look. Sam was her third child. Her first love was out of the picture years before Sam came along.'

'But did he stay out? Just because she married Clemens on the rebound. If she hadn't stopped loving the guy who broke her heart – and number one shows up again – we have new odds, haven't we?'

'Possibly. But there's no way of knowing who he was. Certainly nothing to back up a wild assumption that William

Lyon Mackenzie with a wife and family in Canada on trips to the States carried on an affair with . . .'

'According to his great-grandson, the brigadier general – '

'He had just one oar in the water.'

'But did the president of Macmillan? Look. Before Rosemary and I head for Stratford I'd like to go out to the University – full time – and find everything I can on William Lyon Mackenzie. In the meantime let's get in touch with Macmillan in Toronto. If this John Gray was going along with the brigadier general . . .'

'John Gray died ten years ago.'

'All right. Maybe there's something in his papers. Wouldn't that be something! Mark Twain a Canadian! Paternally speaking, of course. After your biography comes out, you're going to be in deep trouble, Doctor, because the CIA will be coming after you.'

'I'll keep a sharp lookout,' he promised.

'That mean you're going to take a run at it?'

'I think so. If only to get you – and Sarah – off my back.'

———

Sorry, Sam. It's just a long-shot possibility, but one that has to be checked out all the same. This William Lyon Mackenzie was your kind of fellow. Like you he was a printer's devil at fourteen. At the same age his son, James, went to work for him on the *Colonial Advocate*, in which Mackenzie kept giving the Family Compact, the Conservative gang who ran things, regular shit. You were fourteen, too, when you became a printer's apprentice. You and James had to get that printer's ink in your veins from someone up the line. Maybe from the same . . .

265

Just maybe.

There's also the matter of voice. Thanks to Nadya, I've had a chance to read a number of Mackenzie's pieces in the *Colonial Advocate*, and I find his style a lot like yours: colloquial, witty, unrestrained. It's a speaking style, and the voice I hear reminds me of yours. His hasn't got soft r's, of course; yours doesn't have a Dundee burr, but again and again you both sound the same derisive note.

He loves the anecdotal too, as in a piece of his titled 'The Un-marrying.' In those days it was tough times in Upper Canada for anybody who wasn't a Tory or an Anglican. Heaven help you if you were Catholic or Methodist or Presbyterian or Baptist; marriages in your own church were counterfeit, had to be validated by civil ceremony if you didn't want to raise a bunch of catch colts. Mackenzie considered this unfair, especially since there was a high price tag on the service as performed by a local municipal clerk, who just happened to be a Tory and an Anglican. Always.

Mackenzie tells us about a young farmer who had managed to scrape up the marriage-licence fee of fifteen shillings, the size of his average cash income for a year, and got married. But a couple of weeks later he decided it had been a bad mistake. His wife agreed. He went to the clerk, asked him if he could un-marry as well as marry folks. The clerk assured him that such power had indeed been vested in him, just come back with the un-marrying fee, thirty shillings. It meant mortgaging the homestead, but the fellow scraped it up.

Now the government appointee customarily conducted all business from his parlour, and when the couple arrived for the solemn ceremony, they found him prepared with a double-bitted axe in his hand, a chopping stump in the middle of the room, and a large black cat. He laid the cat across the stump, asked the wife and husband to take the end of their choice, raised the axe high and brought it down to cut the cat in two, after which he declaimed the well-known Anglican ritual line: 'What God hath put asunder, let no man join back together.'

Isn't that one a real boomer, Sam? The point I want to make is, it sounds to me just like vintage Mark Twain.

Understand, I was reluctant to bring up the matter of your parentage this late in the game, but you will admit that it does have a bearing on understanding the sort of fellow you were. For one thing, I think it might explain why you were so much closer to your mother than you were to your father. You were a mother's boy, just as much as William Lyon Mackenzie and Mackenzie King were. All your lives, whenever you scored for yourselves, all three of you won for mother, too. I'm sure they were proud of you. They had very good reason to be.

However it turns out, I'll keep you posted, Sam.

12

HE HAD FORGOTTEN AGAIN LAST NIGHT TO DRAW THE BED-
room curtains, so window light had wakened him early; for at
least a couple of hours he'd be the only one stirring, and that
was all right with him because he needed time to come up and
out of sleep to rejoin the living whole. Such as it was. Took
him long enough to get used to himself, let alone other
humans. How he could empathize with those frogs, holding
still in their slough soup a second too long as he and Henry
stalked and pounced to trap them by the hind legs, then drop
them into the red lard pail for fish bait. Beginning of every

morning for the past five years anyway, all he'd been doing was wading, and he generally needed two hours at least to make it to shore.

5:49, the clock on the night table was saying.

Today is the day.

All right, Lyon, just you sit here on the edge of the bed and while you're at it, check out your whole body. As a child, in youth, all through middle age, you didn't truly know you were made up of separate physical parts, did you? Except when you were testing how long you could hold your breath under water at the lake with Henry, or when you had a flu attack, you never did take your lungs seriously. Or the brain. Or the heart. With great regularity the uro-genital and alimentary systems called attention to themselves, but only when need of one sort or another insisted. How much nicer to have lived during the childhood of your race, before people became more informed than they cared to be of the existence of the liver, kidneys, the reproductive and nervous systems, and all the other parts of the self whole. In the old days it had been simple: one soul – one complete body. Ghosts and demons and humours and gods had served man well enough back then.

Now. Those are your shoes by the corner of the bed, where you tripped on them in the dark last night, when one of those systems gave you the thirty-second warning. Toe to toe, one turned up on its side, unmistakably yours with three creases grinning over each instep, retaining the bulges made by the arthritic base joints of your big toes. Unique because they're yours, and on or off they'll keep right on announcing they are.

Last time they were innocents abroad, Sarah had picked them out for him in a shop on the Via Po because she was sick and tired of seeing him wear thick-soled British brogues that reminded her of Greek sponge-fishing boats. The gentle Italian leather had been kind to his feet for so many years; must have had them resoled at least three times. So. He'd ended up a foot fetishist, probably been one ever since the sad trip to tidy up after Henry. Then he had held in his hands a pair of shoes that remembered his brother's feet, and he had cried, and made arrangements with the licensed embalmer and funeral director. Closed casket of course, for the shotgun had blown . . . God, Henry – why did you have to do it?

After the sad trip to Los Angeles he had often wondered and asked himself why he had let the brother ties be broken. Not *he* really, *they*. For too few years their mother had kept them informed about each other, then, after her death, just Christmas-card links had been left. He had been best man at Henry's first wedding, but not the second or the third. The last time he'd seen him had been at their mother's funeral, and again there had been a request for 'Blest Be the Tie that Binds.' He had realized then that Henry had a drinking problem. He had mentioned it to him, only to have it denied with all the courtroom skill his brother possessed.

But why! The note had been addressed to him. It was not till he got down there that he found out about the disbarment seven years before. He was appalled by the sleazy one-room apartment with the hot plate, the cot, and the single ceiling bulb. All the note had said was, 'To: Dr. Kenneth Lyon, English Department, Livingstone University, from his brother, Henry Lyon.'

Dear Kenny:
Peanut butter is *not* made from squirrel turds. I am.
Sorry. Goodbye.

Henry

Enough, Lyon, you've got more important things to do than count your dead this morning. Nadya and Rosemary aren't happy about this leave-taking, either, hardly fair to let them see you looking as though you'd been chewing wild horseradish. Nadya was making the best of it, not much protest out of her when he'd said he'd prefer it if they took a taxi without him to the airport for their flight to Toronto. Bad enough one, let alone two farewells.

She'd knocked herself out to make a great dinner for them last night. He'd finished *Peck's Bad Boy* for Rosemary, but she'd come up with only a couple of giggles. He and Nadya had skipped pool, had sat out on the back deck to talk and to remember.

'I have one too?' she said as he took out a cigar.

He promised again that he would come down to Stratford for her opening. She reminded him that Hamilton and the McMaster University Archives were no more than eighty miles away from Stratford, that he could spend weeks with them while he checked out the brigadier general in the cartons of John Gray's papers. Long after conversation and cigars had died, till well after dark, they sat outside.

6:58.

Their flight was for 10:15. Half an hour to the airport; should be out there an hour before flight time, which meant leaving here by 8:45. Cutting it fine; better get shaved and downstairs, put in a call for their taxi, get breakfast started. After he'd made it down the basement stairs to the cold room and back up again to the kitchen.

———

Rosemary had hardly touched her Prairie Maid; he felt no great interest in his either.

'I'll just have coffee,' Nadya said. 'They're serving a snack on the plane.'

Judging from Wrinkles over on the couch, it had been a pretty glum breakfast for him too.

Rosemary did finish her orange juice.

'Come on,' he said to her.

'Where?'

'Over to the fridge.'

'What for?'

'You'll see,' he said. 'Leave Wrinkles.'

At the fridge he handed the bottle to her. 'Take this to your mother.'

When he came back to the table with the champagne glasses, he said, 'You've seen it before. Remember? Christmas time?'

Nadya nodded.

'You brought it up from the cold room and I asked you to take it back.'

'Yes.'

'I didn't tell you why then. I'd like to now. Till you found it behind the mason jars, it had been lying there for almost ten years.'

'I thought it might be special,' Nadya said.

'Very. Sarah got it the year I retired. She put it on the shelf and said it couldn't be opened until I'd finished the Mark Twain biography.'

'I see.'

'Rosemary, will you get me the tea towel from the counter, please. I want to open it now – before you and your mother leave.'

'Just a minute, Rosemary.' Her mother was holding the bottle up to him. 'It's sweet of you to want to do this, Doctor, but I think it should go back up on that shelf in the cold room.'

'Huh!'

'And I would like you to bring it down with you when you come to Stratford and – '

'To celebrate your Joan – '

'No. You are going to check out that old brigadier general, and find out if William Lyon Mackenzie was Sam Clemens's father, and you are going to finish the Mark Twain biography, and *then* we will crack this bottle.'

'I see.'

'So put the goddam glasses back on the goddam shelf, Doctor.'

———

The front-door chimes sounded. Rosemary ran to the living-room picture window. 'The taxi's here!'

He went out with them to the front steps, where Nadya had piled their luggage and where he'd first met both of them, red poppy and yellow buttercup, almost a year ago. They hugged each other goodbye. As the cab pulled away from the curb he glimpsed Rosemary's face, as he had first seen it in the back seat of Debbie's car.

When he went up and into his office, he saw the envelope on top of his typewriter.

'For the Professor.'

He sat down. She must have put it there last night. He opened it.

Dear Professor:
I am sad we are going away from you. When Mom told me about it I cried and so did Wrinkles too. I couldn't get him to stop it until Mom told us you are

273

coming down to stay with us this summer real soon. Then he stopped but he is still real sad about it and so am I.

Mom says you can't live with us all the time down there but she says we will come back to visit you a lot. She promised. I hope so because I love you to read to me in bed and tell me stories that are funny and scary every night and Mom says there are lots of parks down there we can go to. Please bring some good stories when you come down when Mom opens. She is writing down this to you for me and I am crying inside and I think she is doing it too because she has to stop a lot and snuff up a lot while she does it for me.

You and Mom keep telling me not to say any of those bad words the way you guys do, but there is one I sure wish I could say now.

I will always love you, Professor, and so will Wrinkles.

Rosemary

P.S. Mom says that means something you thought about after you finished. Wrinkles says he wishes he could say the bad word too.

P.P.S. The bad word is shit, Doctor.

Nadya

They're gone now, Sam, and I really should bring you up to date on this relative matter. Nadya got in touch with Macmillan of Canada by phone. Ah – ah – I didn't tell her to; she phoned them on her own hook, and they told her John Gray's papers had gone to McMaster University. That's in Hamilton,

just a short Baptist hop from Toronto. She then phoned
McMaster and spoke to their head bibliographer. He said
there were cartons and cartons, and they've got them sorted
out and catalogued only up to the mid-fifties. I talked with
him too, and he sounded quite excited, said you had quite an
association with Canada. He mentioned your six-week residence in Montreal, which isn't all that relevant to the matter,
since it was for purely commercial and international copy-
right reasons, to end once and for all the pirating of your
work by Canadian publishers. It isn't hard to understand why
your relations with Canada were stormy and vituperative.
You sure blew your cork over that illustration on page 283 of
the Canadian edition of Huckleberry Finn, with Uncle Silas's
open fly and exposed john-donnacker, a real dandy, judging
from the way Aunt Sally's eyes are rolled upwards.

What I really wanted to discuss with you, Sam, is something I think you gave a great deal of thought to in your later
years; how brief is the time that we humans are given up on
the platform. I want you to understand that I think you were
one hell of a fine performer on paper or on the boards, playing
to sell-out houses, bringing laughter and insight to readers
and listeners all over the world. The main point is that you
spoke to the whole world, *for* the new world.

Let's be clear about this; not *just* for the States but for
Canada as well. In the matter of literary genealogy, your
grampa is a Nova Scotia Canadian, Thomas Chandler Hali-
burton, the father of American humour. He left his mark first
on Artemus Ward, then on you. Decent of both of you to
have acknowledged this.

You see, I have found the thematic destination of this biography. Finally. Whether or not you had a rebel Canadian
father isn't all that important, but what is important is that
your voice is the voice of *both* our American nations. You

275

fellows down there below the forty-ninth never have been and never will be the *only* Americans on this continent, and we welcome you as one of us in our new world. I know how you feel about the French, Sam, but I have to say, *vive la différence*.

I'm close to final curtain time now, but make no mistake about it, I'll soon be packing to go down east and into rare books and papers at McMaster University. And before this year is out there is going to be a certain champagne bottle popped, and it will be done not in mine but in your honour.

Good night, Sam.

THE PROGRESS OF LOVE *by* Alice Munro

"Probably the best collection of stories – the most confident and, at the same time, the most adventurous – ever written by a Canadian." *Saturday Night*
>> Fiction, 6 x 9, 320 pages, hardcover

FOUR DAYS OF COURAGE The Untold Story of the Fall of Marcos
by Bryan Johnson

"What may well be the best book on the Marcos-Aquino election campaign and on the 'People Power' that toppled a tyrant ... ." *New York Times*
>> Politics/Journalism, 6 x 9, 288 pages, map and photographs, hardcover

THE RADIANT WAY *by* Margaret Drabble

"*The Radiant Way* does for Thatcher's England what *Middlemarch* did for Victorian England ... Essential reading!" Margaret Atwood   *Fiction, 6 x 9, 400 pages, hardcover*

DANCING ON THE SHORE A Celebration of Life at Annapolis Basin
by Harold Horwood, *Foreword by* Farley Mowat

"A Canadian *Walden*" (*Windsor Star*) that "will reward, provoke, challenge and enchant its readers." (*Books in Canada*)
>> Nature/Ecology, 5 1/2 x 8 1/2, 224 pages, 16 wood engravings, hardcover

NO KIDDING Inside the World of Teenage Girls *by* Myrna Kostash

This frank, informative look at teenage girls today "should join Dr. Spock on every parent's bookshelf." *Maclean's*   *Women/Journalism, 6 x 9, 320 pages, notes, hardcover*

THE HONORARY PATRON   A Novel *by* Jack Hodgins

The Governor General's Award-winner's thoughtful and satisfying third novel mixes comedy and wisdom, "and it's magic". *Ottawa Citizen*
>> Fiction, 6 x 9, 336 pages, hardcover

RITTER IN RESIDENCE A Comic Collection *by* Erika Ritter

This collection by the noted playwright, broadcaster, and humorist reveals "a wonderfully funny view of our world". *Globe and Mail*
>> Humour, 5 1/2 x 8 1/2, 200 pages, hardcover

THE LIFE OF A RIVER *by* Andy Russell

This yarning history of the Oldman river area shows "a sensitivity towards the earth ... that is universally applicable." *Kingston Whig-Standard*
>> History/Ecology, 6 x 9, 184 pages, hardcover

THE INSIDERS Government, Business, and the Lobbyists *by* John Sawatsky

Investigative journalism at its best, this Ottawa exposé is "packed with insider information about the political process". *Globe and Mail*
>> Politics/Business, 6 x 9, 368 pages, photos, hardcover

PADDLE TO THE AMAZON The Ultimate 12,000-Mile Canoe Adventure
by Don Starkell, *edited by* Charles Wilkins

"This real-life adventure book ... must be ranked among the classics of the literature of survival." *Montreal Gazette*   *Adventure, 6 x 9, 320 pages, maps, photos, hardcover*